She push *and be* ***kiss and stepped back.***

"Why did you do that?" she asked.

"Because I wanted to."

"And if I didn't want you to kiss me?"

"Then you shouldn't have kissed me back. It's the simple rule of kissing. If someone kisses you and you'd rather them not, then you simply don't kiss them back."

"I'm not familiar with these so-called rules of kissing."

"Did you enjoy it?"

"I beg your pardon? I will not respond to that."

"That certainly answers my question."

She opened her mouth to answer, but stopped. Honestly? She should be uncomfortable, but she wasn't. This was a fault in her, a fault her father would never understand.

Nor would Richard, her fiancé. She was supposed to meet him today, yet here she was with another man.

A man she'd kissed . . .

Other **AVON ROMANCES**

ROBYN DEHART

COURTING CLAUDIA

AVON BOOKS

An Imprint of HarperCollinsPublishers

This is a work of fiction. Names, characters, places, and incidents are products of the author's imagination or are used fictitiously and are not to be construed as real. Any resemblance to actual events, locales, organizations, or persons, living or dead, is entirely coincidental.

AVON BOOKS
An Imprint of HarperCollins*Publishers*
10 East 53rd Street
New York, New York 10022-5299

Copyright © 2005 by Robyn Ratliff
ISBN: 0-06-078215-3
www.avonromance.com

First Avon Books paperback printing: August 2005

Avon Trademark Reg. U.S. Pat. Off. and in Other Countries, Marca Registrada, Hecho en U.S.A.
HarperCollins® is a registered trademark of HarperCollins Publishers Inc.

Printed in the U.S.A.

10 9 8 7 6 5 4 3 2 1

To Mom and Dad,
who never questioned this crazy dream of mine.
Thanks for being my biggest fans!

To Paul—
it seems it took a lifetime to find you—
but you were so worth the wait.

And to Sammy and Mike,
an example of real love.

Acknowledgments

For Pam, the best agent ever, thanks for answering all my incessant questions and for being there whenever I need something. For Kelly, editor extraordinaire, you made my dream come true and it's been amazing to work with you—thank you. Special thanks to Stacy for finding my obscure political scandal.

Chapter 1

London, 1848

Claudia inhaled three deep breaths, hoping to calm her addled insides, but her stomach still churned. If this was the right decision, why did she not feel relaxed and assured? Whether her body believed this to be the right decision was of no consequence. No lady of good breeding and any shred of propriety would continue to hold a paying position, especially with a marriage proposal on the horizon.

Which was why she currently sat in a carriage just outside the office of *London's Illustrated Times*, resignation letter in hand. Of course, learning that her father despised Derrick Middleton and all his paper stood for had aided her decision to resign. Her father would view her employment with the paper as a betrayal. Emerson Prattley expected his daughter to be loyal at any cost, and she was nothing if not loyal. So with feigned confidence, she opened the carriage door.

Derrick Middleton stared at his office door, muttering to himself. One more interruption today and he might fire everyone. Of course, that would only serve to prove to the Conservatives that he was the bastard they thought him to be. Which was not true, at least concerning his employees. His workers regarded him highly—they enjoyed their positions here, they smiled, they came to work every day.

But today had been a bloody mess. All day, one thing after another. One of his journalists broke his leg, and his assignments had to be handed off to another. His wood carvers sat idle, waiting for the delayed shipment of boxwood to arrive before they began next week's woodcuts. They could substitute another wood, but boxwood worked best for the illustrations.

And now last month's books were not reconciling perfectly. The paper still had money—plenty of it—but Derrick wanted his books perfect, down to the last shilling.

He would have to rewrite all the entries and do the calculations himself. Pressure nagged at his temples. He pinched the bridge of his nose to relieve the strain—to no avail.

He poked the quill back into the well, then went to stand at the window. The street below him bustled with activity. People milled about and went in and out of the shops. A well-dressed lady with an enormous hat decorated with at least a dozen flowers exited a carriage, stopped to smooth her skirts, then looked up as if she knew he stood in the window above her. He took a step back.

The pain in his head drummed against his scalp. Perhaps he should tell Mason he was taking the rest of the afternoon off. He could go home and . . . and what? Worry about the goings on from home. No, he needed to get back to the books and figure out the problem. Perhaps his day would get better. No sooner had he taken a seat than Mason opened the door.

"Mr. Middleton, there is a lady here to see you."

The lady from the carriage. "Who is she, and what does she want?"

"She didn't say. Although she did say it was most important she meet with you."

"*She* didn't say? I believe it is your job as my assistant to ask such questions."

Mason just stood there.

He wasn't a very good assistant, but he was literate and came to work every day. Most days he spoke politely to visitors. And Derrick trusted him—that was the main reason he hadn't fired Mason. Trustworthy employees were hard to come by.

"Very well, send her in." He continued to stand behind his desk until she breached the doorway in a flurry of pale blue ruffles and bows. It was indeed the lady from the carriage, and her hat was even larger this close up. Perplexing how a woman of her stature could hold it up, as she couldn't have been much over five feet tall.

"Thank you for seeing me, Mr. Middleton. I apologize for not making an appointment ahead of time, but I didn't think you would see me if you knew who I was."

"I see. Why did you think I wouldn't see you?"

"Because I am a woman."

He let his eyes roam the short length of her. "Yes, I can see that."

She stared at him as if that was the complete answer—she was a woman—as if that explained everything.

He shook his head. "Exactly who are you?"

"I'm so daft sometimes." She came forward,

4

hand extended. "Claudia Prattley. A pleasure to finally meet you."

He took her hand—a warm, plush hand—and squeezed it gently before he remembered his manners and brought it to his lips. "Prattley. That sounds familiar. Please sit." He motioned to the leather chairs opposite his desk, then took a seat himself.

She gave him a tentative smile, then busied herself retrieving something from her reticule. With her head slightly bent he got full view of her hat. Was that a dove? He suppressed a smile. The hat was ridiculously large, and so full of flowers, not to mention the artificial bird, that it distracted one from noticing much else about her. Finally, she pulled out an envelope, which she looked at for a moment, then leaned forward to hand to him.

"For me?"

"Yes." She sat straighter in her chair and tilted her chin ever so slightly, giving him a better view of her eyes. The muted blue of her dress would have matched them perfectly had it been a few shades brighter.

He brought his attention back to the envelope. The wax seal cracked as he pried up the flap of the envelope.

" 'Dear Mr. Middleton.' " He looked up and she

nodded, her eyes wide, as if eager for news in the letter. " 'I am troubled that I must do this, but the time has come for me to resign.' Who is this from?"

She said nothing, merely pointed at the letter.

He skimmed the languid writing until he reached the signature. 'Miss Claudia J. Prattley, C. J. Prattley.' C. J. Prattley. Why did that sound so bloody familiar?

"I apologize for being so thick today, madam, but I've had one problem after another, and while this name sounds very familiar to me, I simply cannot place it."

"I work for you, Mr. Middleton. I am one of your illustrators."

She lifted her hand to her chest, and he couldn't help but notice the ample bosom it rested upon. She was a plump woman with curves in all the right places, and apple-round cheeks with just the hint of an extra chin. A pleasant-looking woman with bright eyes that held the wonder most people lost in childhood.

This creature worked for him? C. J. Prattley. He let the name rattle a bit in his head. And then it hit him—Society Fashion Report.

"Did I know you were a woman?" He said the words out loud although he truly asked himself.

A blush lit her already rosy cheeks. "I don't believe so."

"And you led me to believe you were a man by using your initials?"

Her gloved hands worried the material of her skirt. "I'm afraid so."

"Clever. You did not believe I would hire you if I knew you were a woman."

"No, sir." Her brow furrowed. "Yes, sir. Would you?"

"Probably not." Leaning back in his chair, he thought on it a bit more. "Although that is a shame considering that you are one of my best illustrators. Your fashion pages alone increased my sales in Society by thirty percent."

"My drawings? I had no idea." Again, her hand to that bosom. Remnants of her blush lingered on the creamy flesh of her neck, making him wonder exactly how far down the pretty color traveled. No doubt Miss Prattley had no clue how that simple movement was so tantalizing. He made his glance return to her face.

"Indeed. There is much mystery around your illustrations. I do believe it is the latest buzz in Society—they are all aflutter trying to discover the identity of the anonymous artist. They simply cannot believe the precise detail of the depictions, so they are positive it must be someone in their midst."

She released a low *ooh* noise that sounded far more primal and sexual than it should have, considering they merely discussed illustrations. "How very exciting. I've never been a part of a mystery before." Her eyes were intoxicating, the blue depths tugging at him. Innocence. The kind of innocence that on other people looked more like ignorance and usually had him dismissing them without thought. But something about Miss Prattley refused to be dismissed.

He leaned forward. "I've even been accused myself of being the artist, since I have on occasion attended an assembly or ball this Season with my aunt. I can scarcely remember an evening when someone hasn't approached and probed me with questions of your identity. Since the mystery seemed to fuel their purchase of the paper, I played along."

She tapped a finger on his desk. "Now that you mention it, I have heard some ladies discuss this at recent parties, but Poppy and I always leave their company as I'm so afraid I will give something away. I have a tendency to speak without thinking. It's a bad habit," she added softly as if revealing the darkest of sins.

"I suppose now that the truth is out, you don't

need to resign. Your secret is safe with me, Miss Prattley."

"I'm sorry?"

"Your identity. It's why you wanted to resign, correct?"

"Not exactly. I mean, only my closest friend knows I illustrate for the paper. I hadn't intended to take the position in the first place. I sent in those initial illustrations never imagining that it would lead to anything. It was wrong of me to take more assignments. I'm afraid my vanity got the better of me. It's just that when I saw the advertisement for the fashion submissions, I could not help myself."

"It is understandable. You are quite talented. There is nothing wrong with wanting to share that."

"Oh, but if my father discovered the truth, why, he would surely disown me. I'm fairly certain of it."

"That seems severe."

"He's very old-fashioned, Mr. Middleton. Traditionally speaking, because of my station I'm not supposed to have a paying position. Except if I were a governess or some such. That might be acceptable."

"So you are resigning because you recently realized it is improper for you to have a paid position?"

She shook her head, the flowers on her hat bobbing. "No, I have to get married and that is why I must resign."

"I don't follow."

"I cannot be a wife and have a . . . a job, Mr. Middleton. It would not be appropriate."

"I see. It appears to me that no part of your position with this paper is appropriate. I find life is vastly more rewarding if you live your life as you like it rather than by what Society deems appropriate."

Her eyes widened and her mouth formed a tiny O. "You must live a daring life, Mr. Middleton," she said, her voice breathy. "A very exciting existence. If only I were so fortunate."

He could certainly show her a more exciting life. And he'd start with peeling off that silly hat so he could see what her hair looked like. Then he'd probably want to kiss that silly little mouth of hers to see if she would make that *ooh* noise again. The muscles across his abdomen tightened.

This was ridiculous. "So when is it that you are getting married?" he asked to get the conversation back on track.

"I'm not sure."

"You haven't set a wedding date?"

"Oh, I'm not betrothed as of yet."

As refreshing as he found her, she sent his mind

spinning with her haphazard logic. "I think I'm confused again."

"My father insists that I marry soon, and I thought now would be as good a time as any to resign, so that I could focus on securing a husband."

"I see." No, he really didn't see at all. Perhaps Miss Prattley was mad—stark, raving mad. That seemed less likely considering she hadn't screamed maniacally or set fire to anything. Perhaps this was just a ploy.

"Why exactly did you come all the way down here to resign when up until now our working relationship has been handled strictly through post?" Derrick asked.

"I thought about mailing you the letter, but since I am retracting a promise, I wanted to do so in person. To apologize for inconveniencing you."

"Miss Prattley, I'm prepared to offer you more money. Your illustrations are important to my paper, and I am used to getting what I want. Name your price."

"Are you quite serious?" she asked.

"I don't joke about money."

She eyed him for a moment. "I'm flattered, sir, but honestly, it isn't money I seek. I really must marry. I shall finish up my last assignment to give

11

you enough time to find a replacement." She stood to leave. "Thank you again for your time."

He caught up with her and placed his hand on her arm. "I do wish you'd reconsider, Miss Prattley."

Her eyes fell to where his hand lay, making him all too aware of the impropriety of such a gesture. He pulled back.

"As much as I wish I could reconsider, I simply cannot. Please know that it has been a pleasure working for you, an experience I won't quickly forget."

With that, she exited his office. His day had gotten worse. The Society Fashion Report had become a most desired portion of his newspaper. What awful luck: just when he'd discovered a way to get his paper into the homes of the aristocracy, his best illustrator resigned. Miss Prattley's drawings far exceeded those of his other illustrators, delineating every detail of ribbons and pleats. Her eye for the specific was incomparable.

Surely he could find a way to convince her to stay on. If not, he'd have to find a replacement, and getting one inside Society would be difficult, if not impossible. And without that inside eye, that section would never be the same.

Damnation!

* * *

Claudia climbed into the carriage and released the breath she hadn't known she'd been holding. Gracious. Poppy had said she'd heard that Mr. Middleton was a dashing man. But good heavens. Dashing—that word seemed lackluster now that she'd met him. His presence was nothing short of mesmerizing.

Honestly. Thank goodness no one could hear her thoughts lest they think her straight from the schoolroom. Mr. Middleton was certainly handsome, sinfully handsome, but she had seen handsome men before.

Then again, his looks went beyond handsome. He wore his dark brown hair too long and had to keep pushing it out of his face. It gave him the look of a privateer. No, he would definitely be a pirate, not a privateer. His smile was easy, yet not one of great humor but more of secretive amusement—as if he alone knew the surprise of the joke.

But it was his eyes, Claudia decided, that made him so dashing. So brown they appeared black, framed with arching eyebrows that reflected his intelligence. Unlike most gentlemen, he had looked at her, really looked at her, eye to eye. Not terribly well-mannered, considering they had just met, but necessary under the circumstances. And it made her feel alive, noticed, important. As if he'd really seen her.

13

Feelings that no strange man should ever evoke in a lady. Gracious. More than his dashing good looks, everything about Mr. Middleton overwhelmed her. She had expected him to be furious at her deception and to refuse to pay her for her last assignment. But he'd scarcely blinked when he'd come to the realization that he'd hired a woman. Then he'd gone several steps further and praised her work and offered her more money.

It was ludicrous. Unheard of. Women were hired for factory jobs, not professional positions with newspapers. But he'd been quite serious. Name her price—as if her skill was something extraordinary and worthy.

Well, even if that were true, and she doubted it, she couldn't continue her employment. But oh, was it tempting. In her life she couldn't remember anything she loved more than illustrating. While she was quite accomplished with watercolors, illustrating was her true passion.

If only she could figure out a way to continue working. She'd managed to keep her secret for six months, but now that her father read the paper, too much was at risk.

Illustrating, making her own money these past six months, embodied her dreams as if she'd been living someone else's life. But she couldn't con-

14

tinue living the fantasy, so she'd have to settle for the entire experience being a sweet memory.

She had made the right decision. The only decision. No matter how much she longed to continue drawing and no matter how tempting Mr. Middleton and his offer were, she'd stick by her resignation.

"You shouldn't scowl like that, dear, makes you look dangerous."

Derrick looked up from his dinner and gave his aunt a weak smile.

"Bad day?"

"Rotten." He pushed his food around on his plate with his fork. He still hadn't figured out what to do about Miss Prattley's resignation.

"Your vocabulary is too much for my feeble mind," she said dryly.

Leave it to Aunt Chloe to give him a chuckle.

She leveled her gray eyes to his. Her silver hair piled atop her head like a crown gave her the illusion of being a tall woman. But it was her confidence and boldness that made her regal, not her appearance.

He knew better than to come home expecting to keep his troubles to himself. She was simply too nosy. She certainly loved him, but more than that she had a streak of curiosity as wide as the Thames.

"One of my illustrators resigned today."

"And now you have to find a replacement?"

"It's not likely. It was the illustrator who's been doing the Society Fashion Report."

She frowned. "I know I'm a dreadful aunt for not even glancing at your paper since I've been back in town. So forgive this old woman and be a dear and explain yourself—Society Fashion Report?"

"The Society Fashion Report was my answer to persuading more of the nobility to purchase the paper. A weekly segment featuring illustrations of the latest fashions. I figured even if it was women who initially bought the paper, it would get into the hands of their husbands eventually. This particular illustrator is on the inside of Society and draws her peers. It's quite the rage, as you know how those gossips love to be the center of attention."

"Brilliant plan, dear boy. And I should like to see these illustrations. But you mustn't forget that the paper is already a success. You have plenty of readers."

"Yes, but not enough. At least not enough of the right kind."

"Your paper doesn't have to be like your father's, you know. You've exceeded his success with the first fully illustrated paper. And you've made it available to the common man. Look around you, look at all you've accomplished. Your father would have been proud."

He didn't need to look around. This was his dining room. His house. He knew what it looked like. Tasteful yet simple decor. He hadn't picked any of it himself, because he didn't really care. He only cared that he had a dining table, not that it was mahogany and sat eight. None of the details mattered. The house, the money—yes, he'd done well for himself, and his father would have been proud. But his father had worked to bring political news to the public; for him it had never been about the money.

"My father loved political news," he replied.

"Your father loved you."

She was right, his father had loved him, but Phillip Middleton had lived and breathed for his paper. The paper had come first with him, and then his family. And with one story, that paper had been destroyed, the credibility and honor stripped away. Derrick hadn't penned another story since.

"It's not your fault, and he knew that. It's a shame you can't see it."

17

Derrick took a bite of roasted hen and let the silence settle in around them. He should send for new lighting for this room. It was too damned bright.

"Back to this illustrator," Aunt Chloe ventured. "What are you going to do?"

"I'm not sure. She won't be replaced easily."

"I'm rather intrigued that you hired a woman. You never mentioned that in your letters."

"I didn't know I'd hired a woman. Not until she came into the office today."

"Who is she?"

"Claudia Prattley. She made mention of her father deeming it inappropriate that she have a paid position, so I'm assuming that he's titled and finds men like me who work for our money nothing more than scuff marks on his boots."

"Prattley, you say? Oh, he's titled alright." Aunt Chloe gave him a smile. A slow smile that resembled a barn cat after she'd devoured a mouse. She all but licked her lips.

"Do you know her father?"

"Indeed. As do you, my dear. Prattley is the family name of the Viscount Kennington."

Derrick dropped his fork. This day could not end soon enough. Of all the rotten luck. Had there been a storm, he wouldn't dare go outside, because lightning would surely strike. He eyed the chandelier, surprised it hadn't fallen on him.

By God, he would have paid his entire fortune to keep in his employ the daughter of Kennington. The man who had made it his personal agenda to ruin Derrick's father and the reputation of *The Challenger*.

The bastard hadn't succeeded, but his letters to the editor disputed every sentiment raised. People had listened to him, as he'd been the chancellor of finance at the time. Despite his efforts, Kennington hadn't ruined the paper; Derrick had managed to do that himself.

"I can tell by your reaction that you hadn't made the connection. Don't you think old Kennie would love to know his precious daughter worked for you and your dirty little paper?" Her eyes sparkled with mischief.

Derrick chuckled. "And if it weren't for the fact that I want her to continue working for me, I just might tell him. I'm not sure the girl would fare well if he ever found out. I would wager he's a tyrant in his own home. He certainly raises enough hell in Parliament."

"Did she indicate why she needed to resign?"

"She has to marry."

"That shouldn't stop her. Marriage never

19

stopped me from doing anything." His aunt pointed her fork at him. "You *are* going to convince her to continue working, aren't you?"

"I haven't figured that out as of yet." He shrugged. "I did find out where Miss Prattley will be tomorrow evening. I have secured myself an invitation and will do what I can there to persuade her."

"How did you manage that?"

"I have my sources. Newsmen never reveal their sources."

"You're no fun." She drained her wineglass. "To whom is she betrothed?"

"She's not. It's confusing—at least it confused me. I suppose she is getting pressure from her father to marry."

"If that is indeed the reason she cannot continue working, then you simply need to ensure she doesn't marry. But first you must convince her to work for you until she is safely wed. Then you prevent the latter from happening."

"You are wicked, Aunt."

"I don't mean indefinitely, dear boy. Just until you can convince her to work for you regardless of her marital status. Or until you find a replacement."

That might work. Surely he could convince her to postpone resigning until she wed. He had always been successful at persuading people to his way of thought.

"But how do I prevent her from marrying?"

"Simple. You court her yourself."

Chapter 2

◦◦◦◦

The glittering ballroom fluttered with people and noise. Claudia stood in a circle with Poppy, Poppy's mother, and three of her friends. They chatted endlessly about the weather and the girls who had just been introduced into Society.

The Draper ball, while never a grand affair, not in comparison with some of the others of the Season, was well attended and nicely decorated. Rose topiaries and ferns lined the ballroom, and the wall of opened balcony doors allowed a gentle breeze to drift through the room.

Claudia sensed Poppy's annoyance—she had sent her a note promising details of her meeting with Mr. Middleton, but a day had passed since then, and she no longer wanted to divulge every detail to Poppy. Mr. Middleton had occupied far too many thoughts over the last twenty-four hours, and it was vastly inappropriate. Claudia would not admit to that, not even to Poppy.

It mattered not now. He had left her life as quickly as he'd entered. And while she regretted not meeting him before yesterday, lamenting a missed friendship seemed silly. Besides, married women didn't have male friends. Soon, she hoped, she could call herself a married woman. If Richard *ever* proposed.

Poppy looked over at her and rolled her eyes.

She smiled. As long as the others remained, they protected her from Poppy's inquiries.

"Girls, we're going to the refreshment table. Do you care for anything?" Poppy's mother asked.

Splendid.

"No, thank you, Mother," Poppy said.

Poppy would probably be suspicious if Claudia went with the other ladies to the refreshments. Deep breaths, that's all she needed. She inhaled; the sweet, tangy scent of roses filled her nose. Claudia watched the three women walk away. She bit the inside of her lip.

"Now that we've successfully rid ourselves of company, tell me what happened," Poppy said.

She just needed to remain calm. She wasn't a silly young chit; surely she could mention the man without salivating on herself.

"I met with Mr. Middleton and resigned. He was courteous and didn't toss me out on my ear—just as you said. So now I am officially unemployed."

"And?"

"He didn't know that I was a woman and admitted that he probably wouldn't have hired me had he known. But he did say that my illustrations had contributed to the success of the paper in Society."

"How did he react to your resignation?"

"He wasn't pleased. Offered me more money." So far, so good.

Just then lords Chester and Brookfield and Mr. Collinsworth appeared to secure dances from Poppy.

She handed them her dance card, then whispered, "How much more?"

"He told me to name my price."

Poppy's green eyes widened. "Honestly?" she asked through her teeth, all the while smiling prettily for her admirers. "So what did you do?"

Claudia waited until the men left. "I told him the truth. That it wasn't about money—that I had to resign so that I could marry."

"I see."

"I agreed to complete my latest assignment, and then my resignation will be official."

"Well, that doesn't sound horrible," Poppy said.

Claudia eyed her best friend, who appeared to be carefully considering their discussion. She hadn't said anything else; perhaps her interrogation about Mr. Middleton was over.

"What of Mr. Middleton himself? What was he like? Dashing as all the rumors I've heard?"

Perhaps not. She took a deep breath. "He was handsome." She shrugged and tried to look indifferent.

Poppy's eyebrows raised.

"If you like that type of man," Claudia quickly added.

"What type of man?"

"He's not very polished." She scrunched her face. "He's wild—admitted it himself."

Poppy narrowed her eyes. "So what you're saying is that he's not the type of man you find attractive."

"Correct." She nodded once for emphasis.

"And what type of man do you find attractive? Richard?"

Richard was kind, the perfect gentleman. But was she attracted to Richard? No, not especially.

She supposed he was nice to look upon, but he wasn't precisely handsome. His features weren't sharp and defined; they were softer, gentler.

At least, her heart never raced around him. And her hands never itched with sweat. She'd never been particularly fascinated by his mouth. All things she'd experienced yesterday with Mr. Middleton. "Richard is lovely," she finally said.

"Richard is lovely? Listen to yourself. I'll tell you what Richard is—Richard is not right for you."

"I cannot understand why you dislike him so."

Poppy shrugged. "I don't trust him. He's too agreeable to be genuine. And I don't think he pays proper attention to someone he's supposed to be courting. You know what you need?"

Claudia shook her head.

"A decent husband. Someone who will take you away from here and let you be yourself. Someone who will love you. Like Stephen and Anne—he adores her and allows her to do as she chooses. Look at them."

Claudia turned toward the dance floor. Anne was four and twenty, three years younger than Claudia and Poppy, but they'd all been friends when they were girls. Anne and Stephen had married last year. He did adore her—it shone all over his face. He looked at her as if she were the only woman in the room. The only person in the room. A love like that would be wonderful. More than wonderful—but love like that didn't happen often, and certainly not to women like Claudia.

Claudia raised her chin a bit. She twirled a stray curl behind her ear. "You and my father agree on something, isn't that a miracle?"

"Agree on what?"

"On my needing to marry."

"I don't, however, think Richard is the right man for you. If your father is so fond of him, why doesn't he marry him? He certainly could use someone's love to soften him."

"If my mother's love couldn't soften him, then no one's could."

"True indeed. In any case, you deserve to find a man who loves you—you should have the freedom to marry your choice and not your father's protégé."

"We both know that marriages like Stephen and Anne's are very rare. And might I point out that you are not married either."

"No, but I have plenty of suitors." Poppy flashed her a smile.

A footman walked by with a tray of champagne. They each took a glass. Claudia sipped at the sparkly liquid, enjoying the bubbles tickling her nose.

"You don't like any of them," Claudia said.

"That's not true." Poppy stuck her chin out and crossed her arms. "Why, last month I almost fancied myself in love with Christopher Newman. Then he up and married that girl from the country. He didn't want to marry me." Her voice softened. "None of them want to marry me. Simply because my dance card is always full doesn't mean, when it comes down to it, I'll have my pick. I know my fate. I shall have to marry some old codger like old man Weatherby with yellowed teeth and bad breath."

"It won't happen like that." Claudia took Poppy's hands and squeezed them. "You'll find someone lovely. You're beautiful."

"Sometimes being pretty isn't enough," Poppy murmured.

Claudia loved her friend, but she'd never understood her aversion to her own looks. Granted, Poppy's nonexistent dowry had made marriage proposals nonexistent as well, but why would being beautiful ever be a bad thing? Oh, to know how it felt like to walk into a room and have all the men stop and stare!

"This isn't about me," Poppy said. "We're talking about you, remember? I know you don't want to abandon your illustrating."

"Not this again. Poppy, I have to. You understand about familial duty, I know you do."

"Yes, but my family is supportive of one another."

"Would your father approve of you taking a paying position?"

"I don't know. If my family doesn't figure out some way to get back some of our money, I very well may have to. Claudia, it's 1848, the times are changing. Someday it will be respectable for women like us to have paid positions other than governesses. Being a governess is all I could do, but not you. You're so talented, and you shouldn't have to give that up. Not for your father or any other man. If you found the right husband, someone who would support you . . ."

"It would be nice," Claudia agreed. But it wouldn't happen. "You know something? You and I together make the perfect woman. You with your beauty, not to mention grace, and me with my pretty dresses and dowry. Someone would snatch us up, wouldn't they?" Poppy looked so pretty in that dress, prettier than it had ever looked on Claudia. Poppy, an accomplished seamstress, had taken it up in all the places where Claudia had more flesh than a girl should have, and the bodice fit snugly against her slender body. She'd removed the bows and ribbons so that now it was simple. Just a pretty, sea-green, satin dress.

"Indeed they would. But someone will snatch you up. Look at this hair." She picked up one of Claudia's ringlets. "And you don't even have to use an iron to get these curls. I would wager half of the girls in this town would likely pull themselves bald if they thought their hair would grow back like yours."

Claudia nodded to the scene in front of them. "I hate to admit it," she said quietly, "but I should like to see Francie Barkwell yank all her hair out. Of course if she doesn't marry soon, her mother might do that for her."

They both giggled as they watched Francie's mother practically push her daughter into a passing earl's path.

"I almost feel sorry for her," Poppy said. "But as I was saying, I just don't think you should close yourself off to other suitors. Why should you have to put your life on hold while Richard pussyfoots about? He's not your only choice."

"He's my father's choice. Besides, it's not as if I have a line of men to choose from." Claudia held up her dance card. "He will propose when the time is right. He's merely busy with his career. Like it or not, Richard is my only choice."

"What about Mr. Middleton?"

"What *about* Mr. Middleton?"

"What color were his eyes?"

"Brown." She said that entirely too fast. Cripes. She was supposed to be uninterested in that man. If she was so uninterested, why did she keep thinking of him? And his brown eyes.

"But he's nothing special?"

"Oh, all right, he's handsome. Devilishly so. Satisfied?" She crossed her arms over her chest, then smiled in spite of herself.

"Partially."

"It simply doesn't matter whether or not he's handsome, I'm still not work—"

Gracious, he was here. And dressed head to toe in black, like a walking sin. His hair, tied back tonight, gave him an almost civilized look. But the sharp slant of his eyebrows over those sensual eyes revealed his secret. She popped open her fan and waved it back and forth a few times. Her cheeks blazed as if on fire. Perhaps she had a fever. Where had that pleasant breeze gone? As if even the trees and wind stilled when he entered the room. What was he doing here?

"Claudia?" Poppy waved a gloved hand in front of her face, which brought her attention back to her friend.

"Yes?"

"Care to share your secret?"

31

"That's Mr. Middleton."

"I suspected as much. I could tell by his devilishly handsome face."

"Stop that."

"You'd better stop waving that fan about—you're beginning to make a spectacle of yourself. What is he doing here?"

"How should I know?" Claudia closed the fan and slipped it back on her wrist. "It matters not to me why he's here. We have no relationship, nothing whatsoever to discuss."

"Then you'd better think of something to discuss, because he's headed in our direction."

He saw her standing across the ballroom, dressed in flamingo pink. She looked more like a frosted cake than a woman. How exactly did he court a woman like her? He'd never courted a lady before, not even his former wife. But tonight he didn't have to think of courting. No, tonight he only needed to convince her to continue to work for him. Tomorrow he could start his courtship.

Damn, there were enough ruffles on that dress to distract a man from noticing her womanly curves. A ruffle gathered the entire neckline that dipped subtly off her shoulders. Clusters of rosebuds bunched on the gathers of her two-layer skirt, but it was the rosebuds pinned at her cleavage that grabbed his attention. It was a bosom that men would write poetry about; not him, though, because he didn't write poetry. But if he *were* that sort of man, her breasts would certainly inspire a sonnet.

He glanced at her face. Her sassy expression did nothing to hide her surprise to find him heading in her direction. She turned to the tall, attractive woman next to her and attempted to say something, but her eyes were drawn back to him. When he finally reached her, she smiled tentatively.

"Miss Prattley, what a pleasure to find you here," he said.

"Thank you, sir. Please meet my dearest friend, Lady Penelope Livingston. But everyone calls her Poppy."

"A pleasure." He nodded over Lady Penelope's hand and then brought Claudia's to his mouth for a kiss. Her eyes grew round and a blush colored prettily in her cheeks. She was not a beautiful woman, not in the classic sense, not like her friend, but something about her drew the eye to her face. It was her smile; honest, real, and full of actual joy—not one of the manufactured smiles that most women wore. She was more cute than pretty, in the way that children or puppies were cute. Only those ruffles hinted at a not-so-childlike body beneath. Cute or no, Claudia Prattley was all woman.

"I thought perhaps we might share a dance this evening. That is, if you still have room on your card."

"Well—"

"Of course she has room left." Poppy nudged her friend in the side.

"Certainly. Where are my manners? I apologize, Mr. Middleton. I do believe I must be coming down with something. I'm simply not thinking clearly. It's been agitating Poppy all evening. Why, I was just saying that—"

Poppy nudged her again.

Claudia smiled sheepishly. "I have a tendency to ramble." She handed him her dance card.

Her first waltz was unclaimed. Perfect. Only one other name appeared on her card—Richard Foxmore—and he was on there no fewer than three times. She certainly kept poor company.

"How do you know Richard Foxmore?" Derrick couldn't help but ask.

"He's courting her," Poppy answered.

Claudia shot her friend a look. He couldn't interpret what it meant, but something about divulging that information made her uncomfortable.

"Indeed?"

"Pardon me?" A portly lady, late in her years, patted him on the arm with her fan. "Are you Mr. Middleton of *London's Illustrated Times*?"

"Yes," he said.

"I thought that might be you! I know this is terribly rude, but I'm an avid reader of your newspaper, and I simply must ask you a question. In last week's issue of the Society Fashion Report, there was a picture of what I'm positive was myself— well, it just had to have been me, I mean the dress was perfect, as was the hair. I simply must know who the illustrator is. I would like to solicit him to do a painting of me for my daughter."

It was then that she noticed Claudia and her friend.

"Goodness me, I nearly didn't see you two. Good evening, Miss Prattley, Lady Penelope."

"Lady Springdale," they said in unison.

"Did you see the illustration?" she asked them. "It was simply marvelous."

"I thought the very same," Poppy said.

Derrick met Claudia's glance, her soulful blue eyes pleading with him not to reveal her. "As it turns out, I cannot release that illustrator's name. My illustrators insist on anonymity, and I must honor their request. But I shall certainly pass on your praise."

"I expected as much." She pursed her lips.

"Those artists are a different sort. In any case, please pass on to him what I said. And if he ever wants to do portraits, I can be most discreet." With that, she turned on her heel and huffed off.

"Discreet?" Poppy snorted.

"Is she not?" Derrick asked.

"She stops short of posting announcements in the *Times*," Claudia said.

"If you will excuse me," Poppy said. "I must go find my mother and check on her. She had the start of one of her headaches this afternoon."

"*That* was a prime example of what I am put through nearly every time I venture into town," Derrick said once they were alone. "Your work is highly praised."

"Thank you for keeping my secret," she said.

"I told you in my office that I would always keep your identity a secret. I don't make statements like that lightly. I believe this next dance is ours."

She looked down at her card. "So it is."

"Shall we?" He held his arm out to her.

She eyed him warily, glancing to her right and then her left. She held out her gloved hand, and he led her to the floor.

The music swelled, and he swept her up into the waltz. Her blond ringlets began well below his chin—so much so that she had to tilt her head to make eye contact. The hint of peppermint tickled his nose, and he resisted the urge to lean closer and smell her hair.

"You must promise me that you'll never tell anyone I beg," he said.

"I'm sorry?" Her brow furrowed in confusion.

"Tonight. You mustn't ever tell anyone that I begged—it would ruin my bad reputation."

"I promise." She smiled up at him, and two dimples pierced her cheeks, causing him to miss a step in their dance. He quickly recovered.

"For what are you begging?" she asked.

"For you."

"Oh." A blush spread across her cheeks and down her creamy throat.

"I'm unfamiliar with it; let us see how I do." He cleared his throat for added drama, which caused her to giggle. "My dear Miss Prattley, I must beg of you to continue your position with my paper. My very life depends on it."

She scrunched her face. "I can tell you're unfamiliar with it."

"Not very good?"

"Terrible. You should say something like, I'm a fine illustrator despite my sex, and your days would be darker without my drawings to look upon. Oh, and then add that no matter what, you'd protect my identity at all costs."

"And if I said all of this, you would agree to continue working for me?"

"Probably not, but it sounds good."

Those dimples again. *Focus, Middleton.* "Would you agree to work for me until I find a replacement for you?"

She turned her head so that it was a little closer to him and whispered, "You shouldn't allow people to think they're replaceable. Makes them feel less than special."

"You're exactly right. You are irreplaceable. I should have instead asked if you would work for me until you marry. I'd like to keep your drawings running as long as possible, since I'll have to discontinue that section when you leave. No one will ever be able to do the job as well as you."

She rewarded him with another smile, but this time he was mindful to keep his footing. There was something about Claudia Prattley. Precisely what, he wasn't sure. But he just might be curious enough to stick around and find out.

Her features straightened into an expression of concern. "Would you promise to continue to protect my identity?"

"You have my word on it. Even if they threaten to have me drawn and quartered, I shall not reveal you."

He thought of the old show of promise he had

done in school—kissing his two fingers, then putting them to his heart. In this situation, it would be more rewarding to kiss Claudia's fingers, but she would surely box his ears.

"I don't believe they still draw and quarter people," she said.

"Is that an agreement?"

She chewed at her lip a moment before nodding.

"I believe I shall give you a raise."

"That won't be necessary."

"Never reject an offer of more money, Miss Prattley. It's bad business."

"Yes, of course."

Their dance ended, and he led her off the dance floor.

"I shall call on you soon to arrange the details of our new agreement."

With another kiss of her hand, Derrick left her to her thoughts while he strolled off to find a drink. A stiff one, preferably. Then he could retreat out of this stuffy ballroom. His presence was beginning to warrant stares.

He couldn't remember the last time he'd danced with a woman, especially in proper Society. Well, other than his aunt, but that hardly counted. An assembly of pretty maidens clumped together whispered and giggled as he passed. He wanted to stop and yell, "Boo!" simply to watch them scatter.

The tongues would be wagging that he'd been here and that he'd danced with Claudia Prattley.

She might be his only dance partner tonight, but Claudia would dance with another. One other. Richard Foxmore. He was here tonight. Somewhere. What was he doing with a woman like Claudia? Didn't he prefer simpleminded girls who allowed him to do as he chose? Although Claudia did seem bound by her sense of duty. Perhaps that was what he sought in her. No, that couldn't be it.

He must be drawn either to her money or to her father. Richard was still climbing the political ropes. Despite being out of the majority and out of the cabinet, Claudia's father must still have some leverage he could offer Richard. She probably had no idea what kind of man Richard was.

If Claudia married him, then that bastard would have played a part in ruining both his father's and his own newspaper. Not that the lack of Claudia's illustrations could actually ruin the paper, but it would decrease sales among the aristocratic families. And he wanted them reading when he introduced the new political segments.

Even as he made the argument to himself, he recognized he wasn't motivated solely by his ambitions for the paper. Certainly he didn't want Claudia to resign. But it was more than that. The thought of innocent and lovely Claudia Prattley at the mercy of Richard Foxmore disgusted him.

Not only should he keep Claudia from marrying Richard so she could continue working for him, he should prevent her from entering into a miserable marriage. He knew about those all too well. Besides, it was the honorable thing to do, since he knew Richard's character. Surely she didn't love the bastard.

From one man's arms to the next—that rarely happened to Claudia in one evening. Richard twirled her around the dance floor, but hadn't said much of anything since the music began.

He didn't seem like himself tonight—usually he spent all their time together talking her ear off about all the latest political news. While she had never been particularly interested in his conversation, she'd always felt flattered that he considered her a companion. Since most men never said more than a word to her, Richard's conversations were his most attractive attribute.

"It's a lovely ball, don't you agree?" she asked.

"Most lovely."

Mr. Middleton was a better dancer, she couldn't help but notice—smoother on his feet, with nice, strong arms to lead her about.

She glanced at Richard's face; pink stained his

cheeks, as if he'd spent the afternoon in too much wind. His pale blue eyes stared above her head, watching something behind her. Mr. Middleton was handsomer than Richard—darker and more masculine in every way. His mere presence demanded and dared you to stare, while Richard blended with the crowd.

He'd asked about Richard; perhaps they knew each other.

"What do you know of Mr. Middleton?"

Richard balked. His eyes met hers for a moment, then once again he looked past her to whatever he stared at behind her. "What I know of Derrick Middleton is not for the ears of a lady. You would be well advised to stay clear of him, Claudia. He is a dangerous man."

Dangerous? He hadn't seemed dangerous. Wild. Exciting. Sensual. Her cheeks warmed, and she knew she blushed. Gracious, she shouldn't think such things. Especially in the arms of the man she was supposed to marry.

"He was very gentlemanly with me," she said quietly.

"Any association with a man like that could ruin your reputation."

Splendid. And she'd danced with him. Perhaps she'd yet again misjudged the situation, as her father always accused her of doing. Richard knew so many people; he no doubt knew the truth. She would have to be very careful. Fulfill her agreement to the paper and then move on.

"I saw you dancing with him," Richard said tightly. "I don't think your father would be pleased."

She thought Richard had been playing billiards at the time. And no doubt he would tell her father. "It would have been rude of me to say no when he asked."

"How did you meet him?"

Think quickly. "Poppy introduced us. He's an acquaintance of her father's." She hated lying, but she couldn't very well tell him the truth.

"I see. Perhaps in the future, Poppy will dance with him instead. I realize that we are not officially engaged, but you know that is my intention. I'm just waiting for the right moment."

She smiled at him. "Yes, Richard, I know. I'm waiting for that moment as well."

"As is your father, I suppose. Has he mentioned it again?"

"Briefly."

"It will happen in good time, my dear. Once we marry, you can get out of this damp city and live in Westfield Hall and paint all the watercolors you want. Won't that be nice?"

"Well, yes. But I don't want to live in the country

the entire year. I enjoy London. Father and I have lived here since Mother died. It's my home."

"You've just forgotten how wonderful country life can be. The air is much cleaner, and I will feel safer if you are there. I worry about you running about the streets like a common person. You don't consider the dangers, and you trust people that you shouldn't trust."

How many times had she heard this speech? That he worried endeared him to her, but, honestly, she could take care of herself. It was not as if she wandered the East End alone. "I suppose we can discuss that more once we're married."

"I'm sure your father will agree with me. I believe he would like to see you settled and safe in the country."

And that epitomized the very thing she liked the least about Richard. He cared too much for what her father thought. She'd spent her entire life fretting about her father's perception of her and fantasizing about marrying a man who would free her from that.

Richard would never be that man. But he was all life had offered her. Women like her didn't get to pick any man they wanted. They married the first man who asked, because chances were he'd be the only one to do so.

If her father got the deciding vote about where

she would have to spend her remaining days, he would most definitely put her in the country. After all, how much trouble could she get into out there? She wouldn't be close enough to embarrass him in front of his friends in Parliament. Marrying Richard would ensure she had to quit her job at the paper.

Richard was a kind man, and he wanted her for his wife, but it wasn't the life full of love she'd dreamed of. It was the life she would learn to love.

Chapter 3

Claudia peeked out from her bedcovers. Never had she lain in bed all morning, but today she was desperate. "Is he still looking for me, Baubie?" She eyed her maid, who stood across the room hanging up dresses.

"Not at the moment, but he'll be looking for you again directly. You cannot hide from him all day."

"I know." She flipped to lie on her stomach with her head propped at the foot of the bed. "But he's going to want to discuss all the details of last night's ball, and I'm not sure I want him to know all the details."

Baubie's eyebrows shot up, and she leaned against the armoire. "Do you have a secret, dearie?"

Not precisely a secret, but right then it certainly felt like one. Like when she was a child and her mother would buy her a trinket, and together they would hide it from her father so he would not get angry. It had been their little secret.

But this was different. This was not an issue, not anything that should even occupy a thought. Yet the dance with Derrick Middleton had consumed her thoughts since she had left his arms. She caught herself before she sighed.

Baubie cleared her throat.

"It's nothing. Really." She tugged at an errant thread on the quilt. "I danced with a gentleman last night, and I'm not certain that Father would approve of him. I *know* Father wouldn't approve of him. He despises him, in fact. Thinks he's the worst sort of man."

Her maid crossed her arms over her abundant bosom. "How daring of you," Baubie said. Then concern crossed her face, and she took a step forward. "Is he the worst sort of man? You don't want to go and get yourself into trouble."

"He was very gentlemanly with me, and Poppy as well. Polite and not at all discourteous."

"He doesn't sound too bad then. Was he handsome?" Baubie asked in a casual tone.

Claudia rolled over onto her back. "He's undeniably the most handsome man in London." She tilted her head and met Baubie's gaze. "I'm relatively certain every woman at the ball would have agreed with me."

Baubie's smile widened. "Is that so?"

"Before you fancy something more, it was not a regular dance. We danced only to discuss something important." She sat up, moving into a crosslegged position. "Business, nothing personal."

"I just asked a question, dearie."

"It was a dance, nothing more. Still, Father would not be pleased, and I'd rather not have that conversation with him. But he will ask as he always does after I've attended a party. He'll want to know who attended and what was said." She frowned. "I don't even think he's interested in what I say, as he always probes for more, then decides to ask someone else. But he'll inquire about the evening nonetheless."

"Well, I told him earlier that you were still asleep." Baubie busied herself with the clothes again. "He said you, like all women, were content to laze about their beds all day."

Claudia snorted. "Wouldn't he be surprised to know that I wake before he does practically every morning? Of course, if he did know that, I would have to eat breakfast with him, and I'm not positive I'm prepared to do that." Guilt gnawed at her stomach. She shouldn't say such things about her father. He had raised her on his own after her mother died. And while he might not be overt with his affection, surely he loved her. He was her father.

Claudia shook her head. "Listen to me. I don't mean to go on and on about him; you know he's not a dreadful man. He's simply strict, and he wants me to honor our family name. I just tire of hearing how I never manage to do that."

"Listen here, dearie," Baubie pointed a knobby finger at her mistress. "Never you mind about what you say about your father in front of me. I saw how that man treated your lovely mother, and how he treats you is no different. There is nothing dishonorable about you. He's the dishonorable one, and if it weren't for the fact that he pays my wages, I'd tell him that myself."

Claudia smiled. "No you wouldn't. You're too kind. But I appreciate the gesture."

Baubie hung all her dresses according to their color. It was the first time Claudia had noticed how many pink dresses she owned. Various shades of pink—coral, orchid, rose, blush—too much pink. She frowned; she wasn't even sure she liked that color. If only she could wear something bold like red or a deep violet.

"What are you going to tell him? About last night, I mean."

"I don't know. I'd rather not lie to him. Perhaps I'll simply withhold some of the details. That's not the same thing as lying. Is it?"

"Not in my eyes. I think you do what you have to do to make yourself happy. That's what your mother would have wanted for you." Baubie brought her hand to her breast. "Bless her soul, that woman adored you. It was as if she didn't start breathing until the day you were born. You made all the darkness in her life brighter." She leaned in and kissed Claudia's forehead, then held her face. "You look just like her, you know. Simply beautiful."

Claudia's eyes misted, and she hugged her maid. Baubie had been the only mother she'd had for so many years.

"I had better get back to work. I can tell your father that you're not feeling well if he asks about you again."

"Don't bother. I'll have to talk to him eventually."

Once Baubie had left, Claudia retrieved the drawing she'd been working on earlier that morning. Derrick Middleton's handsome features stared up at her. She'd not intended to include him in the drawing and wouldn't send this one in, but when she set pencil to paper, he'd been the first image she'd created. Thank goodness, she'd only sketched on paper and hadn't started on the wood.

There was something not quite right in the likeness. It looked like him, but something was missing. Perhaps she'd gotten a feature wrong. His eyes, she realized. On paper, they didn't burn with sensuality and intensity. But how did one capture the subtle change in the shade of brown? Or the way his right eyebrow lifted in silent question?

She laid the drawing aside to begin another. One without Mr. Middleton. He probably wouldn't want himself featured in his own newspaper. And if she presented him with an illustration of himself, he would no doubt think she was smitten, which, of course, she was not.

Putting pencil to paper, she began another drawing. This time, a couple dancing. Amid faceless other dancers, the primary couple took shape. Sharper and sharper their features became, until . . . Mr. Middleton and herself.

She sucked in her breath. She'd never before drawn herself. And there it was, plain as the image on the parchment; while dancing with Mr. Middleton had made her feel pretty, the truth could not lie. No woman who looked as she did would ever catch a man like Derrick Middleton.

She paused over the picture, considering the

number of thoughts Mr. Middleton had consumed since she'd first encountered him. Gracious, some might think her a harlot.

She needed fresh air—time to clear her thoughts and then return to her drawings. Perhaps she should work on her watercolor in the garden. It was a lovely day.

Claudia donned a simple gown of the palest of lavenders, but opted to leave her bonnet inside. Feeling the sunshine on her face would be nice— and she would only do so for a little while, so as to not burn her skin. She'd been hiding inside her bedroom for hours. If her father remained in his office, she could easily sneak out into the garden without his seeing her.

She opened her bedroom door and peeked into the hall, listening for any sounds. All was quiet. Tiptoeing down the stairs, she caught sight of Baubie and waved. Opening the garden doors, she stepped out into the crisp air and took a deep breath.

Her mother had loved the garden. The garden at their country estate had been the most beautiful one in all of Avon. Flowers of every shape and color had surrounded the grounds, and she'd never been able to walk into it without smiling. She didn't even want to think about what that garden must look like today. After her mother's death, they'd moved here and hadn't been back to the country since.

She sat on a bench and looked at the tiny enclosed space. A lovely garden, but so very small. Her mother would have hated it here in London—that was an area in which they differed. Claudia loved it here. Loved the bustle and the streets full of people.

Closing her eyes, she tilted her face up and reveled in the warmth of the sun bathing her skin. The breeze fluttered through the plants around her, while a pair of pipits chirped above her head.

She stood and set up her easel, then went to work on the painting of fruit. As she shaded the cluster of grapes, her mind wandered to a now familiar face. Derrick Middleton. Just the mere thought of him quickened her heart and shortened her breath.

Last night the most amazing thing had happened while she was dancing with the handsome devil. She'd felt almost pretty. Beautiful, if she was completely honest—the way Cinderella must have felt after a visit from her fairy godmother.

But she had no fairy godmother, and Derrick was no prince.

And it didn't matter how she'd felt in his arms.

"Honestly, Claudia," she said aloud to chastise herself. *Forget about him.*

She needed to cease her daydreaming of Derrick Middleton. It was a tiny fancy, that was all—merely because he was so very handsome. And he'd almost flirted with her. It was for that reason and that reason alone that she was attracted to him.

Richard was whom she would marry. Shouldn't he be the man occupying her thoughts? Richard was steadfast and kind. Derrick, on the other hand, embodied a wilder and more impulsive nature. While that sounded vastly more interesting than a life in the country painting fruit bowls, she would marry Richard because her father had asked her to. Demanded was more the word, but that sounded so harsh.

Derrick would fade from her mind once she married Richard. Years from now, she'd remember the night she'd danced with the handsomest man in London.

"Claudia, I thought I'd find you out here." Her father approached her with his I'm-more-important-than-everyone attitude cloaking him like a king's coronation robe. He did not look pleased.

"Yes, well, I came out to get some air and a little sunshine. It's a beautiful day, don't you agree, Father?"

He glanced up at the sky and shrugged. "Looks

like all the others." He sat on the stone bench. "Come and sit and tell me about the Draper ball last night." The multicolored flowers behind him gave the air around him a deceptively calm look. Everything looked better in the garden, she supposed.

She set her paintbrush down and joined him. "It was a lovely evening. I danced with Richard three times. Poppy and I played piquet with Lady Forrester and Lady Primrose. We left early because Poppy's mother was feeling ill."

"How is Richard?"

"He's fine. He mentioned that he would probably be by to see you today. Something about a discussion he had with Lord Dryer."

"I'm going to the club. I'll send him a note, and he can meet me there. What are your plans today?"

"I'm going to stay home. Perhaps paint here in the garden. It's so beautiful today."

"Yes, beautiful," he said absently. "Just be sure you stay out of trouble. I don't like all the time you spend with that Poppy. She puts wrong ideas in your head."

"Poppy is a wonderful friend. She's from a good family. Even you can't deny that."

He snorted. "The Livingston name was tarnished when that brother of hers lost all their money. And the whole lot of them are too liberal.

This country will be destroyed with all that reform."

He puffed out a breath and stood. "I'll see you for supper." He turned to go, then stopped. "I nearly forgot. I received a bill for pencils from some shop on Bond Street. Do you know anything about that?"

She had wondered what had happened with that bill. Next time, she would just pay instead of trying to set up an account. "Yes, Father, I ordered those. I tried to pay for them myself; they must have set up the account incorrectly. You can take the money out of my allowance."

"I'm not worried about the money. What concerns me is your need for pencils. As I recall, I've instructed you on more than one occasion that you are not to be drawing. I'm assuming that this will be our last conversation about it. Unless you're ready to relocate out of London."

"No, sir."

"You paint, that is all, Claudia. Do you understand me? There is no place for a woman in the art world—it is dirty and dangerous and full of . . . Frenchmen. Watercolors is the only acceptable art for ladies of good breeding. I will not have my daughter fancying herself an artist." He straightened his coat. "Remember: everything you do reflects on me. We will not discuss this again. Is that understood?"

She nodded, and he turned and left her alone in the garden.

The butler looked surprised to see him. The skin on the servant's too tall, too thin frame stretched taut, barely covering his old bones. "May I help you?" he asked in a severe tone.

"I'm here to call on Miss Prattley. Is she available?"

"May I have your card, please, sir?"

Derrick handed him his card, and the butler eyed it cautiously, then turned on his heel. "Please wait here," he said as he retreated down the hall.

Derrick did not have a long wait before the butler reappeared.

"She's out in the garden, Mr. Middleton. This way, please."

Derrick followed the hollow-looking man down a long hallway, around a corner, and then out double doors into the small garden.

"Miss Prattley, a Mr. Middleton to see you."

She stood at an easel, paintbrush in hand, her eyes wide. "Mr. Middleton."

Derrick nodded at the butler.

"Jacobs, has my father left for his club?" she asked.

"Yes, madam."

Her shoulders relaxed. "You may leave us."

Jacobs stood for a moment as if unsure if he actually could leave them, then he nodded and returned inside.

Today she wore no hat, so her honey-blond curls glistened in the sunlight. With her eyes wide and her smile bright, she looked surprised to see him. Pleasantly so. He took a step forward.

"What are you doing here?" she asked.

"I came to see you."

"I apologize, that must have sounded rude. It's a surprise to see you." Her brow furrowed. "Is there a change in the assignment?"

"No."

Her simple lilac gown was devoid of any ruffles, bows, or other ornamentation. The clean lines of the bodice cupped her breasts, then hugged the rest of her torso, hinting at a narrow waist and nice round hips.

As if she could read his thoughts, her hand moved to her abdomen. Her head tilted to the right, and her features scrunched. "Then why are you here?"

"I already answered that."

She chewed her lip and thought for a moment. "To see me?" She smiled.

"Yes."

"I wasn't expecting guests." She motioned to her gown. "Or I would have dressed more appropriately."

"I see nothing inappropriate about your clothes, but I do apologize for interrupting. I could come back."

"No. Now is fine."

"What are you working on?" He came to stand behind her at the easel to view her painting up close. It was a typical watercolor, the kind of painting appropriate for a young woman. The tingle of peppermint teased his nose—he had noticed it when they danced, but wasn't sure it was she. He leaned in slightly and sniffed her hair. How fitting—subtle yet refreshing and energetic all at the same time.

"A watercolor. I'm working on shadows." She took a step back and stepped right on his boot.

"Gracious. Did I hurt you?" She looked truly concerned.

He had to laugh. "No, you didn't hurt me. You paint well, but your drawings are much better." He took her hand—it was warm within his, her small round fingers tipped with short-cropped nails.

She gazed up at him with her huge blue eyes, and he nearly forgot everything. Why he was here. Why he needed to court her. Everything but how deep and blue her eyes were and how he wanted to get lost in them and see what else Claudia Prattley could make him forget.

He led her to the garden bench, and once they were seated, she pulled her hand away and set it in her lap. Her movement broke the spell—it was a damned good thing. He didn't need to be getting lost in anyone's eyes. He'd done that once before and been played the fool. He wouldn't be that careless again.

Courting Claudia was a business move and nothing more. It didn't matter how blue her eyes were or how kissable those lips of hers looked.

He needed to focus on the task at hand. "Do you have any illustrations you can show me?"

She looked down at her feet as if inspecting the ground for something. "I've sketched a few ideas but haven't started on the wood."

"May I see them? The sketches?"

"No. They're not ready yet."

"Do you always start with paper?"

"Yes, I often need to draw a few ideas before I'm sure of which one is the best. So I use the paper to work until I feel I have the right image. Then I work on the wood for the final drawing."

Her mouth was fascinating as she talked. Her perfect, pink lips wrapped around each syllable in a caress. Damnation. He sounded like a fool.

"I've never seen one of my illustrator's preliminary works. Let me take a peek. I will not pass judgment."

She chewed at her lip. Such full lips, it was a shame only she nibbled at them.

"I'd rather not. I should have the finished product soon, and I can send that to you."

"I shall have to wait, then." This was going dreadfully. How could he save matters? "I intend to court you." *Charming*. He had to force himself not to wince. He certainly wouldn't knock her off her feet with that kind of clumsiness.

"I beg your pardon?"

Damnation, he'd never courted a proper lady before. He'd never courted any kind of lady before. He and Julia hadn't even had an official courtship, just a few tumbles, a sudden pregnancy, and a hasty marriage. Ever since then, his relations with women had been confined to the bedroom—simple, no complications, no emotions, just touching. So why was he so bloody nervous now?

Uncharted territory, that was all. Nothing about Miss Prattley should make him feel insecure in his intentions. If Richard was her only suitor, then she didn't have much to compare him to, so he needn't worry. And surely he could do better than Richard. *Be courteous and romantic*. That's how men courted proper ladies.

"I do apologize for the abruptness of that. I meant to say it much more . . . that is to say, I only wanted you to know that I came today to notify you of my intentions. I would like to court you, Claudia."

She gawked at him as if he'd sprouted a second head. She opened her mouth to say something, then promptly shook her head and closed her mouth.

"Do you not have anything to say?" he asked.

"I'm not certain what to say." She frowned, then the lines in her forehead smoothed and she gave him a little smile—two dimples pierced her cheeks. It was a most becoming smile. Genuine. She really was quite fetching.

"That is quite amusing, Mr. Middleton, but I should think you had better use of your time than teasing a girl like me."

"I don't follow."

"Well, since you cannot be serious, it must mean that you are playing a joke on me, and while I'm sure you find it vastly entertaining, I do not share your humor in the situation." She tilted her chin up ever so slightly. "Were I not the kind of woman I am, I might have my feelings hurt by your mockery."

Damn. He hated to lie, but he had no choice. He needed her. For his paper. "I assure you I am not mocking you. I came here to express my honest intentions of courting you. You mentioned a need to marry, and I find you utterly charming." Well, at least that wasn't a lie—she was charming. "I thought if you would have me, I would like to throw my hat, as it were, into the pile and try to win your hand."

She released a giggle. The throaty sound played havoc on his nerves. "Into the pile?" she asked.

"Correct."

"I don't believe there is an actual pile, sir."

"Richard Foxmore is courting you, is he not?"

She nodded curtly. "He is."

"And are you engaged?"

"Not officially."

"Has he ever proposed marriage?"

She smoothed her hands across her skirt. "No, he has not. But I believe he and my father have discussed it."

Richard was a spineless bastard. He no doubt was dragging his feet, waiting for a better offer elsewhere. All the while, he strung Claudia along. "If he has not proposed to you, then he lays no claim on you. I am free to court you. Isn't that correct?"

"I suppose that if a girl is not engaged and is not necessarily in love with one suitor, then she is in a position to accept other suitors."

Interesting. "So you admit that you do not love Richard?"

She visibly bristled. "I did not say that. I was speaking hypothetically. Whether or not I love Richard is, frankly, none of your concern."

A sharp tongue too. She became more fascinating by the moment. A breeze fluttered a stray curl to rest on her cheek. He fought the urge to reach up and tuck it behind her ear.

"Why is it so hard to believe that I would court you when you have one suitor already?"

Her eyes narrowed, and tiny lines fanned out in the corners. "You and Richard are . . . different."

"Aside from our birth positions, how exactly are we different? We are both men who obviously share similar taste in beautiful women."

She stiffened. "Do not mock me, sir." Her words came out slow and tight.

He'd hit upon a sore spot. She wasn't beautiful in the fashionable sense—she was shorter and fleshier than most women, but she had a beauty all her own. Her blond curls whispered for a touch, and her perfect mouth begged for a kiss. And her breasts—he didn't even want to think about what her breasts needed.

What he had to do was convince her she was desirable. Considering his half-aroused state, that shouldn't be too difficult.

"I was not trying to mock you." He let his words settle a bit before he continued. "So tell me, what is it that Richard does to woo you? How has he won your heart?"

She frowned. "You'd like to know what, precisely?"

"What does Richard do—how does he court you?"

She opened her mouth, then shut it.

"Let me take a guess. I would wager he recites poetry."

Her head snapped up.

That was so like Richard Foxmore. To ensnare people with words. Not his own, he would guess.

"So he probably quotes poems that mention that your hair is the color of sunlight on a warm day. And that your skin resembles the smoothest of creams. Or perhaps he declares your eyes to be the color of the bluebells growing on the hillside." Those bluebell eyes widened, but she never looked away. "Your mouth, oh, your sweet mouth—he would say it was shaped like the most perfect of rosebuds." Her teeth worried her bottom lip. "Am I getting warmer?"

"He's said some things like that. Only I don't believe I've heard those particular phrases." Her brow furrowed. "Who wrote them?"

He leaned in closer to her. "No one. I just said them."

"I see," she said in a near whisper.

"I cannot court you like that, Miss Prattley. I hope you don't mind. But when I look at your hair, I don't think of sunshine."

Her frown deepened. "You don't?"

"No. I think of thick, rich honey that I want to pour onto my tongue."

"*Oh.*"

"And when I see your skin, I don't think of cream."

"No?"

"No. I think of the finest of satins that I want to glide my fingers across."

"Oh my."

"Your eyes."

"My eyes?"

"Yes, your eyes, I don't think of bluebells. I think of the bluest of water and the way it's slippery against my skin when I dive beneath the surface."

She licked her lips and nodded slightly.

"And your mouth. I don't think of rosebuds or any other flowers when I look at your mouth."

"You don't?"

"No. The only thought I have when I look at your mouth is of warm, slow kisses that last all afternoon."

"Oh my goodness." She leaned in a little closer, and it was all the encouragement he needed.

With one arm, he pulled her closer, then dropped his mouth to hers. It was a kiss meant to prove that he was serious about courting her. A kiss meant to show her she was desirable. But the instant his lips touched hers, he forgot all about his intentions.

Her lips were soft and pliant beneath his. With only a tiny amount of coaxing, he was able to open her mouth and explore inside. Her warm breath mingled with his. When he swept his tongue in her mouth, she stiffened slightly, but then released a throaty moan that sent blood rushing to his groin.

He knew he should stop the kiss and get the hell out of here. But she felt so good. Tasted so sweet. He deepened the kiss and felt her fingers lace through his hair. Her tongue tentatively moved against his. Her lack of experience was evident, but her clumsiness only fueled his arousal. Damn, but he wanted her. Right here, right now on this bench in her father's garden.

He fought the urge to groan and forced himself to end the kiss.

Her eyes remained closed, and her breath came in shallow puffs. Finally she opened her eyes and smiled at him.

"I don't believe you have a future as a poet, sir."

Was she serious? That was her response? While his pants pulled tight across his erection, she thought of poetry. "I should think my poetic words the last thing on your mind."

"Yes, well, I merely thought that likening my eyes to bluebells is frankly not that clever. I believe I've read that in many a poem."

The kiss, meant only to make an impression on her, had missed its mark and instead made a big impression on him. Devil take it! He needed to get out of here.

He pulled out his pocket watch and glanced at the time. "Claudia, it has been a pleasure seeing you today, but I'm afraid I'm late for an appointment. I do hope you'll allow me to call on you again sometime."

She only nodded, then stood and went to her painting.

He watched her back for a few seconds, then turned to leave.

Damnation! He hadn't come to her house intending to kiss her or he sure as hell would have ... Would have what? Prepared himself? Never would he have thought he'd have to prepare himself for kissing Claudia Prattley.

Yet kissing her had proven a serious temptation and had done things to his body that a mere kiss hadn't evoked in years. Perhaps since he was a young man in school. And she hadn't been affected at all. Which made no sense. His kisses generally had even the most tarnished of women swaying in his arms. But not Miss Prattley. No, she merely blinked at him, then dismissed him as if he'd done nothing more than shine her shoes.

Derrick mounted the carriage steps, then sat with a huff. More than bloody likely, he'd just been caught off guard. Or, rather, he'd spent too much time staring at her bosom and he'd been aroused before the kiss. None of it made sense.

But she wouldn't get off this easy. No. Now it was war, so to speak. He would do whatever it took to make Miss Prattley weak in the knees. She would swoon over him before this was done. After all, if he was courting her, he might as well teach her the way a real man acts. Poetry! Imagine spending all his time with a willing, desirable woman and doing nothing more than spouting poetry. Richard was a buffoon.

* * *

Oh my goodness.

Claudia sank back on the stone bench and brought her hands to her cheeks. Her face felt warm, indicating she blushed, just as she suspected. She'd never before kissed a man, and still she knew *that* had to be the kiss to end all kisses. Her entire body felt jiggly, as if someone had taken her apart and put her back together wrong.

She trailed her right index finger along her lips. They were slightly swollen. She didn't feel like herself. She'd never been the girl that men stole kisses from in the garden. Especially not men like Derrick Middleton. He was as handsome as she was plain. It just didn't fit.

Courting her. Indeed. He was funning with her. And she didn't find it the least bit amusing. Her stomach clenched. What could possibly motivate a man to toy with a woman's emotions like that? Surely he wasn't heartless. He seemed the very image of a gentleman.

Well, perhaps not a gentleman in the strictest of terms, but he was kind and well-mannered even if he did steal kisses from unsuspecting women in their gardens. There had been nothing gentlemanly or well-mannered about that kiss.

Or about her response. Heavens.

He had certainly left rather suddenly. As if

something in the kiss had reminded him of something. More than likely, she'd done something dreadfully wrong, and he'd immediately come to his senses. Men like him could have any woman of their choosing. And they rarely dallied with innocent women like her.

In fact, no man had ever ventured a dalliance with her of any kind. She knew it was because of the way she looked. She was plump, and men didn't like plump women. It wasn't as if she'd asked any of them, but it was quite evident. She could count on her hands how many times men had asked her to dance.

But she made the most of her situation. She didn't need a line of men asking her to dance. She'd found her future husband; she was simply waiting for him to propose.

Her mind wandered back to Derrick's kiss. Tingles spread through her body. Gracious. And the simple way he said her name—it seemed to roll off his tongue as if he'd been saying it forever. Her name had never sounded as good as it did in the deep timbre of his voice.

Precisely what was she to do with another suitor? A charade of one or not, Richard was bound to notice sooner or later.

She had one suitor who said he intended to propose, who had never so much as let his mouth linger on her hand. And another suitor who wasn't really a suitor at all, who'd just this afternoon done amazing things with his tongue in her mouth.

What was she supposed to do now?

Chapter 4

⁓◦◯◦⁓

"Poppy, have any of your suitors ever kissed you?"

Poppy looked up from the chessboard and eyed Claudia suspiciously. "On occasion, I suppose a few have stolen tiny kisses behind a plant or on a darkened balcony."

"Real kisses?" Claudia ventured.

"What do you mean, real kisses? They kissed me. That's real, isn't it?"

"Absolutely," Claudia said, with more enthusiasm than she'd intended. "Yes, those are real."

"No, that's not what you meant." Poppy's eyes

narrowed, and she pointed her pawn at Claudia. "What are you hiding?"

Claudia shrugged, trying to look nonchalant. "Well, I . . . I overheard some girls talking, and they were most explicit about the way one of them had been kissed." She scooted her chair closer and leaned forward. "She said that the man put his tongue in her mouth." She sat up quickly. "Can you imagine?"

"I've heard of such kissing. But I've never experienced it."

It was scandalous even to discuss such a thing in the Livingstons' front parlor. She should be ashamed of herself. But curiosity had gotten the better of her, and she'd simply had to ask Poppy. Poppy had so many suitors, but of course she had never been kissed in such a way. She wasn't a tart, as some people clearly were.

Claudia squirmed in her chair and tried to focus on her play. "I'm certain it's not the thing decent people do," she added.

"I don't believe kissing has anything to do with decent or not-so-decent people. Why the sudden interest in kissing?"

"I was merely curious. That's all. It's your move."

Poppy moved her knight, then her head snapped up. "Did Richard kiss you?"

74

"No! Of course not. He's never."

"Never?"

"No."

"Not even on the cheek?"

"No. Is that not normal?"

"I don't know, Claude. I don't think so. Perhaps Richard is afraid of what your father would say."

"You're probably right." But she wasn't so positive. A sickening feeling lay in her stomach like day-old bread. "It's not me, is it?"

Poppy shook her head. "Absolutely not. Not possible. Perhaps he's waiting until you're officially engaged."

Claudia sipped her tea, but the lukewarm liquid did nothing to soothe her anxiety.

"You could ask him," Poppy offered.

"Ask him what?"

"Why he hasn't kissed you."

"Are you mad? I could never do that."

"Well, then you could kiss him."

"Gracious, no."

Poppy shrugged.

"Have you ever kissed a man?" Claudia asked.

"Once. I was fourteen, I think, or was it sixteen? Jared Hendricks. We were staying in the country, and he came to visit his grandparents who lived nearby. He spent the entire summer chasing me, and one day I let him catch me, and then I kissed him. Just to see what it was like."

"And?"

"It wasn't that memorable." Her nose wrinkled. "I recall he smelled funny."

Derrick hadn't smelled funny at all. He'd smelled rather delicious, if she remembered correctly, like sandalwood and mint. But it did not matter what he smelled like. Richard was her beau.

"Suppose I want Richard to kiss me. Short of having him chase me around the garden, do you have any suggestions?"

"My mother always told me that you know if a man wants to kiss you because he looks at your mouth. Does he ever do that?"

"Your mother told you that?"

"She wanted me to be prepared."

Claudia couldn't recollect Richard ever looking at her mouth. But Derrick certainly had. She'd never been so aware of her own mouth as she had been in the presence of Derrick Middleton. If Poppy had only told her this piece of information yesterday, she could have been more prepared for today's kiss. She could still feel his lips on hers. And the thought of running her fingers through his hair—he must think her a complete harlot. That was probably why he left in such a rush.

"Claudia?"

"What?"

"Does Richard ever look at your mouth?"

"I don't think so."

"Hmmm . . . well, that's at least somewhere to start. From now on you'll know that if he looks at your mouth, he wants to kiss you."

"That's only helpful if he wants to kiss me. How do I get him to want to kiss me?"

"Be more friendly with him, not so formal. Touch his arm when you talk to him. Lick your lips. Make sure you look in his eyes when you're talking."

"How do you know all of this?"

"I read a book on it once. And my mother. She's been tutoring me in the ways of catching a husband since I could talk."

"I think the first thing I must do is figure out a way to get him alone. That shouldn't be too much of a problem. I'll simply select a time when Father is out of the house and invite Richard over to sit in the garden. No. That's no good. I'll invite him over for tea."

"What's wrong with the garden?"

That was where Derrick had kissed her. "Richard prefers the indoors."

"How positively shocking. Are you certain you want to marry him?"

"We've been over this. It doesn't matter much if I want to marry him." She took a deep breath. It didn't matter, but it should. She should want to marry Richard. Her father wanted her to, and she should be loyal to that. She met Poppy's gaze, then said, "Yes, if Richard wants to marry me, then I want to marry him."

"All right. So you invite him over for tea. And then what will you do?"

"I'm not certain. I suppose we will have a talk. Richard likes to discuss the latest with Parliament. I'll listen attentively and wait for my opportunity. And then I'll ask him to kiss me."

"You can't do that."

"Oh." She couldn't? "Why is that?"

"Because—"

"It isn't proper," Claudia said, interrupting her friend before Poppy made her look a complete fool. "What was I thinking?"

"No, that's not what I was going to say. I was merely thinking that if you're bold enough to ask a man to kiss you, then you're bold enough to simply kiss him," Poppy said.

"Simply kiss him," she repeated. "I'm not positive I'm bold enough to do either." She straightened in her seat. If she could kiss a relative stranger like Derrick, then she could certainly muster enough nerve to kiss her beau. "But it's time I became that way. I'm going to be Richard's wife. I should be able to have a kiss when I desire one."

"Absolutely. Although, and I know you don't want to hear this, but if you're going to be bold and steal a kiss, I would think Mr. Middleton would be a better candidate."

Claudia all but dropped her teacup. "Why?" She practically shrieked the word. She needed to have better control of her emotions before Poppy discovered the truth. "I mean, I can't imagine why I would be kissing Mr. Middleton. I scarcely know him."

Poppy shrugged. "True, but he's so dashing and seems the kind of man that would heartily appreciate a woman bold enough to kiss a man. And he seems to like you."

She should keep that thought in mind. For what? So she could kiss him the next time they were alone? There wouldn't be a next time.

"That's ridiculous. We have a business agreement, nothing more."

From now on she had to keep a professional distance from Mr. Middleton. Lest her father and Richard find out he'd been "courting" her. She almost chuckled out loud. Courting.

Where was he? It wasn't like Richard to be late. Not even to the theater.

Claudia scanned the theater lobby again and still found no sign of him. She stood with Poppy, although Poppy was surrounded by young gentlemen all eagerly awaiting a smile or something. Poppy was as friendly to each of them as she was to every person.

Poppy was gloriously beautiful, and men always took a second look. Claudia, on the other hand, was not unattractive; she was what men often referred to as charming. But charming didn't keep a man by your side. Charming didn't give you more than one man to choose from. Two if you were lucky. Or extremely wealthy. Both things Claudia had never been. She had a dowry—a nice one, but certainly not enough to warrant a line of suitors.

Claudia sighed. What would it feel like, even for a moment, to have men fall all over themselves to get your attention? She shook her head. It was a silly thought and deserved no more attention. She wasn't that kind of woman, and she never would be.

Poppy said something, and her entourage guffawed. Claudia tried not to roll her eyes. She pitied her friend. So beautiful, but since she had no dowry, not one of those men would ask for her hand. Claudia wasn't certain which of the two of them was in the worse situation.

She glanced around the room again, searching for a sign of Richard, and instead found someone staring at her. That never happened. But there he was, Mr. Middleton, standing across the room, simply watching her. He held his glass up in a silent toast and smiled in a manner that made her shiver all the way up her back. A smile for only her.

He made his way to her, and before she could protest, brought her hand to his lips. She felt his soft breath caress her through her gloves. Trapped in his gaze, she almost forgot where she was. Almost.

"I hoped I'd see you here tonight. You look lovely, Miss Prattley, as always."

She nearly snorted. Lovely. He certainly was giving this courting thing all he could. But she was too clever to fall under his spell. He might be sinfully attractive, and perhaps he had given her a knee-weakening kiss, but that did not mean he was seriously in pursuit of her hand.

With that in mind, she pulled said hand away. "It's certainly a surprise to see you." She tried to sound cool, disinterested, but doubted she was convincing, as he didn't turn to leave.

"Come riding with me tomorrow," he said.

It didn't sound like a request. Her heart quickened. Regardless of how utterly thrilling it was that he wanted to spend more time with her, had sought her out this very evening, she could not encourage his charade. "I cannot."

"Oh, but you must. I have a gentle mount just perfect for a lady such as yourself."

"That's very kind, but I really mustn't."

"You mustn't. That doesn't sound the same as you'd rather not. I'd hate to think my company is that unpleasant."

"Oh no, it's not that at all. Your company is quite pleasant." She shouldn't have said it, but it would have been rude to allow him to believe otherwise.

He was silent for a moment. His gaze wandered to Poppy and her group, and he studied them for a while before he spoke again. "Tell me about all of those men around your friend. Is she some sort of enchantress who has bewitched them?"

"Her beauty bewitches all men. Frankly, I'm surprised you're here talking to me instead of over there with her."

"There's no one else I'd rather be talking with. I'm positive Lady Penelope is a most entertaining converser, but to warrant a crowd of five men? I'm not so certain."

"Look at her."

She watched him glance over at Poppy. His eyes roamed the length of her. Claudia's breath caught in her chest while she waited for his reaction.

She'd seen it in men time and again. This was where he'd see how foolish it was to stand here talking with her, and he'd walk away. But to her surprise he shrugged and turned back to her.

"She's very pretty," he simply said.

"The most beautiful woman in all of England."

"That's a heavy statement. And I'd disagree. I think there are prettier women and some equally pretty." He met her gaze. "A woman's beauty does not lie only in her face. You have to look at the entire body. The graceful curve of the neck." His eyes moved down her neck, and his words burned like fingertips. "The delicate skin of the wrist, the way her body moves when she walks. All of those factor into whether or not a woman is beautiful."

She didn't know how to respond to such a comment. She could scarcely catch her breath. Did he think her beautiful? How foolish. No man thought her beautiful. Even Richard with all his poetic words of love had never uttered anything that so much as suggested she was beautiful.

So rather than face the awkward, she changed the subject.

"Do you enjoy the theater, Mr. Middleton?"

She thought she heard him chuckle, but his expression never changed. "Most of the time. I admit I do not attend that often. I see now that that is

a mistake. I suppose had I been attending more often, I might have met you sooner."

"You flatter me, Mr. Middleton, but surely you
came this evening with a party. Perhaps a paramour?"

"I came this evening because I had a feeling you
might be here, and I wanted to ask you to ride
with me tomorrow. You have not given me the answer I came for. And I must point out that I would
not be courting you if I had a paramour. Obviously
you think me an utter cad."

"I did not mean to offend you. I simply cannot
believe—"

"That I'm truly courting you. Tell me, Miss
Prattley, do you ride?" he asked.

"Horses?"

"Yes."

"It's been a while, but yes."

"Then come riding with me tomorrow and I
shall prove that I am indeed courting you."

With the last of that simple phrase, the hairs at
the back of her neck prickled. How she wished she
could say yes, but she could not encourage a relationship with this man. Her father would be furious. Richard himself had said that Mr. Middleton
was the wrong sort of gentleman—honestly, not a
gentleman at all, he'd said—for her to befriend.

"I can assure you, Miss Prattley, I'm not a man

who settles for less than what he desires. And I desire you . . ."

Then he paused as if that was the end of his statement, as if he simply meant to say he desired her.

". . . to go riding with me."

That was the rest of his statement. He didn't desire her. He was toying with her.

And then she saw him, the pale blond–haired man who strolled into the lobby. Richard. If he saw her with Derrick, he would certainly tell her father.

"I really should get to my seat. I believe the show is going to start directly."

He held his arm out to her. "I'll escort you."

"No!" She practically shrieked the word. "I can manage on my own, thank you."

Then he followed her gaze and gave a little nod. "I see that Lord Foxmore has arrived. Is that why you're scurrying off? You don't want him to see me with you, do you? Well, he should have secured your engagement, if he didn't want you with another man."

"That's not it at all. And I am not scurrying. I simply like to get to my seat on time."

"I'll make a bargain with you—I'll leave you to your own devices and keep old Richard from seeing us together if you agree to go riding with me."

She brought her hand to her throat. Richard took a few steps forward and began to scan the room. "Yes, I shall go riding with you."

"I'll have someone pick you up tomorrow morning at eight. You do rise that early?"

She nodded.

He placed a kiss on her hand that burned through the glove to her skin, then left her standing in the lobby with not a single thought in her head.

Claudia watched Derrick walk away, then found Richard to see if he looked in her direction. He was engaged in a conversation with a gentleman she did not recognize. Perhaps he hadn't seen her exchange with Derrick. But he would find out about them riding together. Surely people would see them.

Truth be told, that thought thrilled her. She would be the talk of the town if it became known that dashing rogue Derrick Middleton was courting her. But her father would never approve, and she had Richard to consider. Riding that early should keep her from most of the gossips' eyes, as most ladies wouldn't be out until after noon.

She would go riding with him, do her best to remain unseen, then cut her ties with Mr. Middleton. For the time being, she should focus on Richard.

She had a plan for their next meeting. Since Richard insisted on playing the gentleman even this far into their courtship, she would take matters into her own hands and instigate their first kiss. Yes, that would work perfectly.

Once she kissed Richard, she would forget her kiss with Mr. Middleton. *No, she wouldn't*, a voice inside her said. No matter if she kissed every man in London, perhaps in England, she'd never forget the way Derrick Middleton's lips felt melted against hers. Or the way his tongue had moved seductively through her mouth. No, she would never forget that. But kissing Richard might spur him to propose sooner, and the sooner he proposed, the sooner Claudia's father would cease his badgering.

"So what was that all about?" Poppy's question startled her out of her reverie.

"Gracious, Poppy, you scared me."

"What did he want?"

"Who?"

"What's the matter with you? Mr. Middleton—I saw him here speaking with you only a few moments ago."

"Oh him. Well, he came to invite me to go riding with him."

"And?"

"And I accepted. I had no choice," she added quickly. "He practically blackmailed me."

"Blackmailed? With what material?" She wiggled her eyebrows. "Have you been holding out on a delicious secret?"

"Of course not." Except the kiss, but she couldn't very well tell her that. "It was Richard. I didn't want him to see us speaking, and Mr. Middleton used it against me. I'm not quite certain why he asked me to go riding with him."

"Perhaps you've captured him with your charms."

Claudia released an unladylike snort. "That must be it," she said dryly. "Be serious, Poppy. I'm in a dreadful situation."

"How is it remotely dreadful when a man that looks and charms like Derrick Middleton is paying attention to you?" Poppy released a tiny shriek and brought her hand to her mouth. "*Oh*! He's courting you."

"Shhh! Not so loud. He is doing no such thing." Claudia winced and leaned closer to her friend. "He claims that he's courting me, but it simply cannot be the truth."

"Why not?"

"Honestly, Poppy. Have you seen him? What on earth would a man like that want with me?"

"There's no reason why every man on earth wouldn't want you."

"You are biased because you are my friend."

"I am biased and I am your friend, but I'm also being truthful. There is not one single reason I can think of as to why Derrick Middleton or any other man wouldn't want to court you."

Claudia opened her mouth to speak, but Poppy cut her off.

"Unless . . ." Poppy frowned.

"Unless what?" Claudia asked.

"It could be your father."

"My father? What does my father have to do with anything?"

"Your father isn't exactly warm and inviting, Claudia. Perhaps men are afraid of him, and that is why Richard is your only suitor." She raised one finger. "Until now. I think it's splendid."

Claudia rolled her eyes. "You would."

"Nobody said you have to marry him. Although given the choice between Richard and Derrick . . . Look at it this way, perhaps a little competition will spur Richard into action."

"Heavens no. I don't want Richard or anyone else knowing that Mr. Middleton is playing this charade. But I do want to spur Richard into action as you say."

"How are you going to do that?"

"I'm not certain."

"I cannot for the life of me understand why Richard is dragging his feet. He has your father's permission and yours. What is he waiting on?"

"How should I know? Maybe he doesn't want to marry me."

"That's rubbish."

"The waiting is not sitting well with my father either. I can't be certain, but I believe he instructed me to seduce Richard."

"He did no such thing!" Poppy said incredulously.

"I believe that is precisely what he meant when he said, 'Claudia'—she deepened her voice—'use what God gave you.' And when I asked for clarification, he boldly proclaimed, 'Your womanly wiles.'"

"He said that? 'Your womanly wiles'?"

Claudia giggled.

"I can't believe he said that. As far as my father is concerned, I have no womanly wiles," Poppy said. She made a face and shook her head. "What a horrible conversation to have with one's father. How embarrassing."

Embarrassing was right. It had been. Humiliating too. Poppy's father had it right. He encouraged his daughter to marry, but not in a dishonorable or deceitful way. That's the way it should be, wasn't it? Whose father encouraged his daughter to seduce men?

Only hers apparently.

She would try to encourage Richard to propose, but she wouldn't put herself in a compromising situation to ensnare him. She might not be high on Society's list of marriageable girls, but she'd rather be a spinster than resort to dishonest tactics to secure a husband.

Chapter 5

A wake at eight indeed. Claudia had been awake since six, if not earlier. Her mind was alert with thoughts of Mr. Middleton's dashing smile and the things he'd said to her. She'd successfully avoided being seen with him last night, but what of this morning while they rode? Would people not see them in the park? People that she knew?

She scrambled to her feet, then rifled through her closet searching for the perfect bonnet. A hideous bonnet, one so large it was sure to hide her from other riders. She found it below her other hats—it was a tad squished and wrinkled, but a few shakes should take care of that.

It didn't match her riding habit, but it would have to do.

Perhaps not, but this was a desperate situation. She couldn't very well break her promise to ride with Mr. Middleton, but she certainly couldn't parade about with him as if he was actually courting her, and she was allowing it.

If her father ever discovered all the time she'd spent with Mr. Middleton, he would likely ship her off to live in a convent somewhere. Especially since most of that time they'd been alone. And part of that time, they'd kissed.

She was a ruined woman. Richard would wed her thinking she was a complete innocent, which she was not.

Her cheeks burned with the thought. Instead of fantasizing about kissing Derrick, she should turn her torrid thoughts to Richard. Should not a wife desire her husband? She closed her eyes and gave it a try, but as much as she wanted to think of Richard in that light, there was nothing torrid about him.

She'd never actually entertained torrid thoughts about anyone until that first kiss. Perhaps once she kissed Richard, all feelings for Derrick Middleton would leave her mind forever and be immediately replaced by desire for Richard.

Only part of her actually believed that, but she kept the thought in her mind in an attempt to persuade the rest of her.

She finished tucking her curls into the oversize bonnet. She would have to be careful walking in such a contraption lest she fall over, as it completely hindered her ability to see anywhere but straight ahead. The color, she noted, did match her eyes perfectly, but you couldn't much see her eyes once the bonnet was in place.

Well, if nothing else, the ridiculousness of this hat would send any suitor in the other direction, so by this afternoon she should be rid of Mr. Middleton and find herself in Richard's embrace.

She allowed that thought to swim around a bit, trying to warm up to Richard's arms, but found that when she thought of kissing, only Derrick's face came to mind. A person needed to take only one glance at Derrick's lips to know they were created for kissing.

How would she get through the morning looking at said face and lips? Ah, yes, the bonnet—she would simply keep her focus straight ahead and never even notice he sat beside her.

Which is precisely how she should be living her life. Looking straight ahead to Richard instead of her continual dalliances on the side with another man. This was the perfect reminder.

She checked the clock; only fifteen more minutes. Grabbing her reticule, she tiptoed out of her room. She peeked out of the hall window and was pleased to see the day shone brightly with not a cloud in the sky. At least it was a pleasant day for a ride. And she hadn't been riding in so long.

A black brougham pulled up and stopped. She slipped out of the front door just as Derrick stepped from the carriage. It was a stately carriage, the black so shiny you could see your reflection, and the wheels were apple-red.

"You're early," she said.

"You're ready." He helped her into the carriage.

"This isn't a customary vehicle for riding in the park," Claudia said as he climbed in beside her. The plush seats welcomed her, and she ran a gloved finger against the velvet cushion.

The carriage lurched forward.

"I never said we were riding in the park."

"Where are we going?" She turned so quickly, she nearly whacked his face with the bill of her bonnet.

"That is a . . . lovely bonnet, Miss Prattley. If memory serves me correctly, it is the exact shade of your eyes. I must use my memory, however, as I cannot see any part of your face but your nose and mouth." He leaned down to peek at her. "Won't you come out?"

He was an irritating man. But blast it, he was as charming as he was handsome.

"You're missing all the lovely scenery."

"I shall consider removing my bonnet once you tell me where you're taking me. This could be considered kidnapping, you know."

"Kidnapping?" His left eyebrow cocked. "Indeed? Perhaps I shall ravish you."

She pulled her mantle tighter around her.

His laugh filled the carriage. "I'm only teasing you. I wouldn't ravish you. Unless, of course, you asked me to," he added in a low voice.

She sucked in her breath, not from horror as a proper lady should, but rather from sheer excitement. He would ravish her if she asked him to? Tingles scattered through her veins like fireflies, the feelings pooled somewhere between her thighs. She shifted in her seat.

"We are going to my home. It's only a short distance from London. I have a large stable and nice land on which to ride. I thought it would be more freeing for both of us. Especially since you don't seem too keen on being seen with me in public."

His words stung. It was the truth, but it was such an ugly truth. It wasn't him—there was nothing wrong with him, but it would only tarnish her father and Richard to explain their feelings about him. And she owed her loyalty to them. They loved her. Mr. Middleton only . . . only what? She wasn't certain what he wanted from her. So rather than make silly excuses, she said nothing.

She untied the ribbon beneath her chin and pulled off the bonnet. She reached to pat her hair, but he stopped her, holding her wrist with his hand. Her pulse leaped beneath his touch.

"Your hair looks fine."

She smiled. "Thank you." While nothing he'd said so far had appeared dishonest, she knew in her heart he wasn't being truthful, yet his words sounded completely sincere.

He released her wrist.

"How long of a drive is it to your estate?"

"Not more than half an hour." He turned slightly so he could face her more. "I think your last drawings were among your best. Whom do you plan to cover next?"

"The Paddington sisters. I've been watching them all Season. They have a unique flair when it comes to their fashions. They're bold."

"And yourself?"

"What about myself?"

"Are you bold?"

"I should say not. My tastes run more with the

subdued—I like to blend, Mr. Middleton. It is never my intention to stand out in a crowd."

"Oh, but you do."

Well, that was nasty. She knew she had a rounder, plumper figure than most girls, but there was no reason for him to point that out. She looked out the window.

"Some things cannot be helped, sir, and I think it quite rude of you to mention them."

"I simply meant that you have a different way about you. Your very presence makes you stand out among women who look and act as if they were cut from a pattern."

She knew her mouth hung open, but she'd never before been around someone who seemed to surprise her at every turn. She found herself speechless with him, which was quite rare. Ordinarily she knew precisely what to say. Or rather she had a tendency to say whatever popped into her mind, whether it was appropriate or not. But with Derrick, she found he filled her mind, yet stole her words.

"Thank you, I suppose," she said.

The rest of the ride was spent in silence. Shortly thereafter, they arrived at his estate. The large stone manor house sat upon an open green expanse. Ash, oak, and birch trees completed the picture. It was simple, yet utterly beautiful.

They parked at the stable and found their mounts were already prepared for them. Her mare was a pretty chestnut and seemed docile enough. It had been a while since she'd actually been on a horse, and her nerves were on edge. But with the help of the groom, she managed to get up into the saddle without embarrassing herself.

They rode for a while in silence. It was nice, and her nerves began to subside. She'd always loved riding and didn't realize until now how much she'd missed it.

"I can't even remember the last time I rode out in the country. It's beautiful."

"I rather like the solace from London. I come out here often." He nodded at her. "You handle a horse well."

"Thank you. My mother loved horses, so as a child I rode a lot. When she died, Father closed our estate, and we moved to London permanently. I love London, and I don't believe I'd want to live in the country. But I miss having a place to get away to."

"You're welcome to come here anytime to ride. Privilege as my employee. Now that I know you're comfortable on a horse, come. I'll show you the rest of the property." He kicked his mount into a gallop.

She followed suit and soon found herself with

the wind blowing through her hair and caressing her cheeks.

She and her mother had ridden like this, fast and wild. It had made her father angry—he thought they should have had more control. But her mother would simply nod and go off to her room. Claudia had forgotten what it felt like to let go and ride freely.

And before she knew it, she was laughing out loud as the horse ran faster and faster, chasing after Derrick. Wind whipped through her hairpins, pulling her curls free.

Finally Derrick stopped, and she reined her horse up next to him. In front of them sat a clear pond surrounded by a handful of willow trees.

"This is my favorite part of the property. It is what made me purchase this estate." He helped her down off her mount. They walked to the edge of the water.

"It's lovely."

"Do you swim?"

"Oh no. That is to say I can, I suppose, prevent myself from drowning, but I haven't been in water in years. Well, I bathe, which I don't suppose we should discuss." She bit her lip. "You can gather what I meant."

He smiled, then motioned to the water. "Want to give it a try? The water should be warm."

"Mercy no. I didn't bring anything to swim in. And it would be highly inappropriate for us to swim alone together."

"Ah, yes." He nodded. "We must always do what is appropriate." He took a step closer to her and gently tucked an errant curl behind her ear. "If you continue to live your life like that, you will miss all that makes life grand."

"Is that so? And I suppose your life is grand?"

"I am my own boss. That makes my life grand."

"What of family?"

"I have my aunt. She and I are close."

"I meant a wife and children. Don't you want to have your own family?"

"I was married once."

He'd been married? Now he wasn't. That could only mean one thing. How dreadful. She didn't even know what to say, how to proceed. Perhaps he still grieved for the loss of his beloved wife.

So she said the only thing she could think of, "I'm sorry, I didn't realize."

"No need to be sorry. You didn't kill her."

He didn't sound like a grieving husband. He sounded sardonic and rather bitter.

Her curiosity got the better of her. "What happened?"

"It is not a story for today; perhaps someday I'll tell you." He picked up a rock and tossed it out into the water. The rock skipped three times, then sank, leaving rings in its wake.

"What was her name?"

"Julia."

"Will you marry again?"

"Perhaps. Right now my newspaper and my employees are my family. I devote all my energy to them."

"And to being inappropriate."

A tiny smile quirked his lips. "When the mood strikes me."

"You get in a mood to be inappropriate?"

"Absolutely." He glanced sideways at her. "Don't you ever get that feeling? That urge to do something that may be wrong, but for the moment it feels right?"

"Like what?"

"I'll show you." And just like that he closed the distance between them and cradled her face in his hands. He first kissed her gently, an innocent kiss. Then he proceeded to place sweet kisses all over her face. Her eyelids. Nose. Each cheek. Everywhere he touched, she wanted him to find a new place to put his lips.

Then his mouth met hers, and he moved across it slowly. Ever so gently, sweeping his tongue across her bottom lip and then the top. She opened for him and felt his tongue enter her mouth. Tentatively, she moved her tongue forward and brushed it against his. The sensation radiated from her mouth to the tips of her breasts and then ended between her thighs. Bolder, she continued the tongue play until she thought she would lose her footing.

This was wrong. But, oh, did it feel right. Still, it was wrong. She should be kissing Richard this way, not this man whom she barely knew and whose motives she didn't completely trust and who, she'd only recently discovered, had been married before. She pushed at his chest, and he broke off the kiss and stepped back.

"Why did you do that?" she asked.

"Because I wanted to."

"And what if I didn't want you to kiss me?"

"Then you shouldn't have kissed me back. It's the simple rule of kissing. If someone kisses you and you'd rather them not, then you simply don't kiss them back."

"I'm not familiar with these so-called rules of kissing."

"Claudia, I'm beginning to think that your so-called fiancé has not taken advantage of your sweet mouth."

She felt herself stiffen. He might not have properly proposed, but Richard was her intended. Everyone knew that. "My relationship with Richard is none of your business."

"That certainly answers my question."

"You didn't ask a question, and it does not."

"Did you enjoy it?"

"I beg your pardon? Did I enjoy what?"

"The kiss."

"I will not answer that."

"Again you answer."

"You are infuriating."

"So I've been told. Why is that, do you think?"

"Because you clearly find it amusing to make those in your company uncomfortable."

"Are you uncomfortable?"

She opened her mouth to answer, but stopped. Honestly? No, she wasn't uncomfortable. She should be, though. Wasn't that the point? Nothing about their time together had been proper. So why didn't she feel uncomfortable as she accused? That was a fault in her.

A fault her father would never understand. Nor would Richard. Richard. She was supposed to meet him today—to test the waters and see if she could persuade him to kiss her. Yet here she was with another man. A man whom she'd kissed. Twice.

"I believe it's past time that we returned. I have an appointment this afternoon."

"Very well."

They rode all the way back to London in silence.

He knew her appointment was with Richard. Knowing that annoyed him. And the fact that he was annoyed annoyed him even more. What did he care if she ruined her life with a bastard like Richard Foxmore?

Derrick acknowledged that it was his pride more than anything that was hurt. She'd kissed him—more passionately than any other woman he'd ever kissed—and yet the entire time she'd been thinking of another man. A man who, Derrick would wager, had successfully hidden his true colors from Claudia and her father.

He climbed back into his carriage after delivering Claudia to her doorstep. This courting business was more difficult than he had anticipated. Not only was he honestly attracted to Claudia, which both complicated and enhanced the situation, but he was beginning to feel guilty about misleading her.

Yes, he was doing an honorable thing by dissuading her from marrying Richard, but wouldn't he still be courting her to save his paper regardless of her relationship with Richard?

The truth of the matter was he didn't want to hurt her. He knew firsthand what betrayal felt like, and he wanted no part in inflicting such pain on someone. He simply needed to ensure that Claudia didn't have real feelings for him. Attraction, yes, but nothing deeper than that, and all would be fine. He couldn't break her heart if she didn't give it to him.

It disgusted him that he'd resorted to trickery to save his paper. He despised all sorts of deception after his marriage with Julia, and he'd wanted no part of another charade. Yet here he was playing the lead role in a major production.

He pushed his fingers through his hair. Damn, he wanted Claudia. Wanted to yank off that ridiculous bonnet of hers and run his fingers through her golden curls. Wanted to peel that riding habit off her lush body and cover her with kisses. He wanted to see if the blush that stained her cheeks also stained her breasts. Hell, he wanted to lose himself inside her until she screamed his name.

He couldn't remember the last time he'd wanted a woman the way he wanted Claudia.

It wasn't as if she'd never been late before, but being more than a quarter of an hour late, she'd be surprised if Richard was still here. She'd been less than kind to Derrick, but that was surely a good thing. If kindness in any way encouraged his attentions, she should be outright nasty to him.

She ran into the house and began her search for Richard. She found him three doors later in the library, newspaper in hand.

"I do apologize for my tardiness, Richard. I can't possibly expect you to forgive me."

He set the paper aside. "It is awfully inconsiderate of you, but I suppose I shall find it in my heart to forgive you." He looked up, and by the expression of horror on his face, Claudia realized her hair and clothes were probably not in perfect order. He came to his feet. "Good God, Claudia, where have you been?"

"I went out for a morning ride, and I'm afraid my horse got away with me, and, well, that is why I look a fright."

"Did anyone see you?"

"I don't believe so. I'm not injured if you're concerned," she added more tartly than she'd intended.

"Of course. I'm glad to see you're all right." He sat. "So tell me what was so urgent that I had to come over today? It must not be too urgent if you couldn't even be here on time."

She came and sat beside him on the settee. "I wanted to spend some time with you. Alone."

"I see."

"Do you have anything you wish to discuss with me?"

He uncrossed his legs, shifted slightly, then recrossed them. "Not that I can think of."

"What did you do this morning?"

"Nothing too interesting."

He recounted his morning events, which consisted of breakfast at his club, and then a meeting with some fellows. "That's very interesting." She situated herself slightly closer to him so that her leg touched his. It was through layers of clothing, but nonetheless, it was the most contact she'd had with Richard aside from dancing.

She listened to him drone on about the last session, all the while contemplating how to get him to kiss her. Poppy had said that if she wanted to kiss a man, she'd do it herself. Well, if Poppy could do it, then so could she. And as fortune, or whatever, would have it, she'd had a lot of experience kissing lately, so at least she was somewhat positive that she'd do it right.

She took a deep breath, closed her eyes, then leaned in and planted her lips on his in midsentence. Even with all her newfound kissing expertise, she'd never started a kiss and wasn't certain how to go about it, so she simply pressed her lips to his.

Richard pushed against her and stood. She must have done something dreadfully wrong.

"Claudia, what has gotten into you?"

"Nothing. I only wanted us to be closer." She stood too. "Richard, we've been together for a long time, and you've never so much as kissed my hand."

"I was waiting until we were properly engaged."

That certainly proved that Mr. Middleton was not a proper gentleman. He'd said that any man who'd been courting her as long as Richard should have kissed her countless times. And now she'd gone and offended Richard.

She would never learn.

"I'm afraid I must go. I shall see you later."

"Richard." She put her hand on his arm. "I wanted to be closer to you. Don't you ever want to kiss me?" She asked the question without realizing that the answer could be something she wasn't prepared to hear.

He glared at her hand resting on his arm, so she pulled it away. "I will not have this discussion with you. Proper gentlemen and ladies do not discuss such things. Good day, Claudia."

He couldn't have made her feel any worse if he'd laid a shilling by her side. She'd worked several scenarios over in her mind of her and Richard's first kiss, and none of them had played out like this.

This led her to two conclusions. One, this had nothing to do with propriety and everything to do with Richard not desiring her. Second, if Richard didn't desire her, there was no way that Derrick did. Not really.

Chapter 6

~~~oOo~~~

Claudia waited in the hall for Derrick's assistant to see if Derrick was busy. Perhaps she should start making appointments before arriving. That wouldn't be necessary though, she reminded herself, as this was a one-time meeting. She'd never before shown anyone her preliminary illustrations, but he'd been so curious to see them in the garden. It was so freeing having someone to discuss her illustrations with.

She felt the heat of shame color her cheeks. Derrick was deceiving her, pretending to court her. And allowing herself to be deceived in such a

111

manner was foolish. But the vanity regarding her drawing was too much of a pull.

It felt as if he truly understood, truly appreciated her talent. Pride swelled in her chest, and she bit her lip to keep from smiling like a fool. It was unusual, this feeling of being recognized. Of course, he did have financial reasons to appear enthusiastic about her talent.

From this moment on, it would be strictly business between them. No more stolen kisses. No more fantasies about stolen kisses. She had a problem with Richard she needed to sort out, and she didn't need Derrick Middleton and the girlish fantasies he evoked getting in the way.

She would show him the illustration, get his opinion, then be on her way. She tilted her chin and gave herself a little nod of approval.

Mason opened the office door and held it for her. "He'll see you now."

"Thank you."

She walked in and noted for the first time how orderly his office was. A bookshelf lined the right wall and was filled with leather-bound volumes. Derrick sat behind a large mahogany desk that was clean of everything but the papers he was currently working on. He gave her a crooked smile.

"That will be all, Mason," he said. "What can I do for you today, Miss Prattley?"

"Such formalities. I don't recall you being quite so formal the last time I saw you, Mr. Middleton." She hated to be haughty, but perhaps if she acted the prude he would cease his attentions.

He leaned forward. "Are you flirting with me?"

She couldn't even successfully pretend to be a prude. "Heavens no." She walked forward and sat across from him. This was a business meeting, and the sooner he realized that, the better. "I brought my preliminary drawing in. It's only a sketch, but you expressed interest. I know it's not customary for me to bring my work in personally; I usually send it by courier, but I was in the neighborhood."

He walked around the desk and sat next to her. "You don't have to make excuses to come see me, Claudia. My door is always open to you."

His breath warmed her arm when he spoke. He was too close.

"I'm not making excuses." She was, and she knew it. He knew it too, which made the entire situation embarrassing.

Her vanity, how little she had of it, would get her into trouble. She should keep her distance from him, but while she recognized that, she didn't want to. She enjoyed his company, enjoyed their conversations. She also very much enjoyed their kisses, but she tried not to think about that.

She retrieved the drawing from her bag and handed it to him.

She watched him examine the parchment. He took the time to really look at it, didn't merely glance at it, then put it aside.

"Excellent. Your detail gets better with every illustration."

"Thank you."

"I'm hoping to incorporate color into the paper soon. I believe your illustrations would be a perfect place to start."

"Color? Oh, that would be marvelous. Of course, then I'd have to make detailed notes to ensure the right color was used. But wouldn't it be splendid?"

He started to hand the drawing back to her, then stopped and fiddled with the edge of the paper. It separated, revealing another sheet beneath. He peeled the top drawing off and placed it on his desktop.

Heavens no! The drawing she'd made of them dancing. How could she have been so foolish? The pages must have gotten stuck together. It had happened a few times before with this particular parchment, and she'd neglected to check. It had never been a problem before, as she'd never shared her initial drawings with anyone. She reached for the illustration, but he pulled it away.

"I want to look at this."

She should have burned it. "But that's not an illustration I'm submitting. That was a mistake," she added quietly.

He looked at her, raised his eyebrow, then looked back at the picture. "Yes, it was a mistake."

Now he would know she was an utter fool. Fantasizing about him when she ought to be thinking about Richard.

"This is not your best work," he said.

His words pinched. "I realize that. I didn't intend to draw you, but it just happened, and the likeness is sadly lacking. I think it's the eyes, but I've never been quite sure."

"It's not *my* image that's lacking." He frowned. "It's yours. This is you, isn't it?" He pointed at the lady in the picture.

"Yes."

"It doesn't look anything like you. It's like a caricature. A badly done cartoon from *The Strand*."

"What do you mean, it doesn't look like me? It looks exactly like me. See, that's my dress." She tapped on the page.

"That might be your dress, but this is not you. Look at the features. The only thing you got right was the hair, and even then the texture looks off."

Texture. What was he talking about? Her hair was curly. Too curly. That was the texture. And the features—she'd gotten them perfect. Right down to the extra flesh that hinted at a second chin. She looked back at him and still he stared at the drawing, his brow furrowed.

"You weren't supposed to ever see this drawing." She tugged on the edge, but he wouldn't release it. "No one was," she added softly.

Derrick shook his head. "If I could draw, I would show where you went wrong. Sorry to say that my illustrating skills are sadly lacking."

"Hand it back to me, and we'll forget about it." She certainly didn't want this to affect his opinion of her talent. "Not all of my illustrations are perfect, that's why I draw more than one before I turn them in. This one was for me, merely a sketch. No one was supposed to see it. Least of all you."

"Claudia, it's not the quality I object to. Look at this. Look at your face. Do you see the difference in the way you drew yourself and the way you drew me? Or how about this?" He grabbed the other drawing from his desk, "The twins. Those girls are not what you would deem beautiful, yet you highlighted their best features in this illustration."

She glanced at the drawing of the twins. He was right, they were not particularly handsome women, but she had taken careful consideration to not draw attention to their overly large noses or poor complexions. She looked over at the image of herself. It might not look exactly like her, but it was close.

"It's not mine but rather your eyes that are lacking in this image. They have none of your sparkle and inquisitiveness." He brushed his hand down the side of her cheek. "It's difficult to capture the glow in your cheeks without color, I realize, but you could have hinted with some shading."

Her cheeks were red all the time, as if she were an actress who had gone too far with the rouge. She found them to be yet one more thing to hate about herself. Yet he thought it was a glow.

"Had I drawn this, I would have focused on the subtle arch of your eyebrows." He moved his thumb across her right eyebrow. "And that mouth of yours. The perfect and intoxicating mouth." One finger feathered a touch across her lips, and she clenched her jaw to keep herself from giving in to the urge to nip them.

His finger trailed from her lips, down her jaw, across her collarbone to the top of her dress. "Where is your tempting cleavage?"

"I beg your pardon?"

"In the picture. Where is your tempting cleavage? Or your waist, for that matter?" He met her gaze, but didn't wait for a reply before he continued. " 'Tis a shame, the way you see yourself,

Claudia." He leaned in so that they were merely a breath away. "I have a mind to strip away those clothes of yours, stand you in front of a mirror, and show you what I see."

Chills scattered over every inch of her body. Her heart beat so rapidly, she was certain it would jump right out of her chest. She brought her hand up to hold it in if necessary.

She needed to leave. This conversation had become highly indecorous. She stood. "I should leave."

He grabbed her arm. "Please don't."

"I only stopped to show you that drawing. I need to be on my way."

"All right, I'll let you leave, but only if you agree to meet me tonight." He stood to face her.

She swallowed. "I cannot meet you. Someone might see us."

"Of course they will! Tonight I'm going to an art showing for a friend." He retrieved an envelope from his desk.

How humiliating. She prayed the floor would open up and swallow her whole. She'd thought he invited her for a rendezvous, and he was offering her a legitimate invitation. She truly was a harlot.

He handed her the invitation. "You would enjoy it."

She *would* enjoy it. But she was so embarrassed right now, she wasn't certain she could ever face him again. "I don't know," she finally said.

"Bring Poppy along. I promise I'll behave. But there is something there I would like you to see."

"I'll talk to Poppy and see what she says."

"Do you want me to send a carriage after you?"

"No. I can manage on my own, thank you."

"Then I shall see you tonight."

"Perhaps."

He took her hand and brought it to his lips, all the while his eyes locked on hers. His warm mouth lingered a bit longer than was necessary, and a shiver went through her.

"I look forward to it," he said and dropped her hand.

Excitement and trepidation swirled through Claudia's stomach, battling for dominance. She shifted on the carriage seat and fought to keep her hands still.

"Where did you tell your father you were going?" Poppy asked from across the carriage.

"To the Petermans' soiree."

"This early?"

"Well, he wasn't home when I left, so he won't know I left several hours before the soiree begins. If he asks, I'll simply tell him I went to your house

119

to get dressed. It's not as if he'll speak to your parents to verify my story."

"True. What kind of art exhibit is this?"

"A private one, by invitation only. I'm not positive what that means, but nonetheless Mr. Middleton secured us an invitation. It's a private society of painters. I can't recollect what they call themselves."

"Sounds mysterious," Poppy said.

Claudia let her gaze fall to the window. The afternoon sun lingered, giving the street an ethereal glow. The calmness of dusk was in sharp contrast to her nerves. Her mind wandered back to what Derrick had said in his office. Strip her clothes off to show her what he saw? What did that mean?

It was utterly scandalous, that much she knew. No one had ever spoken to her in such a manner, and she knew she should be offended, but she felt nothing but shock laced with curiosity and something she could only label as intense desire. What did he see when he looked at her?

"He's still courting you," Poppy said. "I thought you were going to tell him you weren't interested."

"I'm not. I did. Well, that is to say, I told him he mustn't court me."

"Then why did he invite you to a private art showing?"

"Because I'm an artist and he appreciates that."

"Did he invite all his illustrators?"

"I don't know. Perhaps."

Poppy narrowed her eyes. "I don't think you're being completely honest with me." Then she smiled. "But if you want to keep your little secrets, I'll be content to speculate from a distance."

"What is that supposed to mean?"

"Nothing. You never told me how your meeting with Richard went. Did you kiss him?"

Perfect. As if she wasn't nervous enough, and Poppy had to bring up that dreadful incident. She recounted the story of her failed attempt at kissing Richard. Poppy simply sat across from her, staring with mouth agape.

"He pushed you off of him?" Poppy asked incredulously.

"Yes. He was quite offended." Claudia shook her head. "It was a shameful idea. I shouldn't have even thought it, much less attempted it. There is a reason men are the instigators in relationships. It's the way it's supposed to be."

"That's foolish, Claudia. He's a wretched man. There is no rule, unwritten or not, that says that only a man can instigate kisses. Richard is your beau—or is supposed to be. He's been courting you for a year, for heaven's sake, with the intention to marry you. There is absolutely no reason why he wouldn't let you kiss him. Except pure meanness."

"I don't think that's it, Poppy. I think he was affronted that I even attempted it. I think the thought of kissing me repulses him."

Poppy smacked her hands onto her lap. "Well, that's simply ridiculous. And even if it were true, then it's a testament to how wrong Richard is for you."

The carriage rocked to a stop, which was perfect timing because there was no reason to discuss Richard with Poppy. Her friend would never approve of the match.

"I suppose that means we're here," Claudia said, eyeing the carriage door.

"Yes, I suppose it does. Are we going to get out?"

Claudia put her hand on the door, then stopped. "If my father knew about this, he would kill me."

"If you always did as your father instructed, your life would be dreadful. I'm here with you. I realize that doesn't offer you much of a buffer, considering he doesn't exactly approve of me, but it's only an art exhibit."

"I don't know, Poppy."

"Come on, it will be fun." Poppy stepped down from the carriage and began climbing the steps to the town home.

Claudia quickly followed Poppy up the stairs,

then handed their invitation to the butler who opened the door.

"The ballroom is on the second floor," he said in a severely nasal tone. "That is where the majority of the paintings are hung." He took their cloaks. "You will also find some hanging in the drawing room, the study, the library, and the billiard room."

Claudia shivered from the lack of her cloak; the cap sleeves of her pale pink dress barely covered her shoulders. She and Poppy climbed the wide staircase. Poppy stopped in front of the marble statue on the landing. It was a man. A naked man—holding a lute or some sort of string instrument. Claudia felt her cheeks warm, so she quickly averted her eyes, only to find Derrick standing behind them.

"Ladies, I'm glad you could come," he said.

Poppy turned and greeted him.

He kissed both their hands, lingering a little longer on Claudia's—which pleased her.

"Tell me, Mr. Middleton, who are these artists?" Poppy asked. "Claudia couldn't remember."

"They call themselves the Pre-Raphaelite Brotherhood. I've known one of them since he was a scrap of a kid. I went to school with his older brother."

"Pre-Raphaelite Brotherhood," Poppy repeated. "That's quite a name."

"Yes, well, they fancy themselves as anarchists against the Royal Academy. They've only just formed their group, and this is their first showing."

He led them to the ballroom where they began their tour. A variety of paintings hung from the walls and sat upon easels for display. There were only a handful of people in the room. Claudia recognized a few, but wasn't certain of their names. A young man with wavy blond hair waved at Derrick, then walked toward them.

"Derrick, who are these two lovely ladies?" he asked.

"Alistair Lambeth, may I present to you Miss Claudia Prattley and Lady Penelope Livingston."

"What a pleasure." Alistair kindly bent over each of their hands, but his hazel eyes remained fixed on Poppy.

"Alistair here is one of the painters in the brotherhood," Derrick said.

"Yes, well, we must do what we must for our art," the young man replied. "Lady Penelope, might you allow me to escort you around the ballroom? I could give you some background details on the paintings."

It was rare for a man, no matter how charming and attractive, to make Poppy blush. But there it was, just a hint of color blooming in her cheeks.

"I would like that very much," she said.

"It is a pleasure meeting you, Miss Prattley."

Claudia nodded and smiled at him as he led Poppy away. "He seems charming," she said to Derrick once they were left alone.

Derrick merely shrugged. "Shall we look at the paintings? 'Tis why you are here, correct?"

"Of course."

He stood too close to her. She could tell because she could feel his warm breath on the back of her neck. If she wanted, she could lean back and feel the strength of him against her. But leaning against him would be most improper, regardless of how few people were in the ballroom with them. She stood straighter and tried to study the paintings in front of them.

"These are quite lovely," she said, trying to sound as if her entire focus was on the artwork.

"They seem to have an eye toward chivalry and the Arthurian legend," Derrick commented.

She tilted her head. The painting in the center featured a round table with knights, their swords placed on the top of the table. The paintings on either side also depicted knights, one with a knight atop a horse holding a lady's ribbon, while the other painting portrayed a knight kneeling beside a grave.

"So they do," she said.

They were well-done paintings, full of emotion,

with deep, rich hues of gold, purple, red, and green. But they were oh, so much more than that. Claudia's heart clenched with longing.

These paintings depicted men in love.

Men so in love, they wielded a sword to protect their ladies. Claudia certainly held no fantasy about a man using a sword in her honor, but she very much wanted to be that special lady who was loved so grandly.

Derrick's hand pressed into the small of her back to lead her forward. The heat in his touch was so intense, it was as if no material separated his hand from her skin. Her cheeks burned, and she wanted more than anything to lean into his touch, or to turn and lean in for a kiss.

He led her around the ballroom, stopping at each painting and allowing her time to look and study as long as she desired. All the images were beautifully crafted by true masters of their art.

Twenty years from now when she'd married and was living out her days in the country, she'd remember Derrick as the only person who'd ever seen her for the person she truly was.

"I want to show you one over here," he said softly. He led her out of the ballroom and down the hallway, right past the statue of the unclothed man.

She tried not to look, but couldn't help herself.

And she couldn't help but wonder if Derrick looked like that without his clothes. Would his chest and arms be as chiseled, his abdomen as perfectly carved to outline each muscle? Would his legs be as sinuous? And what of that middle area? Well, obviously Derrick had one of those and presumably they all looked the same. Didn't they?

They stopped right outside the billiard room. "Tell me, what do you think of that statue?" he asked as if he read her mind. Which it often seemed he did. Were her thoughts that transparent?

"It's a lovely piece of art," she said, trying to sound worldly and confident.

"Art?" He braced his hands on either side of her against the wall. They were alone in a poorly lit hallway. "Does art always make you blush like that?" His eyes trailed down the front of her.

"Am I blushing?" She released a weak giggle. "I do find it a little warm in here."

"No, you're blushing. You blush often, and I must say you have me wondering." His finger trailed up her bare arm and landed on her collarbone.

"Wondering what?" she asked, her voice sounding strange and breathy.

"Just how far down that blush goes." His finger left her collarbone to snake its way to the edge of her bodice, where it slipped just a snippet inside and tantalized her sensitive flesh. "And precisely what is on your mind that evoked such a blush."

"Oh my."

He leaned in and kissed her hotly on the neck, just below her left ear, then grabbed her hand and pulled her into a room.

"The painting I want you to see is in here."

Painting. Right, that's why she was here. Not to be fondled in the hallway in front of everyone. Granted no one had been there, but someone could have been. They entered the room, and thankfully were no longer alone, else she feared he might take advantage of her on that billiard table. But what scared her even more was that she doubted she would stop him.

His hand was warm over hers, their fingers laced together like those of lovers, and something in her heart swelled. He was touching her in public. Aside from dancing, Richard never touched her in public. He'd held her hand once when they were sitting in her garden, but that had been a long time ago. Derrick seemed not to care whether something was appropriate. Despite how much she enjoyed it, she pulled her hand from his.

He didn't seem to mind, and instead put his hand at the small of her back again. "It's this one right here."

She looked up at the painting, and her breath

caught. The size alone made it magnificent, but the portrait shocked her. It was a woman, fully nude and reclining on a chaise longue, her blond hair hanging loosely.

Most of the paintings she'd seen that evening had women in them, but all had been fully clothed, and all had been looking off to the side or with a downward gaze, but this woman faced the front boldly. She had looked straight at the artist while he painted her, proud of her body, daring him to look. Daring everyone to look.

Derrick's hand slid from her back around to her waist, and he pulled her so that she leaned against him. "I thought of you when I saw this portrait. Look at her body." His words brushed against her cheek.

How could he see such a creature and think of her? She was physically perfect, the kind of woman all other women secretly wished to be. "There is nothing about her that resembles me." Her mouth had gone dry and words seemed hard to form. "Except perhaps the color of her hair."

"It's not her body. It's her passion. Look at her eyes. See the boldness there. I see that in you, simmering just below the surface." He leaned in closer and nipped at her ear. "I long to release it."

Shivers danced through her blood and pooled at the apex of her thighs. Oh, to be that bold.

"She's proud of her body, Claudia. Comfortable with it. That's what makes her beautiful, not the shape of her breasts or her narrow waist."

She fought the urge to close her eyes.

"You would see your own beauty, if you saw yourself through my eyes."

No words found their way to her brain or her tongue. She simply stood there staring at the painting and feeling Derrick's hands and his breath and his heartbeat. It would be so easy to believe him, but wouldn't it also be foolish? As tempting as his words were, she knew that if she believed them she'd be gambling with her heart. She could not afford to lose her heart to Derrick Middleton, as she was certain she'd never recover.

She needed some distance before something happened they both regretted, because all she wanted was to find a secluded room and see if he really could unleash her simmering passion.

She closed her eyes and allowed herself a moment to relish his embrace. She inhaled his scent, willing it to brand itself on her senses. But too much more of him and she wouldn't be able to walk away.

"I think I should go," she said.

"All right. We'll find Poppy, and I'll have a coach take you to your soiree."

Very shortly, she found herself sitting next to

Poppy in the carriage. Poppy chatted nonstop about Alistair and his many wonderful and interesting attributes, but Claudia heard none of it.

Her mind wrestled with Derrick's words. Did he really think she was beautiful? How could he look at a painting of a woman like that, a woman who no doubt was not untouched, and think of her? The thought exhilarated and confused her.

If he was right, and she was beautiful and had that simmering passion, why was he the only man ever to see it? Why hadn't Richard taken the opportunity to release it? Didn't he see it too? If one man could see it, couldn't anyone?

Perhaps Derrick saw it because Derrick was looking.

Chapter 7

It had been two days since the art exhibit. Two days since Derrick had kissed her. Two days in which Claudia had given the current situation a great deal of thought.

So she stood her ground and waited for the inevitable.

Claudia watched from the corner of the ballroom as Derrick crossed the floor toward her. She desperately wanted to turn and run the other direction. But she couldn't very well do that without making everyone around think something was going on between them.

He looked the very picture of the proper gentleman. Clean and crisp and dashing in his black suit. His smile made her catch her breath, and it took her a minute to remember to inhale again. She was certain that if the other women in the ballroom were watching, they must be positively jade with envy.

His determined swagger toward her said he was a man who knew what he wanted, and it very much looked as if he wanted her. Her heart wrestled to accept the possibility, while her mind struggled to comprehend it. Regardless of if he wanted her and regardless of if she wanted him in return, she had other people to consider.

Her entire relationship with Derrick hinged on impropriety. It had potentially damaged her future with Richard, and her father would never forgive her if Richard refused to marry her.

"You don't look happy to see me." His voice smoothed over her skin.

She would not allow him to ruffle her tonight. Surely she could control herself and not fall prey to his flirtatious behavior.

"I have something I wish to discuss with you."

"You sound serious."

"I am. I'm concerned. But we cannot discuss it here. You'll have to meet me outside." She turned to go, but he followed. She stopped short. "You cannot simply follow me. We mustn't make this look as if we're planning a rendezvous."

"But we are."

"It's not a rendezvous. It's a serious discussion."

"I see. If I cannot follow you, what then shall I do?"

"Allow me to go first. I'll wait for you on the balcony. You should walk to the refreshment table first and have a drink and then follow. That way it will not look as if you are going after me."

"Quite a serious plan you've developed."

"I'll meet you outside." She left him standing there and slipped out the balcony doors. The moon was not particularly bright that evening, leaving the long balcony less lit than she would have preferred. She leaned against the railing and inhaled the sweet night air.

She'd never before waited for a man on a balcony, but knew ladies did so often. It was the polite way to steal kisses without their watchful mothers interrupting. These interludes never lasted long, at least from what she'd been told, but nonetheless it seemed quite risky. And she wouldn't admit it to anyone, but quite exciting as well.

"I'm fairly certain I snuck out unseen."

She turned and found him smiling broadly. He

thought this was all a joke. He probably thought she was a joke.

"I don't find that amusing."

He frowned. "I apologize. Now what did you want to discuss with me?"

She took a deep breath and squared her shoulders. "Our relationship. I find the current degree of familiarity and affection we've shared to be highly improper. And if we cannot change the direction, then we will no longer be able to spend time with one another. Which I'm certain won't be a problem considering your courting has all been a ruse."

"That again. Claudia, we've had this conversation. I'm at a loss for other ways to convince you that I'm serious."

She searched his face for a sign of humor, but found none. She'd never met an accomplished liar, but had heard people talk of them. It was said that Lord Moncriff was a liar of the worst sort, but she didn't know him. She shook her head to rattle her thoughts, hoping when they settled everything would make sense. It didn't work.

"Precisely what are you having a difficult time believing?"

"I am not the sort of woman that your sort of man courts."

"What sort of woman are you?"

"I'm plain."

That earned her a laugh. "You are anything but plain. Much to the contrary. Look at your dress. You have enough tassels and ribbons to decorate ten other dresses."

"I wasn't speaking of my dress." She frowned. "Do you think it's too much?" She fingered a ribbon at her sleeve. She'd always picked lavishly decorated patterns because she felt the more between her body and someone's eyes, the better.

"I don't believe they're necessary. You don't need all the extra adornments. You have a subtle beauty about you, one that sneaks up on you while you're not looking. And it has nothing to do with your silly dresses."

"Men have never paid me much mind. So why does it matter how I dress?"

"I don't care if other men pay attention to you; on the contrary, I rather hope they do not. Less competition for me. If other men haven't noticed you, they're not paying attention. I find you most becoming. Surely you must have noticed."

She looked around to ensure their privacy before whispering, "If you're speaking about the kisses, then that's precisely the reason why we must stop this charade. You know as well as I that you don't intend to marry me. Step aside and allow me to fulfill my duty and marry Richard. You and I can maintain our business relationship until I'm married, and after that, we can be friendly acquaintances. I find you a most agreeable man and do not wish to be on unfriendly terms with you."

"Men and women are not friends."

"That's not true. Poppy has a dear gentleman friend she's known her entire life."

"All right then. I am not friends with women. I'm not looking for an acquaintance either; I have plenty of those. I picked you because you fascinate me." He took a step closer to her.

"There is nothing fascinating about me."

"On the contrary. I find it absolutely annoying that I cannot simply walk away from you. You are the most fascinating woman I've ever met. Layers of contradiction. You live your life trapped in a web of propriety, yet I'm positive you have more passion in you than any other woman in that ballroom.

"You seemingly have no vanity, yet you garnish yourself in ruffles and bows." He flicked the ruffle at her bodice, sending chills across her chest. "Not to mention you're an extraordinarily talented illustrator."

"Now you're just appealing to my vanity."

"Is it working?"

She smiled. "A little."

"You have very kissable lips." He ran his thumb along her bottom lip. "In fact they're so kissable, I'm not quite sure how I can resist them for much longer."

"Indeed?" His eyes were mesmerizing. Like pools of water so deep, she'd never find the bottom.

"I need to know if Richard ever kisses you."

His words brought back the humiliation of Richard's rejection. "Why?"

"If he's kissed you, then I'll know that he'll marry you, and I will agree to step aside."

She tilted her head in confusion.

"No man who's kissed those lips could walk away from you. I don't think he has. Tell me, Claudia, I need to know." His voice was low and gravelly.

She couldn't say the words, so instead she shook her head.

"Has he ever come close?" He moved so that he stood right before her. "Tried to sneak a kiss and ended up grazing your cheek?" His lips moved close to her mouth, then just as quickly brushed below her right eye.

She could feel the sting of tears against her eyes. Richard had never come close to trying to kiss anything of hers but her hand. And even then his lips barely brushed her skin. Why had

Richard rejected her advances? Would Derrick do the same if she tried to kiss him? She didn't think so.

There was only one way to find out.

She tilted her head so that she met his lips. Her hands ran up the length of his chest and grabbed the front of his coat, pulling him closer. Unlike Richard's reaction, Derrick kissed her back, slanting his mouth over hers.

Deepening the kiss, she darted her tongue out and ran it against his. She was being bold, brazen, and she loved it. Fireworks sparked through her blood, igniting shocks of pleasure throughout her body. A tingle started at the apex of her thighs and increased until she thought she would scream.

Derrick's tongue swirled through her mouth, and she heard herself moan. She tried to situate herself so that something, anything pressed against that ache between her thighs.

He broke off the kiss long enough to pull them farther into the shadows on the balcony. She knew this was wrong, but her body felt so alive that she couldn't stop. Didn't want to. Not yet.

He kissed her again, but this time he let his mouth trail down her neck to right behind her ear, where he placed tiny licks and bites until she thought she would melt into a puddle at his feet.

Across her collarbone, down to the swell of her breast.

Gracious.

She arched against him, giving him more access. His hand cupped her breast through her dress while he continued to lave kisses on her skin. She moaned again.

No one had ever touched her like this. She felt her breasts peak beneath his touch, and she nearly tore at her dress to give him access to her bare skin. Thankfully Derrick was more controlled and was able to appease her without ripping any material. His hand slipped beneath the neckline and brushed against her skin.

He found her lips just in time to muffle the moan that tore though her at his touch. His rough, warm hands moved against her breast, rubbing her hardened nipple. Moisture gathered between her legs, and she bucked against him.

Derrick removed his hand from her dress, but kept her close against him. His ragged breathing tickled her right ear. He gave her one last kiss on her neck, then took a small step back.

"I know what you want. But now isn't the time, Claudia. We'll be discovered. It's too public." He took her hand and pressed it to the front of his trousers and the evidence of his arousal. "But know this. I want you just as badly."

* * *

Claudia leaned into the seat cushion and allowed the events of the evening to swirl through her head. She needed to talk to Poppy, but that would have to wait until tomorrow. What was she supposed to do?

Derrick had successfully proved to her that he was indeed serious about pursuing her. And the irony was that Richard had supposedly been courting her for a year now and had never advanced past sending her poems. Poorly written poems at that.

Not only had she once again failed to end their relationship, she'd entangled herself with him in a most scandalous way. She was shameless and weak.

Her body wanted Derrick. Of that much she was certain. But her father would never allow her to marry a man like him. His station in life alone was enough to send her father into a fit. But the fact that Derrick was the man that her father seemed to hate the most, aside from the majority party leader, ensured he would never bless a union between them.

If he ever found out about the courting, his head would likely split in two. She'd found a man who wanted her, and not for her dowry, because everyone knew Derrick had more money than most of his so-called betters. He seemed to want her because of her.

She almost squealed with the thought of it. It was a heady feeling, almost addictive—knowing that a man wanted her. No wonder Poppy was usually in such a good mood.

The carriage pulled to a stop in front of her house. Her nerves and body were so alert, she probably wouldn't sleep at all. She took off her slippers to climb the stairs so she wouldn't wake her father. It was a silly precaution, because he always went to bed early.

"Claudia, I'd like to see you now." Her father appeared behind her. "In my study."

His voice was tight and controlled. He'd clearly been waiting up for her. That had never happened. Chills shivered up her spine to prickle the hairs at the nape of her neck. He knew something.

Then she realized the obvious. Someone must have seen her on the balcony. It had been very dark, but it wasn't an impossibility.

"Sit down."

She complied and searched his face for any clue to what he wanted to discuss. She found nothing.

"I've heard a disturbing rumor, and I'm expecting you to dispel it."

She nodded, not sure what to say.

"Are you familiar with a man by the name of Derrick Middleton?"

Her blood turned to ice. He knew. "Yes, sir. I've made his acquaintance recently."

"And is it true he's been seeking you out at parties? Trying to . . . court you?" He spat the words out as if the thought made him physically ill. "Is this true?"

"We have danced a few times." She'd been to his office, and to his estate to ride horses with him. All with no chaperone. But if she told her father all that, he'd send her straight to the country to live the remainder of her days.

"But what are his intentions?"

"It's my understanding, Father, that when a gentleman wants to court a lady, he must first consult with her parents. Has he met with you?"

"Of course not. And if he tried, I would refuse to see him. He is no gentleman, Claudia. Do not be fooled by his money. He is nothing more than a scoundrel who's made his riches off the lies he prints in that paper of his."

Well, that answered her question. Not that she expected a different answer. But she'd held a tiny bit of hope that he would consider allowing Derrick to court her.

"I can't imagine what would prompt him to seek your attentions, but you must put a stop to his advances. Do you understand me?"

"Yes, Father."

"No more dances. I don't even want you speaking to him. Don't exchange pleasantries, don't even look at him. Pretend you do not know him."

She would make that promise now and hope life handed her a way not to keep it. She loved her father, and he knew what was best for her, but sometimes she wished he was wrong.

"You will marry Richard. Do you understand me, girl? You will do anything and everything it takes to secure that man as your husband. And I mean anything. Am I making myself clear?"

"Yes, sir."

"Now get yourself off to bed. And figure out a way to make that man propose to you."

Her father had just given her permission to make herself physically available for Richard's pleasure. She couldn't even begin to imagine how she could seduce a man, much less one who didn't even want to kiss her. What would her father say if he knew that?

Her entire life, she'd dreamed of a man like Derrick courting her, and the very night that dream had become a reality, her father callously ripped it from her hands.

Chapter 8

"A Miss Prattley here to see you, sir."

"Send her in." Derrick stood and waited for her to enter his office. She came a moment later in a flurry of pale green. "I wasn't expecting a visit today."

She straightened slightly, looking anywhere but in his eyes. "I can only take one more assignment."

"I thought we agreed you would work until you married."

"We did. And that might be happening sooner than we had expected."

"Claudia, what's going on? What happened between last night and this morning? Because I know you weren't engaged last night."

"Nothing happened." She was hiding something.

"Why won't you look at me?" He walked to her and turned her face to him. "Look at me, Claudia."

She met his gaze. "Nothing happened."

Something was different in her eyes today, a resolve that hadn't been there before. She was serious this time. She'd tried to walk away from the paper before, but he'd been able to convince her to stay. Today he wasn't so certain he'd be able to do that. "You're lying."

"That's not very kind."

"But it's the truth. Did Richard come over this morning and propose?"

She took a step away from him.

"I take that as a no. Then why the sudden change?"

She didn't answer.

"Is this about last night?"

A blush crept up her neck and settled in her cheeks.

They stood a few steps apart, yet it seemed as if a great chasm separated them.

"Claudia, I didn't plan for that to happen either, but there's nothing wrong with our desire."

"I'm not allowed to see you socially anymore, Derrick. I'm sorry. Since we can't seem to separate business and personal, this will be my final assignment. I have no other option, so there can be no further discussion."

"Not allowed? You're seven and twenty. Who decides who you are and aren't allowed to see?"

She squared her shoulders and said firmly, "My father."

"I haven't made my intentions for you public. How does he even know we've been involved?"

"It doesn't matter how he knows. The point is he knows, and he doesn't want me to see you anymore. He wants me to marry Richard, and that is what I intend to do."

"Are you marrying Richard only because your father wants you to?"

"I don't have to answer that."

"I suppose that means yes. You could stand up to your father."

She threw her arms up in the air. "I am a woman, in case that's failed to come to your attention. I can't stand up to anyone about anything. It isn't done. My father decides whom I marry."

"Do you always let him dictate everything you do?"

"This is a pointless conversation. I don't expect you to understand. You're a man; you can do as you choose. Ladies have no choices."

Why was he fighting her? That restless choking feeling that surged through him couldn't be panic. He had no reason to panic. It was an inconvenience to have her resign her position, but it shouldn't affect him one way or another not to see her anymore. His fascination and attraction to her would eventually wane.

Even as he thought it, somehow he doubted it was true. Not completely. And it was less about her leaving the paper than he was ready to admit. He didn't want her to walk out his door with the intention of never seeing him again.

She had become like a drink to him, a drug his body craved. He couldn't get enough kisses, couldn't stop the fantasies of making love to her that plagued his thoughts.

"Your father is a tyrant."

"My father is not a tyrant," she said quickly. "And if he were, it would be none of your concern." Her defense of her father was solid, her loyalty apparently unbending.

"Let's not discuss your father. What do you know about Richard?" Derrick knew he shouldn't care if she married Richard, yet the thought of her doing so drove him insane. He refused to analyze precisely why he cared. He was merely being a gentleman to protect her from a relationship with such a deceitful and manipulative man.

"What do you mean? He's a marquess. He's from a good family. He works with my father. He's a good man. I know plenty about him."

"Richard is not a good man."

She frowned. "You say that with such certainty."

"That's because I know. I know Richard. I know more about him than you or your father. I'd wager if your father knew what I know, then he'd change his mind about you marrying Richard."

"What is it that you know?"

"Suffice it to say, I know what I'm talking about, and Richard is the wrong man for you."

"Now you're giving me advice about men?"

"I don't want to see you involved in something or someone that will ruin your life."

"I appreciate your concern, but truly it's unnecessary. I know this is all really about the paper. You're protecting what is yours, and I respect that. Regardless of whether I marry Richard or someone else, no husband will allow his wife to have a paid position. Surely you know that."

"I know that narrow-minded men feel threatened when women take paid positions. A society that deems it is acceptable for poor women on the East End to earn their wages on their backs, yet feels it is unacceptable for a woman of good breeding to take a paid position, makes no sense. It's wrong. My mother worked, and there was nothing improper about her."

"That's quite forward thinking."

"I suppose it is. But it's ignorant of us to think that simply because someone is a woman she is unable or unqualified to work. You are the perfect example. You illustrate as well as, if not better than, all my other illustrators. You could be an example for other women."

She released a heavy sigh, then her shoulders dropped. "While I would love to give hope to other women, I'm afraid I'm not the person to do so. Derrick, I appreciate your confidence in me. But whether or not it makes sense, it is inappropriate for women to have paid positions. It's a fact of our society."

"You'll just accept that?"

She walked to look out the window. "It doesn't matter what I think about this."

"How can it not matter if it involves your life?"

She spun around to face him. "I don't have good instincts about things," she said with nearly a yell, then quickly covered her mouth. "I apologize."

"No need to apologize. Yell—it doesn't offend me." He gave her a reassuring smile. "You don't have good instincts about what?"

"Anything. Everything. I've learned to ignore my feelings as they tend to get me into trouble. I try to follow my father's guidance. He knows what is proper."

Somehow that bastard of a father had convinced her that her own instincts were wrong. Inappropriate. And he was using that against her—making her feel guilty for her natural emotions.

No matter what Derrick said, she'd never see life his way—or allow herself the freedom to live as she'd like. She was imprisoned.

"Promise me something," he said. "Find out everything you can about Richard before you agree to marry him. Don't do it simply for your father."

"I'll do what I can."

"In the meantime, continue working for me. At least until Richard actually proposes. In return, I will do my best to prevent any more news about us from reaching your father. Rest assured, our relationship, business or personal, shall be a secret."

She chewed at her lip. She wanted to.

"Claudia, I know you love it. Give yourself permission to enjoy life for the time being. We'll cross the marriage bridge when we come to it."

"Very well. But as soon as he proposes, I must quit. And you must accept that."

"You have my word."

"The next time we see each other in public, please don't ask me to dance or bring me a drink."

"Your father may dictate your actions, Claudia, but he will not dictate mine. I will be discreet, as I want to protect you, but I shall court you as long as I want. And until you personally want me to stop, then don't ask me again to stop for your father's sake." His hands clenched into fists at his sides. "Do you want me to stop?"

She looked up at him, her blue eyes glistening with tears. "I told you, it doesn't matter what I want. I should go. My father will only be out for a short time, and I want to be home when he returns."

He let her leave, but he refused to allow some domineering father to tell him he couldn't court a lady of his choosing. He acknowledged that was the rebel in him. But he also knew he would make a better husband for Claudia than Richard.

Regardless, marriage should be about mutual love and respect, and while he respected Claudia, he couldn't offer her love. He couldn't offer any woman love. He wouldn't give his heart to another after Julia casually dismissed him.

But he also knew he couldn't continue to court Claudia unless he was serious about marrying her. It wasn't fair to her. He didn't want to hurt her; she had enough pain in her life with her bastard of a father.

He had a hell of a decision to make.

Instead of having the driver return her home, Claudia gave him Poppy's address. She needed to talk to someone. So much had happened, Claudia desperately needed a friendly face. She was let into the drawing room where Poppy's mother sat mending.

"Claudia, how good to see you."

"Lady Livingston, I trust you are well."

"Aside from worrying about that daughter of mine, I'm doing well. I do wish you'd encourage her to get serious about securing herself a husband. I don't want her left all alone like my dear cousin Abigail."

"Mother, do stop your fretting," Poppy said from the doorway.

Claudia gave Poppy a look she hoped expressed her need for them to talk alone.

Poppy caught on. "I'm glad you're here. I need you to help me pin one of those dresses you gave me." She smiled lovingly to her mother. "Mother, I hope you don't mind us deserting you."

"Not at all. I believe I'd like to take a short nap. We have a busy evening ahead of us. You girls run along."

Once in the privacy of Poppy's bedroom, Poppy asked, "What's the matter?"

Claudia shook her head. They climbed up onto Poppy's tall, four-poster bed as they'd done since they were little girls and settled in for a talk. It was much more difficult than it had been when they were children, as now they couldn't lounge about because of their corsets and other undergarments restraining them.

"I recently heard some news that Richard might not be all he claims to be. Do you think he's a bad man?"

"Richard Foxmore? No. He's boring and arrogant. But I wouldn't say he was a bad man—presuming you mean evil when you say bad."

"It was implied to me that Richard has some questionable activities in his past. And that if my father knew of them, he would not allow me to marry him. Can you imagine?"

"Who told you such a thing?"

Claudia looked away. She wasn't in the habit of keeping things from her best friend, but when it came to her relationship with Mr. Middleton, she hadn't been very forthcoming.

"Tell me."

"Very well. Mr. Middleton. I had a meeting with him today, and we ended up discussing my relationship with Richard. He said that Richard was not who I thought he was, and I should not marry him."

"Did he give you any details?"

Claudia picked at a piece of thread that had come loose from the bedcovers. "No. Other than that marrying Richard would ruin my life."

"Well, I've told you that before. But Mr. Middleton has connections. He has people all over town who give him information for his paper, and my father swears by it. So it is quite feasible that he would know something about Richard that even your father would not know about."

"It seems so unlikely that Richard has a secret life. I don't consider him boring, but he doesn't seem—you can't tell anyone I said this—he doesn't seem clever enough."

Poppy snapped her fingers. "Exactly. But that doesn't prove that he's not involved in something unsightly. Perhaps he does have a dark past. Maybe that's why he's so dull now. Makes him appear more unassuming."

"I can't see it. I think Richard is simply preoccupied with his work. He's very involved politically, and I'm sure some of his decisions in the past have been controversial. Perhaps that's what Derrick meant." She should say more. Defend Richard, but frankly, after their last encounter, she wasn't certain she knew him at all.

"That seems unlikely. People make unfavorable decisions all the time; that doesn't generally warrant bad reputations. Derrick Middleton isn't from our side of town, so to speak. His definition of a bad man is different than ours—a little harsher, I would think. If he has real information about Richard, I think you should be careful."

"Should I say anything to my father?"

"No. He wouldn't believe you, and he'd want to know who you've been talking to. I'm assuming you don't want to tell him of your new relationship with Derrick Middleton."

"He knows."

Poppy's eyes grew round. "He knows what?"

"That Derrick has been paying court to me. He waited up for me after the Finnigers' ball. He said that someone had told him that I was seen dancing with Derrick on more than one occasion."

"I wonder who told him. Richard wasn't even at that ball. I suppose with your father's connections, it could have been anyone."

"I told him that Mr. Middleton had asked and that I didn't want to appear rude. He told me I should have walked the other way."

"I wish my parents would tell me I could walk away from some of my suitors." Poppy toyed with the curls that framed Claudia's face. "Speaking of the Finnigers' ball, I heard some delicious gossip."

"Really?"

"Mildred Blanlard told me and several other girls that she saw a couple pressed against the balcony. She said they were kissing so much, they were oblivious to everything around them." Poppy raised her eyebrows.

Claudia's lunch flipped in her stomach. Actually, she could imagine. If her father found this out, he'd kill her for sure. She licked her lips and wished she had something to drink, as suddenly her mouth had gone completely dry.

"Did she happen to say who the girl was?" If word got out about this, she'd be ruined. Not only in her father's eyes, but everyone's. Poppy's parents would probably forbid their proper daughter to spend time with someone who behaved so disgracefully.

Poppy shook her head. "No, she said it was too dark to see. She tried to wait to find out, but her mother called her away."

"That's a relief. I mean for that girl. Can you imagine if Mildred saw you doing anything inappropriate? She'd put an announcement in the *Times*. She's such a jealous sort. It's no wonder that she hasn't found a husband yet."

Poppy eyed her suspiciously. "You're acting peculiar. What are you hiding?" She gave Claudia a gentle pinch on the arm. "You know who it was, don't you?"

"No!" she shrieked. Well, there was the way to hide her innocence. She was wretched at keeping secrets.

"Oh my God! It was you, wasn't it? You and Derrick Middleton. I suspected as much."

"How?"

"I saw you two at the art exhibit. You certainly weren't being very discreet."

"Oh, this is simply splendid." Claudia dropped her head into her hands.

"Not to worry," Poppy reassured her, "no one else saw you there. Except for Alistair, but he won't tell. Why didn't you tell me?"

"I don't know. I wanted to, but I wasn't certain how you'd feel about it. He's not properly courting me, and my father will never allow me to have a legitimate relationship with him. There's no respectable reason to allow him to kiss me."

"Then why did you do it?"

Claudia couldn't help herself. She smiled. "I don't know."

"Tell me more. You can't expect me to let you go without giving me details of the kiss."

"The kiss was . . ." *Amazing, toe-curling, sensual, heart-stopping.* So many thoughts came to mind, but none of them seemed to fit. So she settled on "Really nice."

Poppy's shoulders deflated. "Really nice? Derrick Middleton presses you against a balcony rail and kisses you for the better part of ten minutes and all you can say is it was 'really nice'?"

"I don't really have a base for comparison."

"Did you feel it all over? I read in a novel once where the woman was kissed by a wicked Frenchman and she felt it all over. *All over.* I can't even imagine."

A month ago it had been hard to imagine. Never in her wildest thoughts had she envisioned a kiss affecting her the way Derrick's did.

"You could say I felt it all over. I felt it in other places besides my lips." She fought the urge to giggle. She lost. "It feels as if our lips were meant for each other. I know that sounds so silly, but kissing him feels as natural as breathing. Yet it feels so deliciously foreign at the same time. It's quite exhilarating."

"I'm assuming the art exhibit wasn't the first time?"

"No. Once before at my house, in the garden,

that was the first. And then again when I went riding with him. Then the art exhibit, and then the Finnigers' ball. I'm shameless."

"And you've successfully kept this from me for that long?"

Claudia expected Poppy to give her a lecture on how they were supposed to be confidantes. Instead her friend merely smiled.

"I'm impressed," she finally said.

"Impressed?"

"That you kept it a secret. You've never been very good at secrets. Particularly your own. Which leads me to believe that there must be more that you're hiding. More than a few kisses."

Claudia shook her head. "No. Only the kisses. We haven't done anything else. I swear."

Poppy laughed. "That's not what I meant. But that's intriguing."

"You think I'm a harlot, don't you?"

"Why would I think a silly thing like that?"

"Because I've been intimate with a man who is not properly courting me. And who doesn't have permission from my father to do so."

"Doesn't have your father's permission to court you, or to be intimate with you?" Poppy asked with a smile.

"Neither. Of course, Derrick said he would not

be dictated by my father. He claims I'm old enough to marry who I choose."

"That's quite bold of him. Has he proposed?"

"No. I doubt he will. I don't believe he truly wants to marry me."

"For someone who's not so serious, he's certainly doing a better job of courting you than Richard."

"Be serious, Poppy."

"I was. Has it not occurred to you that Mr. Middleton might be interested in you because of who you are and not because of your father and his political ties? This might be the one. The one who could free you, who would allow you to continue illustrating. Who would love you." Poppy fell back on her bed. "If I were you, I'd try to get myself compromised with him so he'd have to marry me."

"Poppy! You would do no such thing, and neither will I. That's a wretched thought, trying to snare a husband in such a manner. He'd probably never speak to me again. I know my father wouldn't."

"I was only joking. But I still think you should consider the fact that Derrick is clearly serious in courting you."

"Honestly, Poppy. When you look at him, am I the type of woman you'd think he'd choose?"

"Why wouldn't you be?"

Claudia shook her head. "Don't think of it as me—you love me, so of course you'll say yes. Pretend I'm a girl you don't know. Some girl across the ballroom wearing a silly dress to hide her imperfections. Am I the type of girl you'd see him with?"

"Claudia, you're beautiful. I'm sorry you can't see that. But I'm thrilled he can. There is no reason you should try to hide behind anything. The only reason more men don't court you is because they're scared of your father. Derrick Middleton is not likely to be afraid of anyone."

"Since Derrick refuses to stop courting me, I must handle the situation myself."

"How are you going to do that?"

"I shall clear my social calendar for a few weeks until Richard proposes."

"And what if Richard doesn't propose? Will you go into permanent hiding?"

"I don't know. But Richard will propose."

"Do I need to tell you again that I think it's a bad idea that you marry Richard?"

"No, you do not. And I trust that when I'm married to him and am as miserable as you predict, you will still be my friend?"

"That is a ridiculous question. Of course I will."

Poppy smacked her in the arm. "I have a question for you, though. What was it about the kisses that you didn't want me to know? Was it that you felt you were betraying Richard? Or did you feel that allowing Derrick liberties would make me question your virtue?"

Claudia thought for a moment of how to answer those questions. Why had she kept the secret from her friend? She rarely kept anything from Poppy. Yet she had been reluctant to share this secret.

She didn't particularly feel as if she was betraying Richard, although she knew she ought to feel that way, which made the entire situation all that much worse. She didn't think Poppy would judge her innocence or lack thereof no matter what liberties she allowed Derrick or any other man to take. Poppy would never judge her. So what was it?

"I know what it is," Poppy said, interrupting her thoughts.

"Splendid, because I'm at a loss. I'm certain I had a perfectly good reason. Perhaps I was simply embarrassed."

"No, that's not it," Poppy said as if that were the most ridiculous thing she ever heard. "To admit to me that you had kissed Derrick Middleton would make you have to acknowledge something you'd rather not acknowledge."

Claudia frowned. "What would that be?"

"That you want him. That you're attracted to him, and you thoroughly enjoy kissing him and wish it were him in your future and not Richard."

Claudia opened her mouth to respond, then promptly shut it. Could she refute that? Was it true? Of course it was true. She wanted Derrick in a way she didn't know a woman could want a man. It was as if once she met him, she'd been turned on, like a lantern, and she burned hotter and brighter than she ever thought possible.

"I will assume your silence confirms my opinion," Poppy said. "It's a logical argument. But now that I've said it out loud, it's out there, in the air, and you must acknowledge it. Admit it, Claudia. You wish you could marry Derrick."

Claudia tilted her head and thought for a moment. "I'm not certain I'll admit to that. I want him, desire him, but I don't know that I want to marry him. I've never considered marriage with any other man than Richard."

"What about when you were a girl? Didn't you fantasize about a handsome man coming to whisk you away, pledging his undying love to you?"

"I suppose I did at one time." But her father's

voice had squelched those fantasies before they became too advanced.

His voice rang in her ears. *You'll never be beautiful, Claudia. You need to cultivate other ways to ensnare a husband.*

No, she'd never much dreamed of anything but living a life that would make her father proud. Yet that seemed the biggest fantasy of all.

"Well, you should start fantasizing about that now. Derrick could be the one, Claudia. You're like the princess trapped in the highest tower of the castle, and he is your knight come to rescue from the evil tyrant."

Claudia winced. "I suppose my father is the evil tyrant in this scenario?"

"Yes."

"You've been reading too many adventure novels. We are not in Camelot, and Derrick Middleton is no knight." Although the thought of him rescuing her was vastly appealing. She loved her father, but she longed to be free from his demands.

"How will you ever know if you're happy, if you never dream?"

She was happy. Wasn't she? And she dreamed, or she used to, but her dreams were impossible. Fantasies. Women of her station didn't have paid positions, and they rarely married for love. Then she remembered what Baubie always told her—that when she was born, she brightened her mother's life. As if her mother was born for that purpose, to be a mother. Perhaps that was Claudia's purpose as well.

"I want a family, Poppy. That is my dream. And that will make me happy."

"Even if you do not love your husband?"

"I can love Richard."

"Not real love, Claudia. Not the heart-pounding kind that shakes every fiber of your being."

"Probably not that kind of love. But I would wager that most marriages lack that kind of love, and they survive and those people are happy. You've never said love was a requirement for marriage. You've said yourself many times how you'll end up in a rotten marriage. What is so different now?"

"Alistair."

"The painter?"

"Yes." Poppy scooted closer. "He's so wonderful. I love him. And I know he loves me. We haven't said so, of course, it's far too soon. But I feel it, and I'm positive he does as well. Oh, Claudia, it's so wonderful to be in love. Just like the heroines I've read about."

Claudia forced herself to smile. She was happy for her friend, and she didn't want to strip her of this moment simply because she hadn't been fortunate to find the same kind of luck.

"That's marvelous, Poppy. What have your parents said?"

"Nothing yet. I haven't exactly told them."

"I don't want to be the bearer of bad news, but what of your responsibility to your family? How will an artist's wages improve your family's financial situation?"

Poppy clapped her hands. "That's the beauty of it! Alistair is rich. He's the second son of an earl. His brother only recently came into the title. Alistair even has a holding in Sussex."

"Oh, that's splendid. See, I told you that you wouldn't get stuck marrying some old codger!"

Chapter 9

"**Y**our note said it was urgent, so I came as quickly as I could," Richard said.

Emerson Prattley, Viscount Kennington, eyed the man in the doorway. He motioned him to enter the room. "Close the door. This matter is not only urgent, but extremely private."

"Is Claudia home?"

"No, but she might be soon. I sent for you hours ago when she first left. Where have you been?"

His eyes shifted. "I was in a meeting."

"I see. Let's carry on before my daughter returns. Sit."

Richard obeyed and sat across the desk in the leather wingback.

"When are you planning to propose to my daughter? I assume you have not forgotten your promise to do so."

He swallowed, then cleared his throat. "No, I have not forgotten. But still I am not ready."

"I can't blame you for stalling. I wouldn't want to be saddled with a woman like my daughter. Too much flesh. And far too many opinions, although I've done what every father could to try and break her of that."

He poured himself a drink, deliberately not offering any to Richard. "She's not the pick of the litter, I realize that, but once you're married, you'll have ample opportunity to mold her to the kind of woman you wish . . . or I suppose you could just blow out the candles at night so you don't have to look at her."

"It's not that. I have a bit of a situation."

"Ah, a lady not willing to share you? You can dally with other females after you're married. There's no reason to drag your feet now. You have a nice dowry waiting for you."

"I'm not dallying with anyone. As soon as my problem is sorted out, I will be ready to take Claudia as my wife. I need more time."

"I'm afraid you don't have any more time. I didn't want to resort to drama, but you've left me no choice. Either you propose to my daughter immediately, or the queen will hear of your little embezzlement."

Richard came to his feet. "You must give me more time. I need money now. Give me her dowry now, and I'll marry her."

"Why do you need money?"

"I have a debt that needs to be repaid."

"Or what?"

"Or they'll kill me," he yelled.

"Lower your voice. I don't believe you keep good company, Foxmore. What is the debt for?"

His lips pursed. "Necessities. Living expenses. There is a high price to pay to wear respectable clothes and eat at respectable establishments."

"Idiot."

"Will you front me her dowry? I'll marry her as soon as the debt is paid."

"What kind of fool do you take me for? No, you won't get one farthing of her dowry until after you've said your vows. I don't trust you, Foxmore."

"If you report me to the queen, I'll hang."

"Possibly. But more than likely you'll rot in prison."

"Give me some more time. Two days, that's all I

ask. I'll go see my uncle to borrow the money. He's only a day's ride from here. As soon as I return, I'll marry Claudia. You have my word."

"Your word means nothing to me." He lit a cigar and took a thoughtful drag. "But your fear speaks loud and clear. I shall give you two days. After that I will post the announcement of your pending nuptials in the *Times* myself. Is that understood?"

"Yes."

"One more thing. Leave a letter for Claudia setting up an appointment where you will propose." He held out a piece of parchment.

Richard took the paper and nodded. He reached for the quill and scratched out a note. He let the ink dry, then folded the letter and wrote her name on the outside.

"I'll be back in two days." He held out the letter.

"I look forward to the announcement. And for your sake, Richard, you better be here, or those people to whom you owe your debt will be the least of your worries."

"I thought you were going to stay home this week, not accept any invitations," Poppy said, obviously surprised to see her friend.

Claudia removed her gloves. "My father insisted I come. He said I was not permitted to re-

171

fuse an invitation by Lady Oliver. Besides, it's not likely I'll see Derrick here. Only dandies come to these card parties."

Poppy giggled. "Yes, I see Morris Brimley over there. He is the very picture of a dandy. I was not aware that dots and stripes were complementary patterns."

"Penelope, watch that mouth," her mother said as she walked near. "If I heard you, then there's a chance he did."

"I doubt it, Lady Livingston, he's deaf in his left ear," Claudia offered.

"Regardless, it wasn't kind. Mind your manners, dear, or you'll never find a husband."

That last part Poppy mouthed in perfect unison with her mother. It seemed every chance she got, Lady Livingston reminded her daughter of the importance of behavior and securing a husband. She meant well. It was only because she herself had found such joy in marriage and motherhood that she wanted Poppy to have the same, and she wanted Poppy well cared for.

"Girls, go and find your tables. And behave."

It was nice having a mother fret over her again. Claudia loved Poppy's mother. She wasn't a replacement by any means, but she was the perfect stand-in when Claudia needed one.

"Alistair sent me a poem," Poppy said as soon as they were out of earshot from her mother.

"An original?"

"I believe so. It's not one I've heard before."

"Was it any good?"

Poppy's smile lit her face. "It was wonderfully romantic, with clever rhymes."

"Has he been to see your father, to make his intentions known?"

"No, but I suspect he will soon."

"I'm really happy for you," Claudia said, then gave Poppy a brief hug before they sat at their table.

They hadn't so much as taken their seats when Derrick walked into the room. Claudia's heart fell to her toes. She was certain her mouth dropped open, so she brought her hand to her lips to hold it shut just in case. What could he possibly be doing here? Tea and a card party, in the middle of the afternoon? It hardly seemed the kind of thing a man would enjoy. Especially a man who took great pleasure in living the life of a rogue.

He met her eyes across the room and smiled. The connection between them sizzled. She looked over at Poppy to see if she'd noticed, but she was busy shuffling the cards.

"Poppy," Claudia whispered.

"What?"

"Look over there." She motioned with her head, trying not to look again in his direction.

"What's he doing here?"

"How am I supposed to know?"

"Well, you are the most intimate with him."

Claudia smacked her in the arm. "Not so loud. And we're not . . . intimate."

"You don't have to say it like a curse. There's nothing wrong with intimacy."

Derrick leaned over an older woman and kissed her on the cheek. She said something, and he laughed heartily. The rich rumble sent gooseflesh dancing across Claudia's arms. He asked Lady Oliver a question, and she pointed to their table.

"Goodness, why is she pointing at us?" Claudia asked.

"We shall find out soon enough; here he comes. Oh, and he's not alone, looks like Morris Brimley will be joining us. What a positively splendid afternoon. Perhaps I can marry him."

Claudia couldn't help herself and giggled at the thought of beautiful Poppy shackled to a fop like Morris Brimley. "At least he's not old," Claudia offered.

Poppy poked her in the arm.

"Having fun without me." Derrick clicked his

tongue. "You should be ashamed." Derrick took the seat opposite her and smiled broadly. It was a wolfish grin, as if he planned to eat her up, then lick his chops.

Ordinarily a feeling that a man wanted to devour her might not sit so well, but with Derrick Middleton, it was a nice, although inappropriate, thought.

Morris took the seat opposite Poppy. He smoothed his hair before offering a smile. "Good afternoon, ladies." Claudia hadn't remembered him having a lisp. "I don't believe I've made your acquaintance, sir. I am Morris Brimley, Viscount Felmworth." His face pinched as he looked at Derrick.

"Derrick Middleton, lowly son of a working man," he said dryly.

Claudia suppressed a laugh. "He owns *London's Illustrated Times*."

Derrick shrugged in confirmation.

Morris seemed unimpressed. More than likely he had a lack of knowledge regarding *London's Illustrated Times*; he didn't seem like much of a reader.

"Mr. Middleton, who is that lady over there that you spoke to when you came in?" Poppy asked.

"That is my aunt, the dowager Duchess of Shelton."

"Your aunt is the dowager Duchess of Shelton?" Claudia asked.

"Yes. You know of her?"

"Everyone *knows* of her," Poppy said. "She's legendary. But I thought she'd retired from Society years ago."

"She had, but she's recently moved back to London, and is reacquainting herself with some old friends."

"I'm sorry, why is she legendary?" Morris asked.

"She's married no fewer than two dukes in her lifetime. And she's known for having a complete disregard for convention. She's a force to be reckoned with and a good example for women of our generation," Poppy said.

"I believe, Lady Penelope, that you know more of my aunt than I do," Derrick said.

"She is a fascinating woman. I would very much like to meet her at some point."

"I think I can arrange that," he said.

"Shall we get on with the game?" Morris suggested. "Lady Penelope, I do believe we've been paired together today." He gave her a toothy grin.

"Splendid," Poppy said, although Morris didn't seem to notice her lack of sincerity.

"I suppose that leaves you and me to partner, Miss Prattley," Derrick said.

"Yes, I suppose it does," Claudia said.

Morris dealt first, with hearts as the trump. Fitting.

Derrick eyed her above his cards. As much as she hated to admit it, it thrilled her to be on the receiving end of his attention. She was certain everyone in the room noticed, and while she might have to pay for that later with her father, right now it made her smile. Besides, it wasn't as if she could do anything about his being here—she herself hadn't invited him. And her father had insisted she attend.

Did her father know Derrick's aunt was the dowager Duchess of Shelton? Would it make a difference? Probably not, but it might be worth mentioning the next time they spoke, since Derrick clearly had no intention to cease courting her.

Something touched her shoe.

She looked up and met his glance, and he raised one eyebrow.

Was that his foot? Touching her foot? At a proper tea and card party, full of matronly women and dandies?

He was completely shameless.

She smiled again despite the gravity of the situation. What she should do was get up and leave. But that would only make a scene and draw more attention to them. She tucked her feet in closer to her, trying desperately to stick them underneath her chair, but with her undergarments, that was an impossibility.

Poppy played a seven of diamonds, and then it was Claudia's turn. She glanced at her cards and tossed down a three of diamonds. Then it was Morris's turn, and she realized she still held the ten of diamonds. Clearly she wasn't paying proper attention to the game. She hoped Derrick wouldn't mind if they lost.

When this game was over, she would simply make her excuses and leave early. She could plead a headache or some other ailment.

It was her turn again. She studied her cards, trying to determine the best to play. Finally she gave up and tossed down a four of spades.

Once the game ended, she quickly stood. "I'm afraid I must leave you to find a new player. I've developed a headache and believe it in my best interest to return home and lie down."

Poppy frowned at her, but she could explain to her friend later.

She didn't check for Derrick's reaction, rather made her excuses to the hostess, then stepped into the hallway.

Claudia stood waiting for the butler to retrieve her cloak, when Derrick grabbed her elbow.

"I do hope you're not leaving on my account."

She jerked her arm free. "Certainly not. I'll have you know that very few of my actions are determined by you."

"I see. Then you are not angry that I followed you here."

"You followed me here?" What was it about him that made her want to touch him? A simple placement of her hand on his arm was all it would take, but such a thing was entirely improper. It seemed the more she tried to behave around him, the more her body and mind protested.

He shrugged. "I knew you would be here today, and I wanted to see you."

She tried her best not to smile. It shouldn't please her so that he'd come here only to see her. But it did. It was a heady feeling that tingled all the way to her toes. He'd followed her here. She should stop being such a goose and leave the house as she intended.

She glanced around the wood-paneled hall, seeing no sign of the butler or anyone else. "You've deserted poor Poppy and Viscount Felmworth. You should get back to your game, and I should be going."

"Are you looking for someone?"

"The butler went to retrieve my cloak." She lifted her chin. "And I don't believe it is appropriate for us to be chatting alone."

"We're in the middle of the hall."

"It matters not. Is there something of importance you wish to discuss with me? Or will you leave me here to wait for my cloak alone?"

"Actually there is something." He grabbed her arm again, but this time he pulled her, leading her to an alcove below the stairs. "Now, is this better?"

"No. If people find us here, they will assume the worst."

"The worst?" His eyebrows arched perfectly over his intoxicating eyes. "What might that be?"

She tried to peek around him into the hall, but his broad chest blocked her view. "That you are ravishing me," she whispered.

"Ravishing?"

"Would you stop repeating everything I say? They'll assume we're being amorous."

"I see." He took a step closer to her, so that he stood mere inches away, his chest only a breath away. He leaned down so that his mouth was close to her ear. His hot breath sent a shiver racing down her spine. "So they might assume that we are kissing?"

"Yes." Her whisper came out louder than she intended. She put her hand over her mouth. "I really must go, I have—"

He straightened, but did not get out of her way. "Yes, a headache. I do hope you're not too ill."

She frowned. "What is it that you wish to discuss with me?"

"Richard."

"Again? I shall not listen. I am meeting with him in a few days, and I plan to discuss your allegations with him."

"And you think he'll tell you the truth? Claudia, surely you're not that naïve."

Was she? She hadn't even considered that Richard, were he in fact guilty, would probably lie about that guilt if she pressed him about it. That certainly made her sound naïve. And stupid. She wasn't stupid.

He plucked a curl from behind her ear and fingered it. "You know what your problem is?" he asked.

"No, but I'm betting you think you do."

"You trust all the wrong people. I think inside you know that Richard isn't the man for you—whether he's done the things I claim he's done aside—you know you shouldn't marry him." He trailed his finger down her cheek to her throat and then across to where her heart lay. "You should trust that."

She didn't trust the wrong people. She simply trusted people until they gave her a reason not to.

And she trusted herself. Didn't she? What was she feeling inside about Richard? She didn't want to marry him, Derrick was right, but that was for purely selfish reasons. She didn't want to marry Richard because he would never love her, but more importantly, because she would never love him.

"Think about what I've said; that's all I'm asking," he said.

"Derrick, even if you're right about me not wanting to marry Richard and him not being an upstanding man, it doesn't change the fact that my father has chosen him for me to marry. I must obey."

"We're never going to agree on that. I still think you could find a way out. If I could find proof of Richard's guilt, then your father would release you from your obligation of marrying him."

"But you have no proof, so this is a futile discussion."

"Here you are, miss." The butler was back from retrieving her cloak. "Miss?"

Derrick put his hand over her mouth and leaned into her, so that his body pressed against hers, and her body pressed into the wall. It was a gesture meant to keep them in hiding lest the servant discover them in this precarious position, but all it did was light her body on fire. Every nerve sparked to life and began stirring about her flesh.

Think about something else. Think about hair ribbons or paintbrushes or . . . ducks. Anything else. Anything but Derrick's hard thigh pressed intimately between her legs. It was difficult to think of anything besides convincing herself not to push against him. Disgraceful thoughts. She really ought to be ashamed of herself, but instead she was exhilarated.

"Always changing their minds," the servant muttered, "strange creatures."

Derrick released a breath and removed his hand from her mouth. But he didn't pull back from her body. "That was close," he said.

"Indeed." She should push him off her, but for reasons she dared not investigate, she stood still and simply stared into his eyes.

"I suppose I could ravish you under here. Not a lot of room, but I do believe we could manage."

She realized her hands were grasping material at his sleeves. His glance dropped to her breasts. *Touch them.* She clenched her jaw to keep from saying it.

"You drive me crazy with desire." His voice was ragged. "I've never wanted a woman the way I want you."

It was all the encouragement she needed. She tilted her head and kissed him. She didn't wait for the slow seduction he usually gave her lips. Instead she thrust her tongue into his mouth. Blood thrummed through her body, singing as it went from one body part to the next. She allowed her hands to release his jacket and move up to thread through his hair.

He kissed her back just as forcefully, their tongues rolling and caressing. He left her mouth and dropped kisses on her cleavage. She was ready to tear her dress off, so she could feel his warm mouth on her skin.

His hand crept beneath the hem of her dress; the fabric brushed against her ankle, then her calf, behind her knee, and then she felt his hand on her inner thigh—dear God, where was he going? He stopped at her most private spot.

"God, Claudia, I want you so badly."

He didn't move his fingers at first, just cupped her gently. She rocked against him. He found the slit in her drawers and moved one finger against her skin. She leaned into his shirt to muffle a cry. What was he doing to her? Slowly he moved his finger against her, back and forth, back and forth, until she thought she'd go mad.

Then suddenly his hand was gone as fast as it had appeared, and much too soon as she was certain something big had been about to happen. She almost asked, but then it became abundantly clear why he'd stopped.

She looked at his face, saw him mutter a curse, then he turned around to face the woman who had discovered their hiding place. How could she have been so stupid? She couldn't even bear to think what the woman must have seen or heard. Was that why she'd come—had Claudia cried out? She'd been so engrossed in the feelings, she hadn't even remembered where they were.

She was the worst sort of woman, a woman without a shred of self-control.

"I daresay, Mr. Middleton, I do hope there is an explanation for this," Lady Oliver said, her voice tight.

Derrick put on his best smile. "Absolutely. I'm afraid it's my fault. You see, Miss Prattley has just agreed to be my bride, and I am embarrassed to say I couldn't hide my enthusiasm."

He was lying. For her. Taking the blame in a situation that was certain to ruin her. She couldn't allow him to do this, yet when she opened her mouth to argue, she found she had no words.

Lady Oliver, known for being a romantic, smiled and placed her hand on her heart. "How very wonderful for you two. And I do apologize for interrupting. It's only that Benson, my butler, was concerned when Miss Prattley asked for her cloak and then disappeared. He came looking for her in the parlor, and when he couldn't find her

185

there, I told him I would go find her. Your secret is safe with me," she whispered. "But you really ought to be more discreet." She winked and swatted Derrick on the arm.

Derrick held on to Claudia's hand as he pulled her out from the stairwell. "Let me get my coat, and we can be on our way. She wants to tell her father right away."

"Of course," Lady Oliver offered.

In the course of fifteen minutes Claudia's entire life had changed. How or why wasn't clear, but she knew nothing would ever be the same. She wouldn't marry Derrick; he would never see it through, and her father certainly wouldn't allow it. He'd clearly been disappointed that they were discovered and that he had to do the honorable thing, or he wouldn't have cursed. He didn't want to marry her, and she certainly wouldn't require him to.

She was weak and obviously had no control over herself. Shame heated her entire body, and she wanted to scream. No matter what happened between them now, she'd always feel as if she'd trapped him. As if she'd given him no other choice. No one wanted to be a bride under those circumstances.

And now it no longer mattered if she did or didn't want to marry Richard, or if he was or wasn't all that Derrick claimed him to be. All that mattered was she had been compromised.

Her reputation was ruined. And her relationship with her father would never be the same.

Chapter 10

❧

"You don't have to marry me," Claudia said once they were alone in the carriage.

"Don't be ridiculous, Claudia, of course we will marry."

"My father will forbid it."

"Your father has no choice. I've ruined your reputation, and I will do the honorable thing."

His words pricked at her heart. Honor. It was an admirable trait, but no woman wanted honor to be the reason for becoming a wife. She almost laughed. Were it not so painful, she might have. She remembered as a little girl she'd dreamed of this day—the day she became betrothed—and it never played out in such a manner.

There had always been declarations of love in her fantasies, but the reality held no promise of love. She looked at Derrick, who sat statue-still across from her. He stared out the window, his mouth tight, a frown furrowing his brow. If he'd been courting her the way he'd claimed, he would not be so disappointed right now.

"When we get to your house," he said as he turned to face her, "I want you to wait in the hall while I speak to your father alone."

"Derrick, my father will not be pleased."

"No father is pleased when his daughter is caught in an intimate embrace in public."

"But he is not fond of you."

"I beg your pardon?"

"He does not care for your paper, believes you print lies. He doesn't like you."

"I don't care if he likes me or not. I am going to marry you. It's the right thing to do. And I'll do it with or without his permission."

"Why are you so angry?" she asked.

He released a heavy breath. "I'm not angry. I'm frustrated. With myself. I should have had more control. This wasn't your fault, Claudia, it was all mine. I take full responsibility.

"I want you to remain in the hall until I am finished speaking to him. I think it will be better that way. Unless you can think of something that will convince him to allow you to marry me."

She chewed at her lip. It would not go well. Her father had such a temper. "No," she said softly.

"I didn't think so."

They rode the rest of the way in silence. When the carriage rocked to a stop, Derrick turned to her. He held his hand out to her, and she clasped it.

"It will be all right. No matter how it appears now."

She gave him a smile, then followed him up the stairs to her house. She took a seat on the bench in the hallway while Derrick was announced in her father's study. Her hands were shaking so badly, she had to clutch at her skirt to still them.

She closed her eyes and tuned her ears to the voices behind the door. She could hear them speaking, but could not make out any words. Frustrated, she stood and put her ear to the door. Still nothing.

Derrick had said everything would be all right. She wanted to believe him, but she knew her father, and nothing that happened today would be all right with him.

"No!" her father suddenly yelled.

She silently cracked the door open, just enough to let the sound out.

"Viscount Kennington, I appreciate your anger, but understand something. I did not come here to discuss this with you. I merely came as a courtesy to my future wife's father." Derrick's tone was even, but strong.

"My daughter will not be your wife."

Her father's steps paced across the floor. No doubt he strolled behind his desk as he did every time he was upset. Guilt settled in her stomach. There was no excuse for what had occurred today. No reason that any of the things that had happened with Derrick had happened. No reason other than her weakness and inability to say no. It was a sickening realization that she had so little resolve.

"Something happened today that demands that Claudia and I marry," Derrick said.

"I don't care what happened. You're not marrying her. You're not even from a decent family," her father spat. "Not to mention that piece of garbage you call a newspaper. If my daughter were associated with you, it would disparage my reputation in Parliament."

"Your daughter is already associated with me."

It was evident that Derrick was trying to tell her

father about the compromise, without having to give him specifics. But her father was not listening. He rarely did.

"Nonsense. A few dances mean nothing. She's danced with other men before. She's betrothed to another; she can't marry."

"Richard Foxmore?" The words came out in short, clipped tones.

"Precisely."

"She's not betrothed to him."

"I beg your pardon."

"Claudia said Richard has never asked for her hand."

"Yes, but he and I have discussed it. He's planning to ask her tomorrow. They have an engagement to meet."

"He's too late." Derrick's tone prickled the hairs at her neck. He did not yell with anger as her father did, yet the anger was there. Quiet and controlled, held just beneath the surface.

"Go to the devil, Middleton," her father said, seemingly unaffected by Derrick's words. "I don't have to explain this any further. You may not marry my daughter. Now get out of my house."

"I compromised your daughter today, and I will marry her, because she does not deserve to have her reputation shredded."

"Compromised? What did you do?"

"The details do not matter. What matters is, we announced our engagement at Lady Oliver's house but an hour ago. I suspect everyone in London knows by now."

There was a long pause before her father mumbled, "Compromise. Wrong bloody man. Should have planned such a situation myself." Then he cleared his throat, "Middleton, your honor is surprising. But take heart, I will not demand you marry her to save her reputation. She'll ride out the scandal herself. I'll send her to the country to make it easier on her."

His words sliced into her heart, as clean as the sharpest of knifes. He was a harsh man; she'd always known that, but she suspected he loved her. In his own way. But to do this? To prefer that she be ruined rather than see her marry a man he didn't approve of? She squeezed her eyes shut to keep the tears from falling.

"You would rather see your daughter ruined than allow her to marry me?"

Derrick had put her own thoughts into words. It was worse hearing them out loud. One tear slipped. She allowed it to fall, leaving a cold, damp trail down her cheek.

"Yes. No question about it. My reputation is far

more important than hers. Girls like her have lived through scandals before. She'll be fine. She's sturdy."

"Sturdy?" She heard Derrick take a ragged breath. "I've tried to be patient and polite, but I'm tired, so let us see if this is easier for you to understand. Claudia and I will be married this Saturday. You are welcome to attend, but only if you support her. If not, stay home. This isn't open for discussion. The announcement will be in the *Times* tomorrow."

"Bastard. You can't do that."

"Try and stop me," Derrick said coldly.

"You won't get her dowry."

"I don't give a damn about her dowry. Keep it. Roll in it if you must. Were it up to me, know that Claudia would cut ties with you as soon as we wed, but I know her, and she won't want that to happen. But it is in your best interest to be kind to her. I'd hate to see anything nasty written about you in my paper."

"Are you threatening me, Middleton?"

"No, I'm warning you."

Before she could move from the door, Derrick pushed it open. His gaze met hers, and compassion warmed his eyes, if only for a brief moment.

"Come with me, Claudia. You won't be staying here any longer."

"I can't live with you," she said.

"I know that. I'll take you to Poppy's. I'm sure you can stay there until we wed. I'll send a carriage for your things. You can include a note with instructions for your maid."

She wished she were the kind of person who knew what to say to her father to make this all right. But she wasn't. She took one last glance at the door, then walked to the carriage. They would talk later. Once he accustomed himself to the idea of her marrying Derrick. Once his anger subsided.

They were halfway to Poppy's before Derrick spoke.

"I'm sorry you had to hear all of that."

She couldn't look at him. She simply kept her focus out the window and let the tears stream down her cheeks.

He didn't know what else to say. She wouldn't even look at him. Her tears shocked him. Not because they were unwarranted, she had every right to cry, but because he was used to seeing her vivacious, not beaten down like this. It stirred something inside him. Something that demanded he protect her at all costs. And that scared the hell out of him.

Hell, he hadn't even been courting her—not really—and now he'd have to tell her that. He certainly couldn't go into a marriage with that lie above them. But not today.

He certainly hadn't meant for them to be compromised. He shouldn't have been so reckless. He'd lived through enough scandals—he certainly didn't need to be tied to another. And he couldn't allow Claudia to take the blame. Her father was capable of making her life unlivable.

He'd had doubts in the carriage on the way to her father's house. Her soft words promising to release him from his duty had been tempting. He wasn't ready to marry again. But after seeing her father and hearing the filth he had to say, there was no question of what to do.

While he wouldn't be able to offer Claudia a marriage full of love, he could certainly give her respect and treat her kindly. He refused to give her his heart, but he'd make up for it every other way he could.

What of her heart? Would she offer it freely to him? Probably not. Especially after he explained the truth behind his courtship. It was completely unfair to expect her to love him when he couldn't offer her love in return, but he acknowledged that he desired just that. He was a selfish bastard.

* * *

Once Claudia was settled in an upstairs room at Poppy's house, and after Lady Livingston had fretted over her for a quarter of an hour, she was left alone. But her solitude was brief. Only a moment later, Poppy poked her head into the room.

"If you're not ready to talk about whatever has happened, I'll understand, but you look just awful. Are you all right?"

She had totally forgotten that the tears had probably left her usually rosy cheeks with white streaks and that her eyes more than likely were puffy and red. She gave Poppy a weak smile.

"I'm fine."

"Can you tell me what happened? I obviously know that something happened at Lady Oliver's, but she wouldn't say." Poppy's brow furrowed. "Which is unusual, but I'm assuming since the dowager duchess was there, she censored herself."

There had been a time when Claudia told Poppy everything, but ever since she'd met Derrick, some things seemed too personal, too intimate.

"Derrick and I are engaged, and my father is upset, to say the least."

"Engaged?! How marvelous."

She shook her head. "I don't know. It was somewhat unplanned and very sudden."

197

"Does this have anything to do with your kiss the other night at the ball? Did someone see you? Were you compromised?"

"Not at the ball."

"When?"

"Today. At the card party." How humiliating. It was bad enough that Lady Oliver knew, but to admit to your best friend that you lacked control . . . She buried her head in her hands and waited for Poppy's disappointed reaction.

But instead, Poppy laughed. Not a little giggle, but a full-out chuckle.

She snapped her head up. "What is so funny?"

Poppy smiled widely. "I'm enjoying the irony of your situation. Your father wants you to marry Richard because it will be good for your reputation, so what do you do—go and get yourself compromised with a man your father despises. And at a tea and card party. In the middle of the afternoon. It couldn't have happened any better had I planned it myself."

"Poppy, it's not funny or ironic. It's dreadful. I've ruined my reputation and tarnished my father's in the process. He'll probably never forgive me. This would never have happened to you. You're the very picture of decorum."

"It has nothing to do with decorum and everything to do with the fact that I've never had a man like Derrick Middleton pull me into his arms. I'm not laughing at you, and I certainly don't find it humorous at your expense." She scrunched her nose. "You know, I hate to admit it, but I'm enjoying the fact that this must be awful for your father."

"That's a rotten thing to say."

"I can't help it. He's been a rotten father." She held up her hand to silence Claudia's protests. "I know he's provided for you, and you think he's done his best raising you without your mother. And yes, he's a hard man, but the truth of the matter is, he's not a kind man. There are many people out there hardened by life, but they haven't allowed it to tarnish their hearts. Being compromised with Derrick is the best thing that's ever happened to you."

"I believe your perception is altered."

"I'm serious. He can take you away from your father. No more worrying about every step you take, every word you say." Poppy clapped her hands together. "Oh, and you'll be free to continue your illustrations. How perfect. You can even sign your name. Let the world know that you are the talent behind those drawings."

Claudia shook her head. "No. It would destroy my father to know that I had a paying position behind his back. I can't do that to him."

"One of these days your blind loyalty to him is going to cost you dearly."

"I can't turn my back on him. You should have heard him when Derrick was explaining what happened. He was furious. He'll probably never forgive me, Poppy, and that hurts me. I know he hasn't been the sort of father you think is kind and loving, but he's the only one I have. The only family I have. And family deserves loyalty. I betrayed him."

Poppy sighed and squeezed her hand. "I understand, and I'm not going to tell you that you're wrong for loving and respecting your father, but you cannot continue to live your life trying to please a man who will never approve of you. Instead of thinking about him and how he feels today, you should be reveling in the fact that Derrick rose to the occasion and saved your reputation. He did the honorable thing, and to find a man with honor is a rare thing—he will make you a good husband, Claudia."

"He doesn't love me."

"You don't know that."

Her heart skipped a beat. Could he love her? In time would he grow to love her, once she gave him children? He liked her, seemed to enjoy her company, but ultimately she didn't believe she was the kind of woman who could evoke such a strong emotion in a man. Derrick would never love her. She was being ridiculous even considering it.

"All right, so maybe he doesn't love you. Yet. That doesn't mean he won't or isn't already starting to. He certainly started courting you for a reason. He genuinely likes you. Anyone can see that. He enjoys your company. He obviously desires you, else you wouldn't have found yourself in this situation."

He did desire her. She knew that. Felt it deep inside. She didn't understand it, but she knew it. Perhaps it was simply that she was a willing female, and he'd have reacted that way with anyone.

But he'd said himself that he'd never wanted anyone the way he wanted her.

"He will love you, Claudia. I know he will. How could he not?" Poppy wiped the tears that Claudia hadn't even realized she'd cried. "I'll leave you alone now, but let me know if you need anything."

Claudia smiled at her best friend. "I'll be fine. I promise. This morning my life was headed in a different direction. But I'll be fine," she assured her.

Poppy was a good friend, but there were things she'd never understand. Derrick would never love her; Claudia knew that. But she could certainly see herself falling in love with him, and that terrified her.

She'd resigned herself to a loveless marriage with Richard. With Richard it wouldn't matter if he didn't love her, because she knew in her heart that she would never love him. But a loveless marriage with Derrick was a different matter entirely. She didn't want to love him if he didn't love her in return. Marrying Derrick would break her heart because she was certain she'd begun to love him already.

Chapter 11

❦

The following day Claudia sat in the Livingston parlor waiting for Derrick to arrive and call off the entire thing. Surely after a night's sleep, he'd come to his senses and realized he didn't want to marry her.

"Do stop pacing, Claudia, you're making me ill," Poppy said.

The door opened, and the Livingston butler poked his head in. "Miss Prattley, a Lord Foxmore to see you."

Richard. Claudia stopped wearing a path in their carpet and glanced at Poppy. "What should I tell him?"

"You don't owe him an explanation, Claudia. You weren't betrothed to him. Simply tell him that you and Derrick are to be married. That is all that needs to be said."

Richard entered the room looking more haggard than she'd ever seen him. In fact, she'd actually never seen him look haggard at all. His usually perfectly groomed hair lacked the oil that kept it in place, so it sat in reckless waves on his head. It was more attractive this way, but she thought better of commenting on it. And his clothing was less than clean. Bags sagged beneath his eyes, indicating at least one sleepless night, but probably more.

Gracious, she hoped this state wasn't because of her.

"Hello, Richard."

"Claudia." He forced a weak smile, then nodded to Poppy.

"I believe I shall go and see if our dresses are ready for the soiree," Poppy said, then left the room.

Traitor. She could have stayed for support. Of course, this was something Claudia needed to do herself.

"I suppose my father told you I was here," she said.

He nodded. He clenched his thin lips tightly together.

"And I suppose he told you why I'm here."

He looked at her, and she was almost certain she saw something close to hatred flash in his eyes. "I cannot believe you would do this to me. You were supposed to marry me." His voice was low and soft, too soft to be calm.

Claudia took a step away from him. She didn't owe him an explanation. Perhaps repeating Poppy's advice would prevent her from giving him too much information. She was sorry if she hurt him, but Poppy was right. They had never been engaged. He'd never even so much as muttered the word marriage to her. Not even once.

"You never asked me."

"What the hell is that supposed to mean? You knew of my intentions. I had spoken with your father about it a number of times and planned to ask for your hand when I returned from the country."

"Speaking to my father is not the same as us being engaged. I'm sorry this happened the way it did, but I'm marrying Derrick."

"You're sorry? You're sorry!" His voice rose to an alarming level. He pushed his hand through his hair. "Damnation, Claudia, this ruins everything. All my plans."

Raw rage dripped off him like wax droplets from a burning candle. She'd ruined his plans. She hadn't hurt him.

"Your plans? I ruined your plans? Richard, I am not a plan. Marriage is not a plan. Not in my eyes, anyway. Marriage is a sacred relationship. It's about mutual respect and admiration and sometimes, if you're one of the lucky ones, sometimes it's about love. But never is it about plans."

"Don't be foolish." A cruel smile lit his face. "Did you think I loved you?"

"You told me you did. All those poems. The trinkets. Those are the actions of a man in love. But to answer your question, no, I didn't think you loved me. Not really. I did think you were at least fond of me. I thought you wanted me for your wife. Not simply because you needed me to secure your political future."

His eyebrows shot up.

"Don't look so surprised. I'm not as foolish as you think, just a little slow to see the truth."

"Truth? Do you know what kind of man Derrick Middleton is?"

"Decent and hardworking."

Richard let out a humorless laugh.

How could she have ever looked at this man with favor? True, she had never loved him, but she'd been somewhat fond of him. Had believed he was a kind man. Had believed he'd honestly wanted to marry her.

What a fool she'd been. Perhaps Derrick had been right about Richard all along, and perhaps Derrick would tell her what he'd been reluctant to tell her before. She wanted the details of Richard's past. She needed to know what kind of man she'd almost married.

"If this is the only reason you came here today, then I'd rather you leave. I'm sorry things turned out the way they did for you and that your plans are ruined. But I have no time to listen to your stories."

"My stories? You don't know anything, you foolish chit. Your would-be lover has a secretive past. I'd wager there's quite a bit you don't know about Derrick Middleton."

"You're talking nonsense." She stood and walked away from him. Wanting to distance herself from his lies. "But if you're talking about his previous marriage, then yes, I know about that."

"No, I'm talking about something Derrick wrote for his father's paper and the result of it was someone's death."

"Reporting the truth is the great purpose of newspapers. It does not make him responsible for a man's life."

"I never said the story was the truth," Richard sneered. "Only that it resulted in a man's death."

What did that mean? That Derrick printed a false story? Impossible. Derrick wasn't a liar. She knew him well enough to know that. Didn't she?

Richard closed the distance between them. "How did you meet Derrick Middleton?"

"My relationship with him is none of your concern."

"From what your father said, you've made it everyone's business." He let his eyes roam down the length of her, and it was as if he'd actually touched her. She shivered in revulsion.

"Had I known that you were so willing," he said, "I'd have made advances myself."

With that he pulled her to him and pressed his mouth against hers. There was no tenderness or sweeping passion in his kiss, rather it was filled with anger and spite. She pushed against him, but to no avail. He continued his assault on her, pushing his tongue against her closed mouth.

She wanted to scream, but his mouth against hers and the bile rising in her throat made it impossible to do so. Tears pricked her eyes, and she kicked at him as best she could with the hindrance of her skirts.

Oh God, how could she get out of this?

And then he was gone, off her as fast as he'd advanced. She opened her eyes and found Richard slammed facedown onto the blue carpet with Derrick hovering above him. He held Richard's head by a handful of hair.

"If I ever catch you again with your hands on Claudia, I will kill you. Is that understood?" His voice was low and even-toned, which made it all the more chilling. He meant those words, and fear and pride rivaled in Claudia's blood. She didn't know what to feel.

"Get off me!" Richard said, his words muffled by the angle of his head.

"Apologize to Miss Prattley." Derrick jammed his knee into Richard's back.

"I'm sorry," his words came out in a grunt.

Derrick released him, and Richard climbed to his feet. He wiped at the blood dripping from his jaw.

He gave a chilling smile. There was something horrible in this man that somehow she'd missed. "I know why you're marrying her, Middleton. Got another news story?"

"What the devil are you talking about?"

Richard's eyes narrowed. He looked from Derrick to her and then back again. "You don't know, do you?"

"I don't know what you're talking about. I

don't report anymore. I run the paper; I don't write anymore."

"Well, in that case, if you want the story of your life—let me know. The story that will explain all the mysteries from your last piece. I'll sell it to you."

"Do you think I'm a fool? The last story you fed me was a pack of lies."

Richard nodded. "I will admit to that. But this time, it's the truth. This time, I'm not working for anyone. It's only me." He shrugged. "As I said, if you're interested, let me know."

He left them standing alone.

"Did he hurt you?" Derrick cupped Claudia's face and searched her skin for any markings.

"No, I'm fine." The rush of emotions nearly overwhelmed her. She blinked back tears. "I had no idea he could behave that way."

"Of course you didn't. He was always on his best behavior. And it is not in your nature to see the less perfect side of people."

"The two of you have more of a past than I thought."

"Yes, well, as I told you before, I know things about Richard."

"Clearly you know things my father is unaware of. Perhaps once he's not so angry, you could talk to him, tell him what you know about Richard. Then maybe he'll be more accepting."

He ran his hand down her cheek. "Are you sure you're not hurt?"

She gave him a weak smile. "I'm fine." Tears pooled in her pretty blue eyes. She waved a hand in front of her. "I really am fine, I don't know why I'm crying. I'm just being silly."

"He scared you." He pulled her to him and hugged her close.

"Yes, I suppose he did."

"He won't do it again."

Derrick kissed the top of her hair, then pulled her in front of him. He kissed each eyelid, then her nose, then placed a gentle kiss on her lips.

"I'm sorry I wasn't here sooner."

"It's not your fault," she said. "But I'm glad you came when you did." She paused before asking, "What did he mean that you wanted to marry me for the story? What story?"

"I have no idea. He's angry, nothing more. Pay him no mind." He gave her a smile. "Have you and Poppy discussed the wedding plans?"

"No." She chewed at her lip. "I wasn't positive. I mean, I still want to allow you to back out if you wish. I will be content alone."

"We're not discussing this again. We're getting

married. You and Poppy decide on the plans—I have the ceremony set for Saturday."

"That doesn't give us much time."

"You're right. You had better get busy. One more thing before I go back to work. I came here to give you this." He held out a ring. "To make our engagement official."

The gold band slid easily onto her finger. She looked down at it; three oval sapphires sat between two smaller diamonds. It was breathtaking.

"The stones match your eyes," he said, then averted his glance.

"I wasn't expecting this. Thank you." She leaned up and kissed him.

"You're welcome. Are you positive you're all right?"

"Yes. He took me by surprise, but he didn't hurt me."

"Very well. I'll come check on you later."

Derrick left with the taste of her still on his lips. He knew he needed to tell her the truth. He hated to start a marriage on a lie. But he couldn't risk her backing out now, not after meeting her father. He was a tyrant of the worst kind, and Derrick would be damned if he allowed her to go back into that house.

So he would wait until after the ceremony, when she was safely his, and then he would tell her.

When he'd arrived and found Richard on her,

his world colored red before him. His only thought had been to get Richard's dirty hands and mouth off her. Had he not arrived when he did, there was no telling what Richard would have done to her. The thought made his breakfast turn over in his stomach. Bastard. He'd kill him if he ever touched her again.

Richard had mentioned a story. Implied that Derrick was marrying Claudia to discover the truth of some matter. Derrick had no doubt that Kennington hid a few secrets, most men of power did. It was unlikely though that Claudia knew about any of them, much less would she divulge them if she did. She would protect her father at all costs. Derrick knew that.

And there still remained the truth that Derrick sought no such hidden story. He was marrying Claudia because he'd ruined her. Besides, it was not above Richard to completely fabricate something to take the focus off something else. That something else, no doubt, was the real mystery. But none of that mattered anymore. All that mattered was Claudia's safety.

She was safe now for the time being, and soon she would be in his protection, in his home, as his wife. He certainly hadn't set out to get another wife, but fate had seen to it that he would have one.

It felt strange to be that protective toward someone, but Claudia was to be his wife. She'd bear his children. And he'd do whatever he could to keep her safe.

"What the devil are you doing here?" Derrick asked. Mason must have left for the day, else he'd have announced the visitor.

Richard, snide as ever, strolled into Derrick's office and took a seat before Derrick could offer or decline one. "I have a proposition for you."

Derrick cocked one eyebrow. "Before you waste your breath, I'm not interested."

Richard gave him a snarl of a smile. "Oh, but I believe you will be. You see, it's about your wife-to-be."

"I thought I told you yesterday to stay the hell away from her. Clearly I should have killed you on the spot."

Richard clicked his tongue. "And hang for killing an aristocrat? That's hardly a way to begin a marriage."

"What the hell do you want?"

"Money, of course." He shrugged.

"You are vile."

"Yes, well, I also hold the secrets to the biggest political scandal this country has ever seen."

"I doubt it. And what does that have to do with Claudia?"

"No details, Middleton, not without payment. Do you think I'm daft?"

"Yes, actually. I won't give you one penny without knowing more details. I have no reason to trust this time will be any different from the last."

"There was a time when you trusted me."

"Yes. And I paid dearly for that. I won't make that same mistake again."

"Very well. I'm sure you remember that little piece you wrote a few years back that indicted Edwards on those embezzlement charges."

Derrick fought the sudden urge to crawl across the table and rip out Richard's larynx. Slimy bastard.

"That story was only partially true, as you might have gathered. Although I must say that Society's treatment of you and your father's paper after that incident was quite unwarranted." He sighed dramatically. "But when you have the chancellor of finance against you, what can be done?"

"Get to the point, Richard. I have work to do."

"Yes, well, I have the real story. The complete truth, and believe me, it will solidify your paper's reputation. I thought you knew about it. I thought you'd somehow discovered the truth and that is why you were sniffing around Claudia, but I was wrong. Although I can't imagine you—or anyone—intentionally courting her for no valid reason."

Derrick's jaw clenched. He squeezed the arm of the chair and mentally counted to ten. "You never intended to marry her, did you?"

"It was not my preference, but eventually her father would have seen to it that we married. I was angry at first, but after some thought, I realized that you saved me. I should thank you, really. But without that dowry money, I'm afraid I can't."

"Bastard." Derrick stood. "Get the hell out of my office."

"Suit yourself. But do reconsider my offer. This time you won't regret it." He tossed his calling card onto Derrick's desk and strode out.

216

Chapter 12

Kennington knocked on the door, then waited. After a moment with no answer, he knocked again, this time more forcefully with the end of his cane. Where was the stupid sop?

Footsteps rapped a beat on the interior hall. No doubt Richard himself, since he could no longer afford servants. *Worthless man.*

The door opened. "What are you doing here?" Richard asked.

"That's no way to greet an old friend. Invite me in."

"We're not friends."

"Invite me in anyway. We have business to discuss." He didn't wait for Richard to move out of the way, rather he pushed the door open with his cane.

"I spoke with Claudia earlier. You and I have no more business. Claudia is getting married."

Their business would be finished when Kennington said it would be and not a moment sooner. Kennington waited until they were seated in the tiny study. Papers littered the desk, and books were scattered about on the floor. He never would have suspected Richard was so disordered.

"Lose something?"

"No." Richard smiled smugly. "I found it. Why are you here?"

"You may think our business is finished, but I have another plan." He needed Richard in the family, needed to keep him near lest the truth of Kennington's past be revealed. But in his family, he could tighten the purse strings and ensure Richard kept quiet. "You give up too easily. You're weak. That's always been your problem. But there is still time. We can fix this minor setback in our plans. Go and get her. Take her across the border. Marry her tonight."

"Have you gone mad? Their engagement has been announced in the papers. Everyone is talking about it. Marrying her now would not save anyone's reputation. Besides, I'm rather glad I don't have to marry her. Never cared for her, really."

He stomped his cane on the floor. "We cannot allow her to marry that man."

"The truth of the matter is, I'm glad she's marrying Middleton. I was angry at first; I hadn't realized she was so willing with her favors. But I never really wanted her, you see. I only wanted what your status could give me, but that's over with. No one listens to you any longer. I'm finished with you. I'm free to do as I please."

"What makes you think you don't need me anymore?"

"I am no longer in need of your assistance to better my position in Parliament. I have influence on my own now. People know me; they respect me."

"Don't be foolish, boy. No one respects you. Don't think for a moment that you can walk away from our arrangement. I own you."

Richard stood abruptly. "I sold the story. I told all the dirty little details of what you did." He swallowed visibly. "Now *I* own *you*."

Kennington laughed. "Foolish boy. Do you think I'm an idiot? You have no proof to sell that story. No one would believe you."

"Oh, but I do have proof."

He rose to his feet. "What are you talking about?"

"The letters."

"What letters?" Kennington tried to keep his voice from rising too loud; he wanted to remain in control.

"The blackmail letters you wrote to Edwards. I have them."

"Liar."

Richard reached into his coat pocket and pulled out an envelope.

Kennington recognized his own penmanship instantly. "Where did you get those?"

"I never gave them to Edwards. A verbal threat was all he needed to comply. I figured these might be useful someday." Richard snickered. "I was correct."

Those letters would ruin him. Not only politically, but they could feasibly send him to prison or to the hangman's noose.

"I paid you to deliver those letters to Edwards." He edged his way toward Richard. "You had no right to keep them."

Richard shrugged. "I am first and foremost loyal to myself and my needs. Keeping these letters served my needs, so loyalty to you fell by the wayside. You really should be more particular when you hire people."

Smug bastard. He held out his hand. "Give me the letters, or I'll kill you."

"That's the third time I've had my life threatened this week, and they've come to no avail."

"Don't test me. Hand them over."

"Go to hell."

Kennington would not allow this idiot to ruin all his plans. He swung his cane and heard the metal knob crack against Richard's skull. Shock etched in Richard's features, and blood ran down his face into his eyes. He wavered a bit, then fell to the floor. Pulling back his cane once more, Kennington brought it down with all the force he could. Blood spattered against his pants leg.

He rolled Richard over and reached into his coat pocket and withdrew the stack of letters. Seven of them. They would have destroyed him.

He looked down into Richard's lifeless face, eyes still open, blood pooling about his head and soaking into the Persian carpet. There would be no marriage between Richard and Claudia now, but with Richard dead, keeping him close was no longer necessary.

"Stupid bastard."

He wiped the blood from his hands and the cane on his shirt—he would burn it when he got home. Then he busied himself with making it look as if there had been a burglary. He took what little money Richard had on him and the few bank notes from his desk. He kicked the papers on the floor about and opened all the desk drawers. Then he took his cane and slammed it into the window for the final touch.

With that, he turned on his heel and left through the back door.

Claudia had never seen her friend in such a state. Poppy's pretty eyes were puffy and red. Alistair had proposed, just as Poppy suspected he would, but his proposition had not been one of marriage. Rather, Alistair had proposed that Poppy become his mistress.

He'd been fully prepared to give her every material thing her heart desired. He'd even offered to give her an allowance that would benefit her entire family, but he'd not offered marriage. He'd offered everything but his love and his name. And now Poppy's heart was broken.

Claudia had tried everything to convince Poppy that things would be right again, but there was no convincing her. She supposed she might feel the same way were she in Poppy's shoes, but she was in an entirely different pair of shoes altogether.

Claudia eyed her best friend sitting quietly beside the window. Her shoulders no longer shook, and tears no longer fell down her streaked cheeks, but she looked defeated and worn.

"Is there anything I can get you?" Claudia asked.

Poppy shook her head.

What would happen when Lady Livingston arrived home from her afternoon tea and found her daughter in shambles? How would she react to such a scandalous event? A shiver pricked its way up Claudia's spine at the thought of having to tell such a story to her father. Granted, he hadn't taken the news of her pending nuptials too well either. She could hardly blame him; he must be mortified by her behavior. Despite her intentions, Claudia had made scandalous behavior an art form.

Just then Lady Livingston entered the parlor. "Good afternoon, girls. How are we today?" The stately woman took one look at her daughter's still figure and stopped moving. "Poppy, darling, what's the matter?"

Poppy turned to face her mother and burst into tears.

Her mother immediately took a seat next to Poppy. "Gracious, whatever is wrong?" Mother and daughter embraced, and Claudia watched as Lady Livingston's hand rubbed an even tempo against Poppy's back.

"Whatever is wrong, remember all will be well." She retrieved a handkerchief from her reticule. Dabbing at Poppy's eyes, she looked at her daughter with nothing but love and concern. "Stop crying, love, before you make yourself ill. Now tell me what happened."

It took Poppy a good fifteen minutes to recount the story amid hiccups and sobs. Her mother held her again and rocked her gently.

"Not precisely the question you thought he'd ask you? Well, I can certainly understand these tears. Your heart is broken, my dear, but it shall mend in due time. I know you think he was the only one to make you feel that love, but he's not. A bit more patience and time, and you'll see."

Claudia watched Lady Livingston console her daughter. Envy sat in her stomach like a stone. She felt like the intruder being here during such an intimate family moment. But she couldn't tear herself away. What must it feel like to have a parent not judge, not scold, but only comfort?

There was no mention of a scandal to the family or how this incident would affect her family name. There was no mention of a lack of judgment or reckless behavior. Instead there were hugs and pats and tender words meant to console and express love. Claudia would have given anything to know what it felt like to have that kind of love, if only for a moment.

Chapter 13

◦─◦◦◦◦─◦

She was married.

Claudia sat at the dressing table, brushing her hair. She'd lost count somewhere along fifty-six strokes as her mind worked to absorb all the day's events.

Married.

It was a strange and giddy feeling. It had been a quiet ceremony with only Poppy's family and a few of Derrick's friends as well as his aunt. Claudia's father had not come. She had known he probably wouldn't come, but she'd hoped he would prove her wrong. She would send a note to him later to let him know she was well and would come see him soon.

Derrick was behind her somewhere in the room; where precisely, she wasn't sure, as she couldn't see him. But she felt him, like a warm blanket around her shoulders. Her husband. She wanted to turn and find him, to study his features as she'd never allowed herself to do, but her nerves wouldn't allow it. There was no awkwardness between them, but there was a charge in the air that was palatable. Tonight he would make her his own, and the thought terrified and exhilarated her. Was he as nervous about the marriage bed as she?

Perhaps, but certainly not for the same reasons. She was nervous because she'd never lain with a man before. But even more so, she'd never had any man look upon her while she was unclothed. Or touch the excess flesh that gave her such shame. She put a hand on her belly and felt the softness. Perhaps he wouldn't want to touch her at all.

Try as she might, she didn't believe that. Derrick would want to touch her. Everywhere.

That thought paralyzed the breath in her chest.

The feelings he'd evoked from touching her the few times they'd had encounters had left her shamelessly aching for more. More of what, she wasn't certain. But surely there was more.

She'd always believed what went on between a

husband and wife behind closed doors was an unpleasant thing, but Derrick had made her believe it might be quite pleasant.

Then suddenly he was behind her, his reflection standing above hers in the mirror. He was so handsome, she nearly gasped. And he was hers.

He took the brush from her and gently brought it back through her hair, his hand smoothing a path behind the brush. There was something so intimate about his brushing her hair. No one save Baubie and her mother had ever brushed her hair. He continued his brushing, all the while keeping his focus on her hair.

She allowed herself to study him in the mirror, and for the first time, she saw something other than his handsome face. There was a childlike concentration in his expression as he brushed her hair, and in that moment he seemed lost and vulnerable, and she felt the strongest need to love him. To forget her worries about one-sided affection and simply hand him her heart.

"There's something you need to know."

He stopped the brushing, and his eyes met hers in the mirror.

He set the brush down and walked to the bed. "Come over here."

She chewed at her bottom lip.

He swore under his breath. "When you do that,

I want to throw you down on that bed and kiss you. From the top of your head to your little dainty toes." He shook his head and released a little chuckle. "They're toes, that's all, and yet they're the most erotic toes I've ever seen. And that ridiculous nightgown."

She looked down at her gown, then looked back up at him. She opened her mouth to say something, but he cut her off.

"It covers everything but your head and the aforementioned erotic toes. I have a confession to make, and all I can think of is bedding you."

She swallowed, then tried to speak, but her voice failed her. Clearing her throat, she tried again, "You have a confession? Oh goodness, you want an annulment."

"God no. What gave you that idea?"

She shrugged. "Figured you'd come to your senses."

"Come sit with me." He patted the bed beside him. "I won't bite you, I promise." He flashed her a toothy grin. "Unless you ask me to."

She complied, but sat far enough away from him so that they could not touch without one of them moving.

"Claudia, we're married now. Nothing will ever change that. I meant my vows." A frown creased his brow. "I need to know that you meant yours, too."

"Of course I did."

He shook his head. "All right, I'm going to come right out with it. I've lied to you."

"You didn't mean your vows?"

"No, not just now. I meant that. I lied to you before."

"Was it for a good reason?"

"That was not the response I was expecting. Is there ever a good reason to lie to someone?"

"I've never been certain of that myself. My mother, on occasion, lied to my father. She claimed she wasn't lying, she was merely withholding information from him. I admit I've done the same. Obviously I did not tell him about my position with the paper." She picked an imaginary piece of lint off her nightgown. "I suppose that's horrible. To lie to your father."

"No, I don't think that's horrible. We need to discuss that more. Your father, I mean, but not right now." He rubbed his temples. "I lied to you about courting you."

She felt the color drain from her face. "You were never seriously courting me. You never intended to win my hand in marriage."

He didn't answer, but the expression on his face

said it all. She'd guessed correctly. All along, her doubts had been well founded.

How could she have been so stupid? She knew, deep inside, that he'd never wanted her, not really, but she'd wanted to believe it so badly, wanted it to be true, that she ignored her mental protests and blindly accepted his words. His betrayal scalded her. She wanted to hit him, which surprised her, because she'd never even considered physical violence in the past.

Her second thought was to leave. To simply gather her ridiculous nightgown around her and hail a hackney to Poppy's house. But she was a married woman now, and while she was no longer tied down by her father's command, she couldn't leave Derrick on a whim. He owned her.

So she ignored both impulses and settled on the only words that would come to her. "I suspected as much."

"I had an excellent reason. In the beginning. Or perhaps we could call it a purely selfish reason, but then something changed."

"What was your reason?"

"Your illustrations. You told me that day you came to my office that you would have to quit when you got married. I decided to court you to prevent you from marrying anyone so that you could continue working for me."

"An excellent reason, indeed. A very selfish reason. I would very much like to box your ears at the moment."

"Go ahead. I deserve it."

She closed her eyes to try and ease the anger, but it did not help. And oh, she felt the utter fool. She sent a brief prayer heavenward that the floor would simply open up and swallow her whole. Free her from this mortifying moment.

But nothing happened. She was still here, in his bedchamber wearing her nightclothes and feeling very much like an arse, if a lady could in fact, feel such a way.

"Did you intend to court me forever and never present me with the opportunity to marry another?"

"To be honest, I hadn't really thought about it. I didn't know you then. At first you were merely a means to an end. Do you realize that your illustrations are the reason the aristocracy started buying that paper? Before that it was a paper for the common man."

"Is that not why you created the paper in the first place? To offer a worthy newspaper for the lower educated and lower income people?"

"Yes. But after the sales changed with your illustrations, I saw what I could do. I could make the aristocracy more socially aware. Use the paper to bring issues in front of them that they would ordinarily ignore."

"That's a noble cause, but I don't believe you went about it the right way." It *was* noble. And part of her couldn't really blame him, but the part of her that screamed for him to love her cried silently in the corner of her heart.

"I'm a businessman. It's the way I think. But I haven't finished my story. That is why I initially started courting you, but a couple of things happened. You were more charming than I anticipated, and I found I wanted to spend more and more time with you. And then there was your connection with Richard."

"What about Richard?"

"I'm assuming it hasn't escaped your memory that he attacked you the other day. I knew he was that kind of man. I didn't want to see you get into a marriage with him. He would have destroyed you. Would have taken that part of you that makes you so different from all the other women and he would have trampled it into the ground. I couldn't allow that to happen."

"Noble again. I feel as if I should thank you, but I'm afraid it would not be genuine."

"That's understandable. I'm still not finished," he said.

"Of course not."

"I continued courting you and trying to convince you I was sincere because I was—I am genuinely attracted to you. I enjoy your company, enjoy being near you."

She said nothing for a long while, waiting for his words to settle in around her. He'd been lying. He hadn't been courting her, not really, but he still maintained that physically he wanted her.

"How am I supposed to believe anything you say, considering you've now admitted to lying to me twice? Should I simply believe you and wait for your confession later?"

"All I can tell you is that I had one marriage based on lies, and I'm determined that this one will not be like that. It is why I had to tell you the truth tonight. Every word out of Julia's mouth was a lie, so I know how you're feeling tonight. I apologize for putting you in that position, but at the time, I thought I was making the right decision. Whether or not you trust me from here is up to you. I can't convince you either way."

How had she forgotten he'd been married before? He'd lost his wife and Claudia had completely let that escape her memory. Yet, he didn't seem to mourn her, instead he only mentioned Julia's deceit. It didn't take the sting away from her deflated pride, but it did give him some justification. A person who'd been wounded by another's lies would be more sensitive to lying himself, wouldn't he? Her head was spinning.

"I came in here tonight terrified about consummating our marriage, and instead I get this confession, which, frankly, I did not need. Was it not bad enough that we married under such horrible conditions? You had to further humiliate me?"

"I don't see any of this as horrible, and I am not trying to humiliate you."

"I should have known you were lying."

"Why is that? Claudia, you're not exactly a great judge of character?"

"That's not kind."

"I apologize. I only meant that you see the good in people. There's nothing wrong with that."

"I'd rather not talk about this. It always sounds as if I'm whining, as if I'm pathetic. And frankly I'd rather you not think that of me on our wedding night."

"I don't think you're pathetic. I've never thought that." He turned her face so that she looked at him. "My false courtship was not about you. I know you think this is about you and whether or not you're desirable as a woman, but that's never been what it was about, Claudia. Before I knew you, I decided to court you to prevent you from resigning from my newspaper. I would not have made that decision had I thought you were a toad. I hadn't planned to marry again. But I recognized that if I had to marry, you were who I would have chosen. I think you're a beautiful, intelligent, and funny woman."

"I'm not beautiful. I think it's cruel that you would try to appeal to my vanity with more lies."

"I would never lie about something like that. I know it's hard to see where I draw the line on what I will and won't lie about. I think I'm more qualified to judge beauty in a woman."

"I'm too plump." It came out in a whisper, and she looked down at the bedcovers. She hadn't intended to say that. It was horrible to admit—not that people didn't already notice. But she'd been more comfortable when she'd been angry with him. Somehow he'd diffused her anger, and now she sat feeling like an open wound waiting for him to pour on the salt.

"You're no such thing. Women are all different. Some are tall and thin like Poppy, and many men find her irresistible. Other women are short, some are fleshy, some are—the list can go on. I don't think you're too plump. I think your body is amazing. I would love to strip off every last inch of that silly nightgown and spend the rest of the night proving to you how delicious I find your body."

"You don't know what my body looks like." She

let out a laugh that sounded more like a snort. "And you clearly don't know what a good corset can hide. My breasts are entirely too large, and I have a generous belly. And my hips and thighs . . ." She shook her head.

"Is this why you were terrified?"

She nodded. "I don't want you to touch me."

"We can't consummate this marriage unless you let me touch you, Claudia. But I won't touch you until you're ready."

"I didn't mean it like that. It's not you. It's me."

"I realize that since I've lied to you once, I must work to regain your trust. I'm determined to do that. No matter what my intentions toward you were in the beginning, my desire for you has always been real. I can't fake that. Those kisses were real. The touches, all real. Someday you'll see that."

She didn't know what to think or what to believe. He seemed so sincere, and she wanted to trust him. But he'd lied to her. And he'd hurt her. He'd said the one thing tonight that she'd feared all along. He hadn't really wanted her. He'd only been after her drawings.

It stung, and all she wanted to do was curl into a ball and cry, but that would solve nothing. If she was honest with herself, it wasn't the only thing she wanted to do. It was only one option swimming through her mind. All the others consisted of Derrick stripping off her clothes and kissing her. Everywhere, as he'd suggested.

She wanted to be angry with him. Angry enough to walk away, but she wanted to consummate this marriage despite her insecurities. She wanted his hands and his mouth on her body. And she wanted to explore his body as well.

Her cheeks burned with the thought, and she knew they flushed red. She brought her hands to them and tried not to look at him. He'd once remarked on her blush, wanting to know how far it traveled down her body.

"Care to share those thoughts?"

"No, thank you. I'm very tired."

She lay down on her side, facing the wall, and pulled her nightgown tighter around her. She shouldn't deny him his rights to her body. He'd done the honorable thing and married her, now she should do the honorable thing and allow him to consummate their marriage. As much as she didn't want to admit it, she wanted to. Despite her hurt feelings and wounded pride, she wanted him to make love to her. She wanted him to prove to her that he didn't care that her body wasn't perfect.

"Don't you want to get under the covers?" Without waiting for her response, he tugged at the covers to pull them out from under her. Then he stood and gently covered her. He leaned down and kissed her, a sweet and tender kiss.

It didn't take her long to decide to kiss him back. She opened her mouth to him and slid her tongue across his bottom lip. His throat emitted a low growl. He deepened the kiss, and she buried her fingers in his hair. She loved kissing him. It was turning out to be one of her favorite pastimes, which made it a good thing they had married, since now she could kiss him whenever she liked.

She felt the weight of his body press into hers, and even though the bedcovers separated them, she could still feel his heat. Still feel his obvious desire for her. He hadn't been lying about that.

He moved, rubbing his hard length against her. She opened her legs slightly, wishing the bedcovers were gone, but not wanting to remove them herself. He moved again. And again. Slow and steady.

Those bloody bedcovers.

As if he'd read her mind, he maneuvered his way underneath them. Clothes still barricaded their skin, but the pressure was much greater.

They continued to kiss, deep searching kisses that curled her toes and sent warmth radiating through her body. His steady rocking against her was building something inside her, stronger with every movement. She bucked beneath him, trying to make it come faster, whatever it was.

"I want to touch you." Derrick's words broke the silence.

"Where?"

"Anywhere. Everywhere. Let me take this silly gown off you."

"Put out the lights first."

"Claudia, I'm going to see you eventually. You are my wife."

"Not tonight."

He nodded, then climbed off her. One by one, he doused the lights.

A moment passed, and he still did not return to the bed. He'd changed his mind. This marriage would never work. She should have done as her father suggested and retired herself to the country. She could have painted all day.

"What are you doing?" she ventured.

"Removing my clothes."

"All of them?"

"Yes. It's usually how I sleep. Would you prefer I wore something?"

Sleeping next to a naked man. Sleeping next to naked Derrick. The thought made her giddy, and she nearly giggled, but the gravity of the current situation extinguished her humor.

"I don't want to change your habits," she said.

"You may sleep nude as well."

"I'd prefer not to."

"Whatever makes you comfortable. But I am going to take the gown off you."

She had no response to that, and then he was next to her. On the bed, with his mouth on hers and his hand on her ankle.

He was naked.

The thought excited yet embarrassed her. She didn't know the first thing about what to do with a naked man.

His hand slid farther up her leg, and his mouth continued a slow seduction of her own mouth, neck, and ears. Chills danced across her skin, and her nipples peaked. Her mother had never made the marriage bed sound this pleasant. She had told her it was something she had to bear out of duty, not that it would be something she could look forward to, or enjoy. But she was certainly enjoying this. Kissing Derrick had never been a problem, though. Perhaps whatever came next was the unpleasant part. She doubted, though, that anything involving Derrick could be unpleasant.

Where was she supposed to put her hands? They rested at her sides, wadding the sheets while she waited to see exactly how far Derrick's hand would go beneath her nightgown. At the current moment, he was up to her knee.

His mouth played at her collarbone, and she tilted her head farther into the pillow to give him better access. Oh, the things he did with his tongue. While his left hand continued to play with her knee, his right made its way to her breasts. He cupped one gently.

Cold air hit her thighs, and she realized he'd hiked her nightgown up that high. She grabbed the hem.

"What's the matter?" he asked.

"I'm not positive I'm ready for you to touch me yet."

"All right. You tell me where I can touch you, and I'll only touch you in those places. The rest of you will be safe from my touch until you're ready."

Interesting proposition.

He laid her back down and kissed her again.

"But I need to take this off you."

"All right." She sat and felt him pull the nightgown over her head, then heard it hit the floor. She'd never been naked before except during bathtime. It was surprisingly freeing.

She felt his hand at the top of her thigh, just below where it met with her hips.

"Can I touch you here?"

The warmth of his hand felt nice. More than nice. "I think that's all right."

"Good. Now can I touch you here?" He moved his other hand and cupped her breast again.

"Yes." Her voice was breathy.

"Excellent."

The hand on her thigh slid up and slightly to the right until it lay across her most intimate part. The touch jolted her, and she released a moan.

"How about here?" he asked.

"Mmmmuh."

"Perfect. Let's keep going." He trailed a finger from her breast down her rib cage and landed right on her abdomen.

She grabbed his hand. "Not there."

"All right. You tell me when you're ready. I want to touch you everywhere, but I'll wait for you." He kissed her then, allowing his tongue to play with hers. "We've set your limits, and I promise to stay within them."

"Yes," was all she could manage.

"May I take your drawers off as well?"

"Then we'll both be naked."

"That's the general idea." She heard the smile in his voice. "Relax, I won't do anything you don't want me to. You can trust me."

"All right."

"Do you want me to tell you before I do something?"

"No. I think I'm ready."

"You can touch me too. If you want."

"Where?"

"Anywhere."

She tentatively reached out and ran her hand across his chest. His muscles contracted beneath her touch. It was a combination of hard muscle, soft skin, and traces of feathery hair. She wanted to see him. But in order to do that, he'd have to turn the lights back on, and then he'd see her. That was out of the question. She'd have to wait to see him. Perhaps she could catch him changing or taking a bath someday.

He lay very still while her hand explored his torso. She followed a trail of hair that traveled down the length of his hard stomach, and then she bumped right into his sex. He jerked and moaned, and she pulled her hand away. Perhaps it was painful for him to be touched there. How she wished she'd had her mother to ask about these things, or perhaps a book to read for guidance.

The next thing she knew, his mouth was on her breast, and she was biting her tongue not to cry out. His warm mouth teased and taunted her, moving from one breast to the next. Gracious, she'd never known it could be like this. She wiggled her hips trying to ease the ache that persisted between her thighs.

She allowed her hands to find his back, and she ran her fingernails lightly up and down. He suckled hard on her nipple, and she cried out, arching her back.

He continued to kiss her breasts as his hand slid up her thigh and gently cupped her. No one else had ever touched her there. She'd never even imagined anyone touching her there. And if she had, it wouldn't have been like this. His fingers parted her hair, and she could feel wetness all around.

He slid one finger into her, and she almost lifted off the bed.

"Are you all right?" he asked.

"Yes."

"Is this hurting you?"

"No."

"Do you like it?"

"I think so."

"How about this?" He moved his finger in and out a few times, and she rocked her hips with him.

"Yes."

"You feel so good." He again suckled her breast while moving his finger in and out, then in and out again.

She tried to match his rhythm, but her body felt out of control. She needed something, but didn't know what. Knew something was coming, but wasn't sure what it was. But God, it felt good.

Another finger slid in, and she felt his thumb rub against the tiny nub that hid beneath her hair. She cried out his name, and faster and faster he pumped his fingers into her until something happened, and for a moment everything was still and then the world turned on its axis and ripples of pleasure shook her to her toes. She knew she cried out, but she couldn't help it. Never had she felt such amazing pleasure.

"You're so beautiful," she heard him say through her fog.

He hadn't had his pleasure, of that she was certain. She reached out and placed her hand on his chest. "What about you?" was all she could think to say.

"Are you ready?"

It was her duty as his wife to please him. "What do you want me to do?"

"Give me your hand." He took her hand from his chest and led it down his stomach and then to the hard length of him. "Touch me here."

She ran her fingers up the length of him and felt a bit of moisture at the tip, then down to the base where she found crisp hair.

His breathing became shorter, more shallow.

"Like this," he said as he grabbed her hand and splayed it around his organ. "Now move your hand up and down."

She did as she was told and reveled in the feel of the soft skin. She hadn't stroked him long before he grabbed her hand.

"No more." His voice was shaky.

"Was I doing it wrong?"

"No. Perfect, but I need to be inside you now."

His words tingled down her body.

His hand again found her center, and he inserted two fingers. "I want to make sure you're ready for me. I don't want to hurt you."

"My mother told me it was painful. But if it will bring you pleasure, then I am ready."

"I'll try to be as gentle as I can, but you've got me so randy, I don't know how long I can make it."

He climbed on top of her and kissed her long and hard.

She felt the tip of him inch into her, and then in one swift movement he was inside. Pain burned inside her, and she winced.

"I'm sorry. I know that's painful."

"I'm fine," she lied.

He feathered soft kisses all over her face.

"I'm going to move now. I want you to let me know if it's too unpleasant for you, and I'll stop."

His movements were slow and shallow at first, and it was uncomfortable. His tongue found her nipple, and he suckled her breast until she almost forgot the discomfort between her legs, and then that swirling emotion started again. The climbing feeling that something was coming.

"You feel so good." His breathing was harder now, his words raspy and raw.

Faster and faster he moved, and higher and higher she climbed. She heard herself moaning again. She pulled her legs up higher, so that she could wrap them around him.

Then again it hit her, harder this time, but faster. Her body spinning out of control as she waited for the spasms to pass. He moaned loudly, then collapsed on top of her while his hot seed poured inside.

They lay silently for a moment, him still inside her, her legs still wrapped around him.

He tilted his head so that his chin rested on her chest. She couldn't see him, but imagined he was giving her that smile of his that made her knees wobble and her mouth go dry.

"I'm going to enjoy being married to you," he said.

247

Chapter 14

❧

Derrick eyed the older lady standing in his study.

"I came to see Miss Prattley."

"What's your name?"

"Baubie. I'm her nurse, sir. Well, I suppose I should say maid, but I've been her nurse since she was born."

"Her name is Middleton now, and she's sleeping."

The chubby woman wrung her hands and looked about the room.

"Is there a message I can pass on to her?"

"I'm not sure, sir. I'm concerned about something involving her father."

"Baubie, I want to assure you that I have Claudia's best interest at heart. I don't know what kind of loyalty you have to Lord Kennington, but frankly, he's a bastard, and I would rather my wife cut her ties with him immediately. Seeing as she's rather devoted to him, I don't see that happening. But if you have concerns, please rest assured that you can trust me with them."

Relief washed over her features, and her shoulders relaxed. "You might be the answer to my prayers. I've been praying that Claudia would find someone to take her away from him. He's a horrible man. Mean. I know that's dreadful of me to say, seeing as he pays my wages and all, but he was awful to Claudia's sweet mother, and he's never been anything but hateful to her. But as you say, she's devoted. Never understood why, except that girl has loyalty running thick in her blood. If she gives you her loyalty, sir, you'd best cherish it, as it will be yours forever."

Was Claudia loyal to him? He didn't know. He didn't think she trusted him yet. Not completely. But last night was a start.

"Do you want to discuss your concerns with me? Or do you want to wait for Claudia?"

"I don't think it can wait, sir." She took a few steps closer to him. "I believe Lord Kennington murdered someone."

He'd known Kennington was a thief and a liar, but a murderer? Nothing was certain yet. He would listen to the entire story, and then decide how to approach Claudia with the news.

"Why don't you sit down." He led Baubie to the sofa, then took the chair across from her. "What makes you believe this?"

"He came home late the other night, almost morning. I'm a light sleeper, and I could hear him throwing things around in his study. I couldn't go back to sleep after that and got an early start on my work. I went down to check the fire in his study, and he was passed out on his sofa. He smelled awful of brandy, and the decanter lay empty at his feet. No telling how much he drank. That's when I noticed the blood. All over his fingers. Streaks ran down his pants where he'd obviously rubbed his hands."

"Blood? Was it his?"

"That's what I thought at first. I looked all over as best I could without disturbing his sleep, and there was no other blood in sight. So I looked around a bit to see if there was blood anywhere else in the room. I found a little more on his cane, but that was it. But I did find these, stuffed into the fireplace." She reached into her bag and pulled out some paper. Black edged the papers, and smoke had clouded the coloring.

Whatever Kennington had tried to burn that night, he'd failed at doing so. "You pulled these out of the fire?"

"Yes, sir. He's burned papers before. Important papers. Bills. So I reached in and grabbed them, but this isn't bills. These are letters. I didn't read all of them, but it looks like blackmail to me."

"They're all addressed to a Chester Edwards."

Derrick's heart sped up. Chester Edwards.

"Will you leave them with me?"

She narrowed her eyes. "Will you make certain no harm comes to Claudia?"

"You have my vow."

She leaned forward and handed him the letters.

"You are welcome to come and work here now. To stay with Claudia."

"Can't, sir. She made me promise I'd stay and look after her father. Until she knows he'll be fine without her."

"But if what you believe is true, he could be dangerous."

She squared her shoulders. "I'm not afraid of him."

"If you believe he will harm you, leave and come here immediately."

"Yes, sir." She worried the material of her faded skirt. "What are you going to tell her?"

"I'm going to do some investigating before I tell her. No need to worry her about this until we know the truth. Her devotion to her father will blind her to his guilt, and we need to protect her. I'm going to take her to my country estate for a few days. See if I can convince her to stay out there for a while. Then I'll come back and figure out what to do."

"Oh, sir, you must love her indeed."

He didn't want to disillusion the maid, so he ignored her comment. He would not love Claudia. He refused to do so. They would have a successful marriage without love. People did that all the time, and he and Claudia would be no different.

He desired Claudia, of that he was positive. Last night had only whetted his appetite for her. He respected her. He genuinely liked her and enjoyed her company. But love? He had learned his lesson about that years ago.

It had nothing to do with love. She was his wife, and he'd protect her. That was his duty. "You can be certain that I will do everything I can to keep her safe."

He would keep her safe. And that meant getting Claudia out of London until he could uncover the truth behind the blood and the blackmail letters.

He was itching to read them, but they would have to wait. Claudia's safety was at hand and that needed to take precedence.

There would be time enough to quench his own curiosity. And perhaps ease some of his guilt.

Claudia stretched, arching her back, on the bed. She noted a slight soreness between her legs and felt a blush heat her cheeks. She had been wanton last night. No doubt Derrick thought ill of her. Which might explain why she was in the bed alone.

Thoughts of their lovemaking filled her mind, and she couldn't help but smile. Without ever having other lovers, she instinctively knew Derrick was perfect. He had taken great patience to bring her pleasure, something she'd heard most men avoided.

There was a knock at the door, and then Derrick appeared, carrying a breakfast tray.

"I thought you might be hungry."

She allowed her eyes to roam over him. She'd never tire of looking at him. He was simply beautiful.

"Thank you. I apologize for lazing about this morning. I am generally an early riser."

"I kept you up late last night."

He brought the tray over to her, so she sat up. When the cool air hit her skin, she remembered she was naked. She snatched the sheets and pulled them up to her neck.

"No need to cover yourself on my account. I would love to see you."

She shook her head. "Not at breakfast."

He sat next to her and put the tray on the bed. "What's so special about breakfast?"

"It's daylight and morning. It is wrong."

"Naughty?" he whispered.

"Yes."

He popped a fig into his mouth. "Precisely the way I like it."

She stared at him, somehow unable to absorb everything that had happened in the last week. Like the fact that at this very moment she sat naked in a bed with Derrick Middleton in front of her. Or that last night he'd done amazing things to her. With his mouth, with his hands, with his . . . Oh, she couldn't even think it.

"What are you thinking about?"

She met his eyes, and he raised an eyebrow. So she smiled and took a bite of her breakfast.

"Cheater." He reached out and trailed one finger down her exposed arm. She shivered beneath his touch.

"It's good," she said, taking another bite.

"I'm glad you like it."

It was difficult to eat and hold the sheet up at the same time. She tried to tuck the fabric behind her, but it kept slipping, giving him a peekaboo view of her left breast.

"Can you hand me my nightgown?"

He retrieved it for her, then turned around so she could slip it on.

"I know you think I'm being a goose, but I haven't quite accepted the idea of someone seeing me without my clothes on."

He nodded, then climbed back onto the bed. "Eat. I think for our honeymoon, we'll go into the country for a few days. How does that sound?"

"What about the paper?"

"Mason can handle things while I'm gone."

She eyed her plate and the figs and bread lying there. She wasn't accustomed to eating in front of men either. Her father had once told her that a woman who ate as much as she did was disgusting. Women should eat tiny portions. So she'd resigned herself to rising earlier than he and eating breakfast before he came downstairs. The other meals she'd taken in her room or at Poppy's. And she never ate refreshments at soirees or parties.

But Derrick wasn't looking at her plate. Instead he focused out the window. He seemed distracted.

"Speaking of the paper"—he turned to face her

again—"you can reveal your identity now. It's your choice. The mystery has served you well. But you shouldn't feel like you have to hide now."

"I don't know if that would be a good idea."

He eyed her for a few minutes more. "Unless you want me to strip that shift off you and make love to you right now, I suggest you pack your things for a weekend in the country."

It was a tempting thought, but with the light flooding the room, it was out of the question.

"Be off with you then, so I may dress properly, and we can be on our way."

He leaned over her plate and gave her a sultry kiss. "Very well, I shall have the carriage ready."

Derrick stared at Mason. "Are you positive?"

"Yes, sir. I saw it with my own eyes. I walked right past his house on the way to work. They were carrying out a body. I can only assume it was him. There was blood all over the sheet."

First Baubie's suspicion that Claudia's father had murdered someone, and now Richard turned up dead. Or supposedly dead. What didn't fit was why Lord Kennington would kill Richard. The answer probably lay in those letters Baubie had brought him.

They sat in his coat pocket even now, waiting to be read. He would have taken time to read them this morning, but he'd wanted to ensure the paper was properly cared for before he took Claudia to the country.

"Do you have any idea who did it?" Mason asked, then without waiting for an answer, he added, "or do you suppose he offed himself?"

"I have a suspicion. And I don't believe he did it himself. Richard was far too vain to kill himself. Not to mention too stupid."

"Are you going to tell your new bride? She knew him, didn't she?"

"Yes, she knew him. I don't know if I'll tell her. She has a right to know, but I want to confirm it was Richard before I tell her. Send Blakey down to see if he can't get some information for us."

Blakey had been a wood carver for Derrick since he'd opened the paper. He was the largest man at the paper, possibly in all of London, and he often worked for extra money helping Derrick investigate when the necessity arose. His size alone usually made even the most secretive person spill his secrets. But on occasion he used money to buy the information.

"Mason, I'm going to take Claudia into the country for the weekend. Have a honeymoon of sorts. Can you take care of things here?"

"Absolutely."

"Thank you. Send me a post whenever Blakey

gets back. With or without news, I want to be informed. I'll be within riding distance if there are any problems."

"Yes, sir." Mason turned to leave, then paused. "Oh and Mr. Middleton, despite the current situation, enjoy your honeymoon and your new bride."

Derrick waited until Mason had disappeared before pulling out the stack of letters and tossing them onto his desk. He picked up one and fingered the envelope, then stood and walked to the window. Whatever lay in these letters had been the real story behind Chester Edwards's suicide. The story he'd printed all those years ago had implicated a man on charges that he may or may not have been guilty of, and then that man had taken his own life.

Reading those letters, Derrick realized, might release him of all the guilt he'd felt for the last ten years. Or they might confirm he was partly at fault.

He looked back at the desk and eyed the tempting letters. Now another man was dead, and Claudia's father might be at fault.

Walking back to his desk, he picked up the first letter and unfolded it. Burned paper flaked off the edges, and the smell of smoke lingered on the parchment.

One letter after another, the story became more and more clear. Ten years ago the Conservatives had been in the majority, and Kennington had been the chancellor of finance, the man in charge of all the queen's finances, including the patent office. Claudia's father had blackmailed the patent officer, Edwards, into skimming funds. Somehow Kennington had discovered the truth of a rather sensitive situation with Edwards's daughter. He'd threatened to go public, threatened to ruin her reputation and with it any real chance of her to secure a reputable marriage. Then when he'd tired of the man, or more likely when Edwards threatened to go public with the truth, Kennington had beat him to it by having Richard sell the false story to Derrick.

A story where Kennington had blamed the embezzled funds completely on Edwards. Apparently Edwards hadn't been strong enough to fight Kennington. He'd died, taking the full blame for a scheme much larger than himself, all to protect his daughter's virtue.

How had Derrick been so blind to the connection? Surely there had been clues. He should have realized all this once he discovered Richard's connection with Claudia's father. He'd known there had to have been someone pulling Richard's strings like a puppet. Kennington.

It must have been easy for Kennington to get his snares in Richard at the time. He'd been starved for power and wealth. Richard had probably banked on Kennington's status aiding him in advancing politically.

Everything made sense now. Everything was more complicated now. How was Derrick supposed to explain to his wife that her father was the man responsible for all these crimes?

He couldn't. She wouldn't believe him. Her loyalty to her father was too strong. Derrick needed to wait until he knew Claudia's loyalty to him was secure. To see her father for what he was, she needed some distance. But before she could do that, she needed to learn to trust herself.

Taking Claudia to the country to keep her mind off her father and on her new husband was the only solution. Teaching her to trust him would be easy, Derrick realized. It was teaching her to trust herself that would prove his greatest challenge.

She'd had it practically beaten into her that she was always wrong, no matter the circumstances.

She needed to let herself go, to give in to her feelings and her desires. Once she learned to do that, she would learn to trust herself.

Then he could risk sharing the truth about her father.

Chapter 15

~~~~~~∞∞~~~~~~

Two hours later Claudia found herself in the carriage on the way to Derrick's country estate. She had packed as quickly as she could, eager to see her new home. She'd only seen the house from a distance the day they rode, but if it was in as good shape as the stable, it would be a palace.

"We need to have a conversation about the kind of wife I expect you to be."

Married less than two days, and she'd already done something wrong. Why else would he bring this up?

"I realize you were raised to believe that wives are supposed to behave in a certain fashion."

"Yes. My mother taught me a lot before she died, and my father continued that education as much as he was able."

"I want you to forget everything they told you. This is our marriage, and we'll live it the way we choose."

"But—"

"I know what kind of wife they instructed you to be, and that's not what I want. Mousy, quiet, and without opinions are traits that do not suit you. You're a passionate woman, and I expect to see that fire." He met her gaze. "In the bedroom and out."

"But what if we disagree about something?"

"Then we shall argue about it."

She shook her head. "I don't think arguing solves anything."

"Perhaps not, but after the argument comes the making up, and that is what I'll look forward to." He winked at her. "Perhaps I'll even start arguments for that very reason."

"You wouldn't."

"Is that a challenge?"

She shook her head. "No."

He just sat there grinning at her.

"What?" she asked.

"You're really quite beautiful. I hadn't thought so at first."

She frowned. "I'm not certain that was a compliment," she said.

"I didn't mean that the way it sounded. I always knew you were an attractive woman, but you're more beautiful than I'd first realized."

She knew her mouth hung open, and she tried to close it, but couldn't. So instead she dug for something clever to say. "You no longer have to court me to gain my favor. I'm your wife. You can cease your silly compliments. Frankly, you were never very good at them."

He cocked one eyebrow. "Indeed? I seem to recall my wretched excuse for poetry being quite effective that day in the garden."

It had in fact been quite effective. Enough to lure her into that first kiss.

"It's rather unfair," he said. "The entire courting situation. Women do nothing save look pretty, and men must put forth all the effort."

"Until there is a wedding, and then the women do the work for the rest of their lives."

He narrowed his eyes. "That might be true. But only partially. Courting is difficult."

"How would you know? You were only pretending to court me." The truth of that still stung, but she hoped that joking about it would lessen the pain.

"Touché." He placed a kiss on her hand. "I did

give it my full attention. My intentions were not entirely noble, but I never intended to hurt you, and I meant everything I said to you."

"I might be persuaded to believe that. But I will have to deliberate about it further."

"Fair enough. In the meantime, why don't you give it a try."

"What?"

"Courting. Let's see how you would do if the shoe were on the other foot. How would you lure me in, get me interested in you?"

She shrugged. "That's a silly game."

"But it will be fun. Or do you not think you can do it?"

Two weeks ago, she would have faltered under such a request, but she was a different woman now. Stronger, not necessarily bold, but bolder than she'd ever been in her life. Trying her hand at courting might be fun. She'd often daydreamed about the perfect courtship.

"Very well, but no laughing at me."

"I promise."

"I suppose I would tell you that I find you very handsome."

He nodded. Giving her no indication as to whether that would win him over.

"In particular your eyes. Intense and haunting, eyes that keep me up at night, eyes that feel as if they can peer into my very soul. Sometimes with merely a glance you send shivers dancing across my skin."

He folded his arms across his chest, and his face settled into an expression that very much resembled a cat who'd devoured a mouse.

"There are other aspects of your appearance that I find attractive, but one must not strictly focus on the physical attributes. I find you intelligent and respect the way you run your business. Your dedication to bringing news to those who typically cannot afford newspapers is quite noble. It is one of the reasons I accepted the position. When I saw the advertisement, I knew I must apply. I never dreamed you would hire me, but figured I stood a better chance if you and everyone else thought I was a man."

He gave her a smile.

Her heart flipped in her chest. "Gracious, and that smile. I hate to admit how you affect me. It's not like me to be so bold."

"Come here." He leaned across the carriage and pulled her across his lap. "You be as bold as you like. You affect me, too."

He pulled her face to his and kissed her, his mouth slanting across hers in a full assault on her defenses. She opened to him and swept her tongue against his. She'd never tire of kissing him.

"I want you now," he said.

His hands slid under her skirts, and he found her through the slit in her drawers. His finger entered her, and she released a moan into his mouth. He moved his finger within her, until she could feel the moisture between her legs. All the while, he continued his assault with his mouth. He nipped and licked, until she could no longer focus on anything but the feelings he created. Then he withdrew and began undoing his pants.

"We can't."

"Why not?"

"We're in a carriage?"

"We're married, and we can do this anytime we like. Anyplace we want. Even in a carriage. Besides, no one can see us. Trust me." His eyes bored into her, and she realized she did. Despite his not being completely honest with her in the beginning. He'd promised they'd have a truthful marriage, and she believed him. She completely trusted him.

He finished removing enough of his clothing so that his member sprang up between them. She hadn't seen it the night before, and now that she had, she was amazed it had fit inside her.

"What are you thinking about?" he asked.

She could have lied. Averted her eyes and said nothing, but he'd said he liked her to be bold. And truth be told, she liked being bold. It was exhilarating. So she swallowed her nerves, looked him right in the eyes, and answered.

"Your body."

"What about my body?"

"I'm puzzled by how everything works. How we fit."

"We're a perfect fit," he said, then he lowered her hips down until she felt the tip of him enter her. Then he stopped.

"What's the matter?" she asked.

"Nothing. I want you to be in charge."

"I can't. I don't know what to do."

"Yes, you do. You simply do what feels right."

"But what about you?"

"Whatever you do will feel good to me."

He held eye contact while she slowly lowered herself on him. He filled her, and the discomfort was there again, but only in the background. She stayed still to let her body adjust to the invasion, all the while looking at him. It was shockingly intimate to look him in the eyes while his body was joined with her. Almost overwhelmingly so. She felt tears pull at her eyes, so she closed them and began to move.

Tentative at first, she rocked slowly, until her body hit a rhythm. She moved her hips forward, loving the feel of him buried inside her.

"Look at me, Claudia."

She opened her eyes and met his gaze, but stopped her movement. His brown eyes had darkened several shades, appearing almost black now.

"I wanted to watch you last night." He picked up her hips and moved her up and down a few times. Pleasure etched his features. "I love the feel of you."

She wanted to close her eyes again, or lean into him, so that he couldn't see her. But she enjoyed watching him. The intensity in his eyes touched her deep inside. He was a man of great feeling; she could see that now. Perhaps he could grow to love her.

"Move, Claudia."

She chewed on her lip.

"Don't be embarrassed. I want to watch you."

He reached into the bodice of her dress and cupped her breast. She arched against him and began her movement again. A slow, steady rhythm.

He rolled her nipple between his fingers, and she cried out.

"That's it. Just let go of your mind and feel. Do you like this?" He cupped her breast again.

She nodded, unable to say anything.

"I want to see your breasts." He unbuttoned the front of her dress, and the material sagged, revealing her corset and chemise.

It took some maneuvering, but he managed to loosen the material enough so he could release her breasts from their confines.

"Beautiful." He leaned in and brought a nipple into his mouth and suckled hard.

She bucked against him, trying to reach release. While he kissed her breast, his hand reached beneath her skirts and found the sensitive nub. He rubbed it gently, moving in a slow circle.

"You're almost there; can you feel it?"

"Yes."

"Don't hold back, Claudia. Ride as hard as you like."

She did as she was told and increased her movements. Faster and faster, harder and harder. She threw her head back and moaned loudly.

"I'm coming with you," he said.

And just when the waves of pleasure hit her, she felt him spill into her, and he cried out her name. He closed his eyes and clenched his jaw as he continued to shudder.

She leaned into him. She kissed him softly on the neck and then the chin.

"You're amazing," he said.

"I never knew."

He chuckled. "That you're amazing?"

"No. That this could be pleasurable."

"It would be quite unfair were it only pleasurable for men. Considering the women actually go through childbirth."

She smiled. He had such a unique way of looking at things. She inhaled his scent, earthy and male mixed with the musky smell of their lovemaking.

"We'll be at the house soon." His voice rumbled against her. "I hope you like it."

"I know I will."

Chapter 16

"**S**o that was the grand tour." Derrick led her into the front parlor, which was richly decorated in burgundy and gold. It had always been one of his favorite rooms. It was so warm. Shortly after he'd bought the house, he'd decided that should he ever marry again and have a family, this would be the room where they would celebrate Christmas. He sat next to her on the settee, then leaned back. "What do you think?"

"The house, like this room, is really quite beautiful. Very well taken care of considering only a handful of servants live here full-time."

"I visit often, at least once a month to see that everything is running smoothly."

She rubbed her hand across the brocade fabric of the settee. "Did you select the decorations and color schemes yourself?"

"I decided to stay with the original decor, but had some pieces of furniture restuffed and upholstered. I liked the look and wanted to maintain it."

"How did you acquire the house?"

"I bought it. The Earl of Limewood wanted to live full-time in London and had no heirs for his estate, so he decided to sell it. I'd been looking for someplace in the country where I could get away when needed, so when this property came available, I bought it."

"It's perfect."

"I want to show you the grounds as well. I know you saw them on our ride, but now this is your home too. I had the cook pack us a lunch. We can eat it outside."

"A picnic?"

"Yes. I believe everything is waiting for us by the pond."

She smiled up at him, and his heart nearly stopped. Lately everything she did gave him pause. Making love to her had not quenched his desire for her even a fraction; if anything, he wanted her more.

But she still was holding back, nervous that he might not approve or perhaps that he would reject her. He wasn't sure what stopped her, but he intended to change it. The carriage had been the closest he'd come to seeing her while making love, and they'd both been fully clothed. He had plans to remedy that this afternoon, but it would be a challenge.

He threaded his fingers with hers as he led her outside and across the gently sloping hill. They walked in silence, and he waited for an awkward feeling to settle over him, urging him to break the reverie. But it did not come. Instead, he found a comfortable silence between them as they crossed his lush green lawn. They reached an area covered in trees, and he spotted the pond glistening ahead. Beneath the willow tree, a blanket was spread with the food for their picnic.

"It's wonderful," she said.

He helped her take a seat on the blanket, then sat across from her.

He unpacked their lunch and poured her a glass of wine, then proceeded to prepare plates of bread, jam, and cheese.

"This is my favorite part of the entire estate. I suppose it was the main reason I bought it."

"It's very peaceful." She took a sip of her wine. "Like a painting come to life."

He held a piece of bread out to her, and she reached for it, but he pulled it back. "No. Take a bite."

"You wish to feed me?" she asked, clearly surprised.

"I do." Again he leaned toward her with the bite of bread, and she hesitated, but leaned in and took the morsel.

He held out a piece of cheese for her, and she took it, her lips brushing against his fingers. He dipped his finger in the marmalade.

"Are you going to smear that on some bread?" she asked.

"No." He held his finger out to her. "Lick it off."

Her eyes widened. "You want me to lick that marmalade off your finger?"

"Scandalous, isn't it?"

Try as she might, she lost whatever battle she fought in her mind and rewarded him with a devilish little grin. He was eroding her defenses. His plan was working.

She leaned forward, wrapped her perfect pink lips around his finger, closed her eyes, and then gently sucked the jam off his finger. She was wearing him down as well. He didn't know if he could wait to complete his plan. He wanted her now. Beneath him, squirming with pleasure.

He pulled off his shoes. "Today there are no

worries about appointments or propriety. We are going to swim."

"Right now?"

"Yes, now."

"I don't think so."

"Why? The pond isn't that deep." He tugged her right foot out from underneath her skirts and began unlacing her boot. He pulled it off, then reached beneath her skirts, undid her garter, and rolled her stocking off.

"Derrick, honestly," she said, while swatting uselessly at his hands.

He ignored her protests and removed her left boot and stocking.

"We don't have the proper attire for swimming."

"We don't need them." He stood and shrugged out of his jacket. He began removing his trousers when she suddenly jumped to her feet.

"You don't intend to swim in your drawers, do you?"

"Of course not. I intend to swim in the nude."

"You'll freeze."

"Not this late in the day. The sun has warmed the pond nicely. And I have plans to keep myself warm."

She frowned, thought for a moment, then concluded. "Swimming for exercise? I have heard that is quite popular with men."

"That's not what I meant." He held his hand out to her. "Come with me."

She shook her head. "No, I couldn't."

"Of course you can. There are no more could nots or should nots. With me, you are free. There is no one here but us."

He pulled her close and kissed her, putting as much passion as he could in it to arouse her. She clung to him and released soft whimpers.

"Take my shirt off."

Her eyes flew open.

"Here, I'll get you started." He unfastened the first two buttons, then placed her hand on the third. He grabbed her hands and put them on the next button. "I need to know you want me, Claudia. As much as I want you."

She licked her lips and swallowed. Carefully she released one button, then another, until the material gaped, and all the buttons were undone.

"Now pull it off me."

She pushed the material off his shoulders. Her small hands brushed against his skin. He closed his eyes, enjoying her touch.

"Now, my drawers."

Her eyes widened, and she took a step back.

"You've touched me before, Claudia. You can do this." He guided her hand to the front flap of his drawers. She undid the buttons quickly, and he felt the sun heat his backside as the silk slid down his legs.

He pulled her to him and kissed her again, his erection pressed between them. He wanted to lay her down on the blanket, toss her skirts up, and bury himself inside her. But he needed to be patient.

"Look at me, Claudia."

She met his gaze.

"No, look at my body."

Her eyes traveled the length of him, all the way down, then trailed back up and lingered at his middle.

"Do you see how much I want you?"

"Yes," she whispered.

"Do you want me?"

"Yes."

"Then show me. Show me how much you want me." With that, he turned and waded into the pond. The water lapped around him as he moved out to the middle. He turned around to face her, and she still stood on the blanket watching him.

"Take your clothes off, Claudia. Come and join me."

He had no way of knowing whether this plan would work, but he knew she wanted him. He just hoped it was enough to throw her fears aside and join him in the water.

"I want to see you."

"No you don't," she said. "You won't like what you see."

"How do you know that?"

"Because I've seen myself."

"I don't think it's fair for you to judge what I will and won't find attractive. I think you're beautiful."

She crossed her arms over her chest and shook her head.

"Claudia, I need you. Take one thing off at a time. Start with your dress. Excellent choice, selecting one that buttons down the front."

"You learn to dress yourself when you don't have a lady's maid."

"The dress. Please, do this for me."

She eyed him for a moment, then did as he asked. The garment fell at her feet in a heap, and she stood wearing her petticoat and corset. His pulse quickened. Her breasts rose and fell rapidly above her corset. He longed to release her from all her constraints, the tangible ones as well as the emotional.

"Your petticoat. That can't be comfortable."

"Not so much," she said with a hint of a smile, "but certainly better than the corset."

"Then remove it."

It took her a while to unlace it, but when she finally got it undone, she visibly relaxed. No doubt the damned thing was cutting off some of her air.

"You're so beautiful. Keep going, my love, let yourself go."

She chewed at her lip, then turned to face the opposite direction. She pulled off her chemise, then turned back around with her arms crossed on her chest, blocking his view. The pressure from her arms smashed her breasts against her.

"Move your arms."

A blush crept up her neck and stained her cheeks. She closed her eyes and dropped her hands to her side. Her breasts were magnificent, large and round with a pale dusting of pink at the centers. Her nipples rose proudly. Red marks streaked down her abdomen where the corset bones had pressed into her too tightly.

His heart thrummed wildly against the cage of his chest. A surge of lust hit him forcefully, followed by an equally powerful surge of protectiveness. She was his, and he'd be damned if anyone, especially her father, hurt her again.

"I wish you could see yourself the way I see you," he said.

She opened her eyes, but did not look at him.

"You've only your drawers left. Take them off and join me. Feel the water slippery against your skin. There's nothing like it in the world."

With almost a visible surge of determination, she peeled the drawers from her body. The triangle of golden hair glistened in the sunlight. Her stomach was not flat, and this was obviously the source of her anxiety. Her waist was not excessively narrow, and her hips were rounder than was fashionable, but to him, she was the most beautiful woman he'd ever seen.

His breath caught in his throat. He'd never want another woman as long as she was with him. She was like a golden goddess released from an Italian Renaissance painting.

"Claudia, look at me."

She didn't move.

"Please."

Her eyes met his, and he saw the shimmer of tears edging her eyes. "You're perfect. Now come here."

She came into the pond and stood before him.

He wiped a tear from her cheek. "Thank you. I know that was difficult. But honest, I think you're perfect." He pulled her to him and hugged her, feeling the warmth of her skin pressed against his.

"How does the water feel?"

She gave him a weak smile. "Strange. A little cold."

He scooped water, then poured it against her chest. She inhaled sharply, and her breasts tightened. He cupped them, reveling in the weight of them.

"You have the most magnificent breasts I've ever seen."

"They're too large."

He smiled at her. "Not for me."

"You don't have to pack them around all day."

"No, but I would if you asked me to."

She looked up at him with just a slight movement of her eyes, a glance so subtly seductive he would have thought she'd practiced it. But he knew better.

She really was beautiful, in such an unassuming way it had caught him off guard. She stood before him, water dripping off her perfect breasts, with desire blatant in her eyes. He put his hands at her waist and felt her stiffen.

"Today I want to touch you everywhere. You've let me see you, now trust me."

He kissed her in the hollow of her collarbone, lapping the water droplets off her skin. From her waist, he moved one hand to her hip and then over to her stomach. She flinched beneath his touch, trying to disguise her imperfection. She wanted to be beautiful and desirable for him, and it made him want her more.

Her flesh was soft, and she closed her eyes as he moved from her stomach into the curls at the juncture of her thighs. He'd never touched a woman in the water. It was invigorating, daring, and a little bit naughty—something he hadn't felt in years.

He continued his kisses on her neck and breasts, while his fingers explored her folds. She was hot and wet, and he groaned from the feel of her.

"I've got to have you now."

"Yes."

He lifted her and brought her closer. "Wrap your legs around me."

She did, and he set her down, inching her onto his length. It didn't take either of them long to reach a climax. He cried out her name as he thrust the last few times into her.

It had never been with another woman the way it was with Claudia. His desire for her never wavered. She met his passion with a fervor he had not known a woman could possess. It was as if they were designed to love only each other, as if their bodies were created to fit each other perfectly.

She laid her head on his shoulder, her legs still wrapped around his waist, his member still buried within her.

"I will never tire of making love to you," he told her.

She gave him a shy smile. "Nor I of you. It is like my body craves you now, like a lush with his drink."

Her body craved him, but did her heart want him? Would she choose him when the truth came out?

"Do you promise that you're not disgusted by my body?"

"I promise. I love your body. It's perfect."

He set her down, then grabbed her hand, and they walked to shore. Water drops scattered across their bodies as they lay on the blanket.

"We'll let the sun dry us, then we can dress and return to the house."

A few of her ringlets had escaped their confines during their lovemaking and now sat in tight, wet coils on her neck. He lay on his back and pulled her so that she partially lay on top of him. She put her chin in the hollow spot of his chest. Something swelled in his chest. It was powerful to see someone in such an intimate state. She looked the very picture of a sated woman, and in that moment, he knew he would never regret marrying her.

"This spot was made for my chin."

"Indeed?"

"Yes, it fits perfectly." She placed a kiss on the spot for confirmation, then moved her mouth along his chest, tentatively licking the moisture from his skin.

She turned her head so that she faced the pond, her curls lightly brushing his chin. Her hand rested on his stomach. He absently rubbed her back, soaking in the moment.

"Have you thought any more about what you want to do with your illustrations?" he asked.

"Yes. I would like to continue. I haven't yet decided whether to keep my identity a secret." Her finger made slow circles on his abdomen. "I enjoy the mystery."

"Whatever your decision, I'll stand behind you. I don't want you to make that decision based on your father. He can't hurt you anymore, and whether or not you have a paying job won't disparage my reputation. You've lived your life far too long consumed by what people think about you. It's not a good way to live."

"It's been a fine way to live."

"But what has it gotten you?"

She shrugged. "It's not about me. I have a responsibility to my family and my family's name. I have a duty to uphold my father's reputation."

"If the politicians are driven by the antics of their daughters, then Parliament is in more trouble than I thought."

"That's not precisely what I meant."

"Your father's reputation is no longer your concern. You are my wife now."

She said nothing for a while, just continued to drag her fingers lightly across his abdomen. Perhaps now wasn't the best time to discuss her father. Her hand inched lower, following the trail of hair below his belly button. He felt his blood stir and knew it wouldn't be long before he could take her again.

He enjoyed her curious exploration of his body and didn't want her to stop.

"Did you always want to be an artist?"

"No. I didn't know I could draw until after my mother died." Her fingers brushed against his sensitive flesh. "It had been a hobby of hers, and I suppose I tried it as a way to feel connected with her."

She was watching his body change, and that made it all the more exciting. She would soon know the power she had over him, the power to arouse him, to make him think of nothing else but making love to her again.

Lightly, she moved her hand against him, a feather of a touch with the tips of her fingers, back and forth. She was telling him about her past, important information, but he found he could not concentrate.

"So I painted at first. Watercolors, because that is what well-bred ladies do." Her touch became bolder, rubbing a bit more firmly and moving across his length to the tip.

He closed his eyes.

"I don't recall what made me decide to try

drawing, but I wanted to do something with more detail, more dimension. It was never my intention to end up drawing fashions. I envisioned myself doing portraits." She wrapped her hand around him, and he released a moan. Her boldness was intoxicating. She moved her hand up and down, and he wished he could see her face. But then it didn't matter at this point, because he could barely concentrate on her words.

"But I love doing the fashions. I love the intricate details of the dresses and getting them perfect in my pictures. I especially love hearing about that perfection at balls when the paper has just been released."

Faster and faster she pumped him, and he knew his release was near. He didn't want it to happen like this, as erotic as the situation was. He stilled her hand.

"Did I do something wrong?"

"No. You're doing everything right. But I won't have any control in a few moments, and this can get messy."

She lifted her head. "Oh?!"

He tilted her head and kissed her nose. "But suffice it to say, I enjoyed that very much, and we'll have to continue that again sometime. When things can be cleaner."

"Like in the water?"

"Exactly. I like the way you think."

She chewed at her lip.

"What are you thinking about?"

"That was rather amazing. The way your body works. The way you responded so rapidly and boldly only by my touch."

"I've responded to less than your touch. Sometimes it's something you say, or the curve of your neck, or the hint of your perfume. I've never wanted a woman the way that I want you."

Three days since her wedding, and married life was nothing like Claudia had anticipated. Derrick had what seemed to be an unquenchable desire for her body, and she matched him with every stride.

She wasn't ready to say she was comfortable with her nakedness around him, but there was so little time for thought once he started touching her that she didn't have many moments to fret about it.

He'd said he'd never wanted any woman the way he wanted her. It was a glimmer. Certainly not an admission of feelings, but it gave her hope. He didn't talk much about Julia, but she knew that Derrick's first marriage had ended with his heart broken. Claudia still did not know the full story, only that Julia had broken his heart. Not by her death, but by some betrayal before she'd died. Perhaps once he realized that Claudia would never hurt him, he'd open up his heart to her.

So much for keeping her own heart closely guarded. She tried not to expend too much thought on the matter, but she was fairly certain she loved him already. She wouldn't dare admit to it for fear it would break whatever spell she miraculously held over him.

Chapter 17

The note from Mason had arrived that morning confirming that Richard was dead and the authorities hadn't been forthcoming with specific details, but said they suspected it was murder. Derrick knew he'd have to tell Claudia.

If Baubie's suspicions were correct, her father was to blame, but he couldn't tell her that. Not yet. Not until he had proof.

If her father was capable of such a crime, he might hurt Claudia, and that thought had Derrick feeling rage as he'd never felt it before. He'd kill him. With his bare hands, if the lousy excuse for a father hurt Claudia. It was a sobering thought to find he had so much violence in him, when he'd always considered himself a gentle man. Perhaps marriage had changed him.

No, Claudia had changed him.

The thought of losing her or someone harming her made his thoughts spin out of control.

Which was why he had to convince her to stay here in the country without him. Then he could be sure of her safety. Back in London he could do some investigating and uncover the truth behind Richard's murder. If her father was to blame, he wanted to be the one to tell her.

Publishing the information contained within the blackmail letters would eliminate some of Chester Edwards's guilt in the embezzlement. Give his family a little peace. It would also reestablish Derrick's name as a journalist. It would be the last and final story he'd write, and then he would retire to his job as editor and publisher.

Printing that story would indict Claudia's father, which might or might not pit her against him. If he knew she trusted him, if he could guarantee her loyalty would lie with him, then he could print it with no worries. But he had no guarantee. He knew she trusted him, to an extent. But he wasn't so certain that choosing him over a man she'd idolized her entire life would be easy.

He had called her to meet him in his study. Having both of them fully clothed and on neutral ground might prevent this discussion from becoming a lovemaking session. Not that he wouldn't rather do that, but they needed to have this conversation. She needed to know about Richard's death.

He tried to prepare himself for her reaction, not knowing the extent of her feelings for the man.

A knock sounded on the door, then she poked her head in.

"You don't need to knock, Claudia. This is your house now."

"Oh." She opened the door, then shut it behind her. She looked fetching in a simple gown of lavender. It suited her much more than those frilly frocks she usually wore.

"I like that dress," he said.

"Really?" She looked down on it. "You don't find it boring?"

"No. I like the simplicity. It allows me to see you and not a dress. Which is nice, because you are what makes the dress attractive, not the other way around."

"Thank you."

"You should order ten more just like it when we get back to town. In every color."

"Ten?"

"Twenty then. However many you want. But I

291

much prefer this to the ones covered in ribbons and ruffles."

"I certainly don't need twenty new gowns."

"I can afford them."

She scrunched her nose. "Is this what you wanted to discuss with me?"

"No." He was avoiding the real topic. "It was merely an observation."

"Well, I shall go to the dressmaker when I return and order some dresses more to your liking." She sat across from him. "I rather like the simplicity as well. It's that I felt—"

"Felt as if you had to hide yourself behind those layers? Not necessary. You have a beautiful body that any woman would be lucky to have; you should flaunt it with pride. You should consider wearing bolder colors. They would suit you. Especially a nice, bold red or wine."

She chewed at her lip a moment, then said, "I've always been rather fond of daring colors, but never thought I could wear them. I shall consider your suggestions."

"Excellent. Now we need to get to that thing I wanted to discuss with you. I'm afraid I have bad news. I don't know how you're going to take it, but I wanted to tell you myself before you read it in the paper."

"Is my father well?"

"Yes. He's fine. As far as I know." He leaned forward. "It's Richard. I'm afraid he's dead."

"Richard?" Her brow furrowed, but no tears came. "Dead? Are you certain? How?"

"Murdered. At the moment the police don't have any suspects, but they're doing an investigation."

"Oh my," was her only response.

"Are you all right?"

"I suppose so. I'm not certain. I don't really know what to feel. I suppose I should feel sad." She looked up and met his eyes. "But I don't. Not in a personal way. I mean, I'm sad that he lost his life, just as I would feel reading about anyone's death. But it doesn't feel as though I lost someone I knew. Someone I cared about."

"Perhaps you're in shock."

"Why aren't I sad? I should be sad."

He came around the desk and knelt beside her. "Claudia, you feel the way you feel. There aren't any shoulds when it comes to our feelings. You can't control them."

"But I was going to marry him." She shook her head. "I should feel something, and yet inside"—she tapped on her chest—"there is nothing."

"Give yourself some time." He pulled her to a standing position. "Come sit with me on the sofa."

She followed him, a blank stare on her face.

"His death is simply not real to you yet. Let your mind absorb the information. You knew Richard a long time. But not feeling something is fine too. Let your heart guide you."

"Are you sad?" she asked him.

He took a deep breath. "Richard and I were friends a long time ago. Good friends. The best even. But then we grew up, and things changed. Life was different away from school. Richard made some decisions that drastically changed his life and the man he became. In the end he was not the person I remembered, the person I cared for. He died to me a long time ago. So, no, I'm not sad."

"Thank you for telling me."

"Not knowing who did this, I can't in good conscience bring you back to London with me. I want you to stay here for a few weeks. Until I can be sure that you will be safe."

"What does his murder have to do with me?"

"Perhaps nothing, but I don't want to put you at risk."

"It was probably a burglary and nothing more. I shall be fine in London. I do not want to stay here alone."

"I can send Poppy out here to stay with you."

"Poppy's mother will never hear of that. She

can't miss one single engagement and the opportunity to find herself a husband."

"Well, then I can send my aunt out here. The two of you will get along fabulously."

"No." She folded her arms across her chest and nodded, punctuating her stance.

"What?"

"I said no. I don't want to stay here, and I refuse to do so. You told me that you wanted me to speak my mind, have opinions, argue with you. Well, I'm taking advantage of that. I am going back to London with you. That's my final decision."

"This is not what I meant and you know it. This is a different situation than disagreeing with me on an everyday matter. Your safety could be at risk, and it is my duty to care for you."

"Your duty?"

"Yes."

"Derrick, you suggested I fight you. Stand up for what I want. This is what I want. I don't want you to stick me here in the country and forget about me. I want to go home to London with you. Continue my illustrations. It will be easier to keep me safe when you can keep an eye on me."

Damnation. He had asked for it. He needed some bloody distance from her. Her body was intoxicating, and having it at his disposal was weakening his resolve, and he could not allow her to get to his heart.

So he could make her stay here. But she'd hate him for it. Although perhaps that wouldn't be such a bad thing. On the other hand, he didn't want to destroy their marriage. So if he made her stay here, she'd consider him a liar. He'd told her in one breath to speak her mind and then in the next stifled her because she disagreed with him. He would have to keep her close and possibly hire someone to watch the house to ensure her safety.

He would bring her home, knowing full well that in the end she would probably choose her father over him. He'd ignore the tiny hope that she'd choose him. That in the end she'd fall in love with him and give him her complete loyalty. Why would he need her love? It was cruel to want it when he wouldn't return it.

"All right, my wife, you win. But I am not pleased about this. You will not be able to traipse about London as you are accustomed to doing. I expect you to use an escort at all times. And tell me where you're going and when."

She smiled brightly. "I can do that."

"As it turns out, I need to get back to the paper, so we'll be leaving today."

She stood.

"One more thing." He pulled her down onto his

lap and kissed her. It was a full assault on her mouth; he plunged his tongue deep in her mouth, swirling it around with hers.

God, he wanted her.

He released her. Her eyes fluttered open, and she smiled at him.

"I believe my aunt is planning a ball in our honor. An announcement of our marriage. I hope you don't mind."

She shook her head. "But I will definitely need to go to the dressmaker now." She gave him a quick kiss, then left the room.

She closed the door behind her and leaned against it. She couldn't keep her mind clear for more than a few minutes with him kissing her all the time. It was deliciously fun, but it rattled her, kept her from thinking clearly.

He'd wanted her to stay here. Was he ashamed of her as a wife? Did he not want a real marriage with her even though he claimed he did? He obviously wanted her body, a realization that thrilled her like nothing else, but what about her? She'd spent her entire life waiting for a man to notice her, expecting to find a man who would eventually grow to love her for the person she was on the inside. Instead she married the only man in London who physically desired yet could not love her.

Of all the rotten luck.

* * *

Once they'd arrived back in London, Derrick had left her at home with strict instructions that she was not to go anywhere except to visit Poppy. Which she fully intended to do and was on her way out the door when the butler stopped her.

"Mistress, these letters came for you while you were in the country." He handed her a stack of letters, three in all.

She recognized her father's penmanship immediately. She thanked the butler, then took a seat in the nearby parlor. The wax seal cracked as she quickly unfolded the letter.

All three of them were similar. "Please come quickly." "I need you." "I can't believe you deserted me." Her heart beat wildly in her chest. Her father was reaching out to her the only way he knew how, and she'd left town on her honeymoon. What if he was ill? Oh, please don't let her be too late.

She gave the carriage driver the address. A visit to Poppy would have to wait. She must see her father now. Derrick would likely be upset, but surely he would understand these circumstances. Derrick had made it clear how he felt about her father, but a good daughter wouldn't desert a man in need.

The carriage rocked to a stop, and she didn't even wait for the driver to assist her to the ground. She flew up the front steps and let herself in.

"Father? Father, where are you?"

She met Baubie halfway up to the second floor.

"How is he?" Claudia asked.

"The worst I've ever seen him. He's not eating, only drinking. And cursing and yelling like a madman. I've been tossing the liquor when I can find his hidden bottles. Doesn't seem to do much good though, he seems to always have one on hand."

"Thank you, Baubie. I've got to find him."

She opened two doors before she found him, sitting in his office, a drink in one hand and looking more ragged than she'd ever seen him.

"Father?"

He looked up, his eyes not quite focusing on her. "Claudia, is that you?"

She came to kneel before him. The sharp odor of alcohol almost knocked her over. He looked and smelled as if he'd been drinking for days. "I came as quickly as I could. I've been on my honeymoon, or I would have been here sooner. Are you ill?"

"Ill?" His voice was louder than necessary considering she was right next to him. His breath reeked of brandy. "No, I'm not ill." He dropped his glass, and the contents splashed onto her dress before seeping into the carpet. He grabbed both her arms and shook her. "You've deserted me."

"No, I haven't." She peeled his hands off her and took a seat in the chair across from him. She needed distance, from the stench and from his forceful touch. "I got married, that's all. I'm still here for you."

"You chose that bastard over me. I told him he couldn't marry you. But you did it anyway. Didn't you care that I didn't want you to marry him?"

"Father, I had to. If I hadn't married him, my reputation would have been ruined. You wouldn't have wanted that."

He swiped his hand through the air. "Pah. We could have sent you to the country for a few years, then you could have returned, and no one would have even remembered."

"It's over and done with. I'm married to Derrick."

He reached across and grabbed her knee. "You must leave him, Claudia. He's a dangerous man. You've got to leave him and come back home. I can protect you."

What was the matter with him? She knew Derrick, and Derrick wasn't dangerous. Of course, she'd thought she knew Richard too, and she'd been dreadfully wrong. But still, this was her husband. He wasn't dangerous. "You're talking crazy. Derrick isn't dangerous, and I can't leave him. He's my husband." With all their lovemaking, she could very well be carrying his child right now, but she left that out.

"Who will take care of me?"

"Father, you've always taken care of yourself. You've never needed me." She'd never seen him like this. So defeated, so . . . pathetic.

"I never needed you because you were always there. But now you're gone."

"I would have been gone had I married Richard. I would not have stayed here with you."

"Yes, but Richard would not have controlled you. This Middleton, he'll try to control you."

Now, that was rich. What he really meant was that he controlled Richard, and therefore would have continued his control over her. That's what this was about. It was killing him that he didn't have any more say in how she lived her life. She stood.

"Where are you going?"

"You need a bath. It will make you feel better. And I'll have the cook make some strong coffee. It will get the drink out of your body. I'll be right back."

She came back and found him half sitting, half lying on the sofa. "Stand up. I'll help you upstairs." She'd never before spoken to her father with such force, such charge. It felt neither good nor bad, merely necessary under the current situation.

She lifted him to a standing position, and he leaned so heavily on her, she thought she might fall. She steadied herself and walked into the hallway.

"You must leave him, Claudia. He killed Richard."

The hair at the nape of her neck prickled and she shivered. "What did you say?"

"Richard. Didn't you know? He was murdered. And I think your husband did it."

He wasn't merely drunk, he was experiencing delusions. He'd better hope it was only delusions because she'd hate to have to confront him on an actual accusation of her husband. That was more than even she could take. But clearly her father was not in his right mind.

Because Derrick wasn't capable of murder. He was a kind and honest man. Well, mostly honest. She shook off the doubt. No, her father was completely mad for saying such a thing.

"That's preposterous. Derrick has been with

me since our wedding. There would have been no time for him to go and murder someone. Besides, had he done so, surely I would be able to tell by his behavior. A person who could do such a heinous thing can't very well live normally, pretending all is right with the world. Surely it was a burglar."

"What would a burglar steal from Richard? He was poor as a street urchin."

"Perhaps there was nothing to steal, and the thief was angered, and that is why he killed poor Richard."

"I think you know it was that rotten husband of yours, and you're trying to protect him."

"That's nonsense."

They made it to his room, and his valet was already there readying the bath.

"Father, this bath will make you feel more like yourself. Then you need to get some rest and make sure you eat something. Baubie tells me you haven't been eating properly."

"Baubie talks too much. Always has. I should have fired her years ago."

"You wouldn't dare."

He shrugged. "Probably not. She makes the best shortbread in London."

"Yes, she does. I'll have her make you some

shortbread. I'm going to go home now. Send for me if you need me, but only if it is an emergency. Otherwise, I'll see you tomorrow."

He grabbed her wrists. "You must leave him, Claudia. He'll ruin you."

She jerked her hands free. "I cannot leave him. He is my husband. He's a wonderful man. You'll see once you get to know him properly. Perhaps we can have dinner together." She knelt to pour some scented oil into the water to soothe her father's muscles.

"Do not bring that man into my house." His words dripped with hatred.

She felt her body stiffen. Then she slowly rose to a standing position, put the scented oil down. Let his valet worry about any aching muscles.

"Father, you must accept Derrick sooner or later. He's a part of my life now."

"Foolish girl."

"I shall see you tomorrow. Get some rest. And stay away from the brandy."

She closed the bedroom door and leaned against it. He was like a different man. She'd never seen such pleading in his eyes before. Nor had she heard him plead. For anything. Ever. Something in him had changed.

He'd said it was that he'd finally realized he

needed her, but she doubted that. It didn't make sense. He'd never so much as had a civil conversation with her. Instead he'd spent their time together berating her for poor decisions and challenging her to straighten up. Meaning stop playing with her art and marry Richard.

Now her father was panicking because he'd lost control over her life. As much as she knew that was the real reason for his newfound attitude toward her, she couldn't turn her back on him. He needed her, maybe not for the right reasons, but it was a start.

But she refused to allow him to disparage her husband. She could come to terms with her husband and father never liking each other, but they would have to be civil. She wouldn't be torn between them.

How had her life ended in such a state? A month ago, she'd been content to marry Richard. Had believed she had plenty of time to do so. Granted, she hadn't been in a hurry, because she hadn't wanted to marry him. Not really.

But he'd never seemed as if he'd wanted to marry her either. Or else he would have proposed. Generally if a man was ready to marry and had the girl's father's permission, the wedding date was set. But Richard had stalled. Why, she'd never know.

But now everything had changed. She was free to continue illustrating, but according to her father, she had married the wrong man. And now Richard was dead.

Chapter 18

It was late afternoon, almost evening, by the time she got home, and the sun had already set. She climbed the stairs to the bedroom, eager to wash the stench of alcohol from her body. After her father had spilled the foul liquid on her dress and feet, he'd proceeded to touch her more than he had ever done in her life, leaving in his wake the foul odor of day-old liquor. Week-old, perhaps.

No doubt she smelled of the streets.

Upon entering their bedroom, she found Derrick sitting and staring at the door with a dark scowl across his face. His eyes landed on her, and he immediately stood.

"I'm trying hard not to yell at you right now. I'm very angry, but I do not want to frighten you. You've spent too much of your life being afraid."

She said nothing, simply stood there.

"Where the hell have you been?" His words came out in tight clips, squeezed between his teeth.

"First tell me why you are angry," she cautiously answered.

"Because I asked you to stay here. And if you had to leave the house, only to go and visit Poppy. Well, I know you weren't there, because I checked myself. Where were you, Claudia?"

"I went to see my father. He sent letters while we were away, begging me to come home. He said he was ill, that he needed me."

"Was he ill?"

"Not precisely. Inebriated is more the term, I believe." She pulled her gloves off, then began unpinning her hat.

"I see." He took three deep breaths before he continued. "And what did you discuss?"

She didn't want to lie to him, yet she didn't want to tell him that her father suspected him of Richard's murder. She didn't see any reason to fuel their hatred of each other. "He's still not accepted our marriage. He asked me to come home." She placed her hat on her dressing table and the pins in the crystal bowl.

He laughed a humorless laugh. "And what did you tell him?"

She turned to face him. "I told him no. That I was your wife, and I belonged with you."

He nodded, clearly approving her response. "Did he have anything else to say?"

"Only that he missed me and needed me. Which is odd, considering he's never been an affectionate man. I assume it was the drink that made him act so peculiar. I had a bath drawn for him and instructed the staff to make him eat and rest. I will check on him tomorrow."

"No."

"I beg your pardon?"

"I said no. I don't trust the man. I don't believe he has your best interests at heart, and I can't help but think, with his new attitude toward you, he has an ulterior plan."

"So it is unfathomable that he might have realized he loves me and needs me after I left his life?"

"That's not what I said. Nor what I meant." He led her to the chair and brought her down on his lap once he sat. "I don't want you harmed."

"He would never hurt me."

"You know that for certain? Has he ever struck you?" He began removing the hairpins that secured her coiffure.

"No."

"What about your mother?"

"Not that she ever admitted, but I was always suspicious."

"If a man can strike one woman, he can strike another. Drinking can bring out the worst in a person."

Her hair fell about her shoulders in a wave. Not having her hair tightly bound to her head relieved a throbbing pressure she hadn't noticed before. "I suppose that makes sense. Well, then what do you propose I do? I cannot very well desert him. He was in the worst shape I've ever seen him."

Derrick's fingertips rubbed her aching scalp. "I don't care for your father, we've established that, but I know you will hate me if I ask you to walk away from him. In the future I will accompany you to see him."

"That will not work."

"Why not?"

"Because he will not allow you in his house. Told me so this afternoon."

"Bloody hell he won't. Either he will see both of us, or he will not see you. That's the rule."

"Derrick, he's my father. How can you be so unreasonable?"

"I'm not being unreasonable. I'm being cautious. I need for you to trust me on this. I'm not trying to imprison you. I want to investigate all possible avenues regarding Richard's death."

"And you think my father is a potential avenue?"

"I'm simply not ruling him out. Your father and Richard were more than acquaintances. Arguments happen."

"Well, I'll have you know he said the same thing about you this afternoon. It's so nice to be caught between my husband and father while they toss ludicrous accusations at each other, as if their words have no consequences. Neither of you acknowledges that my heart is in the middle of your childish dispute."

"He suggested to you that I killed Richard?"

"Yes."

"What did you tell him?"

"That you were with me the entire time. That it was probably a burglary."

"I'm only being cautious." He turned her chin so that their eyes met. "I don't want anything to happen to you."

His hand rubbed against her back, soothing her doubts. Derrick cared about her. He might not be in love with her, but he cared about her, was concerned for her safety. That's why he'd been angry. That's why he was suspicious of her father. It didn't make her feel any better about the latter, but she understood.

* * *

Today when he'd come home and she'd been gone, he'd thought the worst. It had terrified him. He'd gone to Poppy's to try to find her, only to be told Poppy hadn't heard from Claudia all day. He should have known she'd go to see her father. Derrick could have gone to check for himself, but he'd wanted to know if she would come back.

She had come home. And she'd been honest with him. He pulled her tighter to him, loving the crush of her body next to his and the smell of her hair as it tickled his nose. He loved the gentle curve of her neck and her big, amazing eyes that nearly made him forget everything else around him. He loved her excited chatter and the passion she saved for only him. He loved her ridiculous hats and the way she bit down on her lip to concentrate. He loved . . . everything about her.

He loved her.

The thought hit him so hard he nearly fell over. His heart raced, and he had to bite his tongue to keep from saying it aloud.

He'd thought he'd loved Julia, but now he saw how limited those feelings had been. With Julia he'd been giddy and starry-eyed and so hopeful for the future. But with Claudia, the feelings had snuck up on him. She'd silently wormed her way into his heart, into his very soul, and the feelings ran much deeper and stronger than the foolish infatuation he'd had for his first bride.

Claudia was different from Julia, and their marriage was different. But still, a man stood between Derrick and his wife.

Which was why he couldn't tell Claudia about his feelings now. Not until he knew the truth about her father. Not until he was able to tell her everything about his past. But he could show her. He took her mouth and kissed her passionately, releasing all the worry he'd felt all day.

She put her arms around his neck and kissed him back. He brought them both to a standing position, and his fingers worked the buttons of her dress, trying to get her undressed as quickly as he could. Finally he was able to free her, and the dress pooled at her feet. They made it to the bed between kisses and the removal of their clothes.

Tonight there wouldn't be slow, patient lovemaking. Tonight it would be hot and hard and hurried. Her hands were all over him, driving him mad with desire.

They were both so ready by the time he entered her that it took only a few thrusts before they both climaxed. Her moans echoed in the room, and he hugged her close.

As much as he'd tried to protect his heart, he'd

failed. He loved her, and now he'd have to do the one thing that would probably lose her to him forever.

Go after her father.

Chapter 19

❦❦

"I do hope he hasn't been drinking today," Claudia said.

The carriage rounded the corner onto her father's street.

"If he has, then we'll leave," Derrick said.

"No, I promised him I would come."

"You are fulfilling that promise. But you're coming to visit him, and if he doesn't have the common courtesy not to get himself drunk as a boiled owl before you arrive, then we shall leave."

They were shown into the front parlor not ten minutes later to wait for her father. She heard the telltale rapping of her father's cane on the floor, and then he entered the room looking more like his old self, although heavy bags sat beneath his eyes.

He stopped short in the doorway. "What the devil is he doing here?"

"He escorted me," Claudia said.

"Well, I don't want him here." He puffed his chest out, looking very much like a country ram about to charge. "You hear that, Middleton, you're not welcome here."

"Then we shall take our leave."

"Leave Claudia here. I'll have a carriage return her later."

"If I leave, she's going with me."

"Stop it, both of you." Both men turned to face her. Derrick nodded. Her father scowled. "Father, Derrick is my husband, and you will have to accept him. Now let's all sit and have a nice visit."

That sat in silence for a good while until she couldn't stand it any longer. "Tell me, Father, how are the arguments going for the new policy you're trying to pass."

He stiffened. "Did he tell you to ask me that?"

"What?"

"That's why he married you." He pointed at

her. "Mark my words, girl. He married you to try to dig up information about me."

"That's absurd," Claudia countered.

"Political stories, he wants them for his paper. You'll see. That's why he came sniffing around you in the first place."

"For your information," Claudia said, "I went sniffing around him, if you insist on such crude language. I introduced myself to him, not the other way around."

"What are you talking about?"

She eyed Derrick, who sat silently watching their discussion. This was as good a time as any to break the news to her father. She didn't want to keep it a secret anymore. She wanted him to know she was a paid illustrator.

Squaring her shoulders, she looked directly at him. "I went to see him to resign from my position with the paper."

"What position?"

Derrick grabbed her hand and squeezed it. Her husband believed in her; she could do this. She could tell her father the truth. He couldn't do anything to her now.

"I am an illustrator for *London's Illustrated Times*."

"A damned good one too," Derrick piped in.

"Thank you." She smiled at him.

"Impossible," her father spat.

"What's impossible? My holding a paying position without your knowledge or my having the ability to be an illustrator?"

He narrowed his eyes at her. "Don't get cheeky with me, girl. How could you have kept this from me?"

She shrugged. "You saw what you wanted to see. It really wasn't that difficult to hide. Only recently did I become nervous you would discover me, which is why I went to resign. That, and I knew I couldn't continue once I married Richard. But now that I've married Derrick, I can retain my position."

"This is ludicrous."

"I had hoped you might be proud," she said softly. "I'm quite accomplished."

"Proud? You thought I'd be proud? Proud of my daughter selling her services like a common whore? No, I'm not proud. I am a viscount, Claudia, and the former chancellor of finance. No daughter of mine would have a paying position. Especially one working for a man like him."

He stood and slammed his cane down onto the floor. "You've always been such a disappointment to me, and now this. Have you no consideration for me? No, of course not. You were so blinded that a man could actually want you, that you did anything and everything to encourage the relationship."

There, he'd said it. Her worst fear put into words right here in front of Derrick. And she hated her father for saying it. She didn't dare look at Derrick for fear of seeing the truth of her father's words in his eyes. She had been blinded by his desire for her. Had allowed him to seduce her with kisses and love words, until she'd been ruined and forced to marry.

"To marry a man like this." A look of disgust crossed his face. "Lowly born, unmannered, and clearly using you to further his career. A commoner only allowed in our circles because of his aunt and his money. If not for that, he'd be no different than the beggars on the street."

For him to degrade her was one thing, but she would not stand for him to talk so disrespectfully of her husband. She stood. "That is enough. I will listen to no more of this. From this day forward, you are not to say another disparaging word about my husband or our marriage. If you cannot adhere to that, then we might as well say our good-byes now, because I will not be back. I'm not asking you to like him or even accept him, but you will not speak poorly of him in my presence anymore. Is that understood?"

She did not wait for a response, but rather took hold of Derrick's hand and pulled him to his feet.

"Let's go home."

He only nodded.

"Claudia! Claudia, you cannot walk out on me." Her father's words trailed behind her as she marched down the hall, Derrick in tow.

"Do not walk out of here, girl; we're not done with our discussion."

She heard his cane and footsteps tapping on the floor behind her, but she didn't stop. She didn't want to discuss it anymore. She didn't want to change her mind. For once in her life, she'd stood up to him, and she felt nervous and excited and sick all at once. Her blood pounded loudly in her ears, and she thought if she stopped walking, she might crumple to the floor.

"If you walk out of here, don't come back. Do you understand me?" he yelled behind her. "Don't you come back. Ever!"

She closed her eyes and stopped walking. She could feel Derrick's breath on her neck. He didn't nudge the small of her back to move forward, nor did he grab her arm and lead her outside, instead he simply stood there, behind her, allowing her to make this decision.

She hadn't wanted any of this to come down to her choosing, but it had. And she couldn't choose her father. She loved him, and she'd wanted her whole life for him to accept and approve of her, but it didn't matter now. She didn't need it anymore. She was proud of herself and her accomplishments.

She chose her husband. She walked the few steps it took to cross the threshold, then closed the door behind her.

"You didn't have to do that, you know. You didn't have to choose," Derrick said.

"Yes, I did."

She didn't speak the entire ride back to their house. Derrick kept trying to think of something to say, something to make the hurt go away, but he was at a loss. Her father was a bastard; that was the only excuse. It wasn't her fault, and she shouldn't have to hurt because of her father's selfishness. She was a dutiful and loving daughter, one any father would be proud of, but for some mysterious reason hers was not.

She cried no tears, but rather sat quietly staring out the window as they rode home. He wanted to comfort her, but didn't know how. He wanted to kill her father for causing her such pain, but for obvious reasons he couldn't do that. She'd chosen him, and he was yet again deceiving her. All for good reason, but what would she say if she knew he was close to accusing her father?

Once they arrived home, he followed her up to their room, not wanting to leave her alone. He closed the bedroom door and turned to her.

"Claudia, I—"

She put her finger to his lips. "No. There's nothing to say. I'll be all right. A little shocked. Although I'm not certain why. I shouldn't be the least surprised. It's not as if he's shown me any warmth to indicate that he loved me and wanted me to be happy." She tried to smile. "Honestly, I don't know what my mother saw in him."

"Perhaps nothing. They could have married for any number of reasons."

"She claimed she loved him. But maybe she only said that for my benefit. I can't imagine someone as gentle and loving as my mother giving her heart to that man. I've wasted so much time trying to please him." She shook her head. "I don't want to talk about him."

"Is there anything I can do?"

She stood silently a moment, then met his gaze. "Yes. Right now I feel so numb, so dead inside. I need to touch you. I need you to touch me. I need to know that I'm alive and can still feel."

He nodded.

She came to him then, her hands already unbuttoning her dress. Her eyes traveled the length of him in a look so seductive and practiced, she looked more mistress than wife.

In an instant, her mouth was on his, hungrily kissing him. Her fingers fumbled with his shirt, and he tried to help her, but she pushed his hands out of the way. She was in charge. Had his mouth not been otherwise engaged, he would have smiled.

She peeled his shirt off and immediately began unfastening his pants. Already partially aroused, he grew instantly hard as her hand grazed him while unfastening his pants.

He tried again to touch her, to cup her breasts, and she moved his hands.

"No," she said. "This time I want to do it."

She needed to be in control, and he understood that. She'd fought her own desires her entire life, and tonight she'd stood up to her father for the first time. It would take more than one night of taking the lead in the bedroom to banish her demons, but it was a step. She finished removing his clothes and led him to the bed. He climbed atop it and turned to face her. Her beautiful blue eyes had darkened to the color of the sky right before a storm.

She gave him a lazy smile, then began removing her clothes. Slowly. Seductively. He was going crazy with want for her. His loins ached for the warmth of her body.

First her dress came off, and she gave a little wiggle. Then her petticoat. Piece by piece, until she stood before him gloriously naked. He wanted to lick every inch of her pale, soft flesh.

His eyes moved to the triangle of hair between her legs, golden like the hair on her head. He longed to part it and bury himself inside her.

"Claudia, please."

"Be patient."

She sauntered to the bed. One hand grabbed onto a bedpost, and she tossed her head back, and her blond ringlets brushed against her plump bottom. He squirmed. She inched onto the bed next to his feet, then got on her hands and knees. Ever so gently, she crawled up his body, only stopping to rub her breasts against his legs, then his member, and then his chest.

She spread kisses up his torso and neck, lingering at his right ear, where she licked and breathed and nibbled until he thought he would lose his mind. He reached between them and cupped both her breasts, and she cried out. If she would but lower herself. He bucked up to meet her, and she released a low giggle.

"Do you want me?" she asked.

"Yes."

"How much do you want me?" This time she looked him in the eyes.

"More than I've ever wanted anyone. Please."

The change in her was dramatic, and it was all for him. He'd taught her to trust him enough that she felt comfortable being the dominant lover. His heart pounded rapidly. He loved her. God, how he loved her.

She lowered her body, and he felt the hot slickness of her rest against him. She moved a little. Back and forth, back and forth. Bloody hell, if she wasn't careful, he wouldn't make it very long.

"Claudia, I need to be inside you."

She leaned in and kissed him while she lowered herself on him. She sat still for a moment before she began to move. Faster and harder she rode, and he thought he would explode, but he kept up with her.

She tilted her head back and squeezed her eyes closed. Tears slid down her cheeks, yet she continued to move. And then it was over, in a flash of pleasure. Her waves of pleasure subsided and still she cried. She collapsed on top of him, her curls brushing his cheek.

"Thank you," she said quietly.

He said nothing, merely wrapped his arms around her and hugged her tightly.

I love you, he wanted to say, but couldn't. Not

now. Not until he could be completely honest with her. Damnation. When she needed to hear it the most, and he couldn't bring himself to say it.

She listened to the steady rhythm of his heart. The crinkle of hair sprinkled on his chest tickled her cheek. She felt exhilarated and free. Never had she thought she would do what she'd just done. She'd never imagined the marriage bed could be pleasant, and Derrick had taught her differently, and now she was instigating their lovemaking.

She giggled.

"What's so funny?" He smoothed the hair at her temple.

"Married life is not at all what I envisioned. I'm not the same person I was mere weeks ago. I can't even believe what I just did."

"You can do it anytime you want." His hand slid down the length of her back and swatted at her behind. "I mean it. Consider me your personal love slave."

Now that was a delicious thought. Every once in a while, it hit her that he was hers and hers alone. "Sometimes it doesn't seem real."

"What?"

"Us. Our marriage. Sometimes I think I'll wake up and it will only have been a dream."

He brushed the hair out of her face. "A good dream?"

"Yes. When we first got married, I wasn't so sure. I thought you were the wrong husband, that my life would be a terrible mess from then on. But the truth is, I married the right man. I'm happy with you, Derrick, and I hope someday you'll be happy with our marriage too."

"What makes you think I'm not happy?"

"I know you didn't want to marry again."

"No, I didn't, but I don't regret it. I'll never regret marrying you."

"What about Julia?"

"What about Julia? She's in the past."

"Do you still love her?"

"No. I haven't loved her in many years."

"You said that day by the pond that your marriage to her was a story for another day. Will you tell me now?"

He shrugged. "There's not much to tell, really. I met her shortly after I returned to London after going to the university and doing some traveling. She enchanted me, and I fell in love with her immediately."

Claudia tried not to wince. She'd known he'd loved his first wife, but she hadn't been prepared to hear him say it.

He idly rubbed her back while he spoke. "It was a boy's love, though, childish and fanciful. We married a few short weeks after we met, and a year later she was gone."

"What happened?" she ventured.

"She got pregnant." He took a deep breath.

"If this is too painful, we don't have to talk about it."

"It's not painful. Julia had an affair, her lover got her pregnant. Julia wanted to run off with him. She made certain that everyone knew the truth, that everyone knew who the father of her child was."

"Wasn't that a little risky with her reputation and yours?"

"Yes, but she didn't care. She'd always been reckless, it was one of the things that attracted me to her. I wouldn't let her leave though. I was self-ish, I didn't want to let her go." He released a deep breath. "She died having that bastard's child and he didn't even come to her funeral."

"And the child?"

"She lived all of three days, then she too died. She's buried at my estate."

"You gave her your name?" Claudia asked, al-ready knowing the answer.

"Yes. She deserved to die with some degree of dignity, even if her parents had none."

"You are a good man, Derrick."

He shrugged. "It is all in the past. I was a boy, it was a long time ago, and it's forgotten. Whatever your worries are about Julia, dismiss them. She does not affect our marriage."

She smiled. "Very well."

"I do have something I've been wanting to tell you, though," he said. "I guess it's a day for confessions." He gave her a weak smile. "There are things about my past that you should know. Twelve years ago, I worked for my father's newspaper, the *Challenger*. I was a journalist. His paper printed mostly political news. The latest of Parliament, scandals, debates, anything regarding politics went into that paper. And it was popular. The sales were great." He was silent for a moment before he continued.

"Then I got the story of a lifetime. A scandal to beat all scandals. My source was reliable, or so I thought, and when I questioned the gentleman, he had no arguments against my facts. So I printed the story. And it ruined him. He was terminated from his position with the patents office and charged with treason. Two days after the paper was printed, he shot himself. His wife and daughter found him."

His voice was lined with pain and obvious guilt. She tried to think of something to say, but found no words.

"I swore I'd never write again. And I haven't.

Eventually the paper was ruined. People didn't take too kindly to us ruining that family—we were blamed for his suicide, me especially."

"But it wasn't your fault. Surely you know that."

"It wasn't completely my fault. But I am partially to blame. As it turns out, the story wasn't completely true."

"But the man. You asked him to comment, and he didn't challenge your facts."

"No, he didn't. I've always wondered why. At the time, I thought he was being a stubborn, righteous old man. But now I know that he was protecting someone."

"Who?"

"He was being blackmailed to embezzle the money. Of the funds he skimmed, he never spent one cent. It all went to someone else. He should have gone to the crown and reported the blackmailer. But I suppose he didn't see any way to do that. To him, the secret he hid was more important than crimes against the crown."

"Do you know who it was? The person behind the blackmail?" she asked.

"I have my suspicions."

"But you won't tell me?"

"Not until I have proof. I don't want to wrongly accuse anyone. I can tell you that my source, the one I trusted who gave me the original story, was Richard."

"So that is your past together, why you didn't trust him."

"Exactly," he said.

"So your father's paper was destroyed by this one act?"

"Yes. He died shortly after that. That's when I started thinking of ways to recreate his success. I wanted to carry on his good name of providing quality news to people. But I wanted to take it a step further and make it available to everyone. It took me eight years to get the formula right, but I'm proud of my paper. And I think my father would be proud."

She touched his cheek. "I know he would be."

"He would have liked you very much."

"Really?"

"Yes."

"You know, that wasn't exactly the first time I'd heard that story."

"You knew about me?"

"No, not precisely. That day you found Richard and me. He'd told me something similar. I figured he was angry and didn't know what he was talking about."

"Why didn't you ask me?"

"I felt if it was important, then you'd tell me eventually."

He was quiet a moment, then asked, "What do you think about it?"

"I'm dreadfully disappointed in myself that I did not see Richard for the man he truly was. Now I understand you trying to protect me from him. As far as the story and the man's suicide, it was unfortunate. Certainly not your fault. I bet you were a wonderful writer."

She tilted her head and kissed his chin.

"So you believe me?"

She searched his eyes. He was serious, concerned. "Of course I believe you. I trust you."

"You're amazing."

She smiled. "I don't think so, but thank you for saying so."

"I'm serious. I've given you no reason to have faith in me, and yet you do. Unwavering, it seems. You walked out on your father for me. I don't even know how to say thank you for something like that." His hand brushed her cheek, lingering by her ear.

"You've given me every reason to have faith in you. Aside from your slight prevarication at the beginning of our relationship, you've been nothing but honest with me. You went out of your way to prevent me from marrying Richard, and while

I'm not certain your tactics were the best, under the circumstances—me refusing to see the truth— it was your only choice.

"As for my father, I realized that I've spent my entire life seeking his approval, and it's never going to happen. No matter who I am or who I become, I will always be lacking in his eyes. I much prefer the way I look in your eyes."

Chapter 20

"**N**ot that color."

Claudia eyed her husband. "What's wrong with this color?" She fingered the fine pale blue silk. He'd talked her into going to the dressmaker this morning. They'd been here a full twenty minutes, and he'd rejected every fabric she'd selected.

"It looks like all your other dresses. I don't want you to buy a gown your father would approve of. I want you to select material that makes you feel like a woman." His voice was a mere breath away, warm next to her ear. "Vibrant colors. Passionate."

She fought the urge to lean into him. What a wanton she'd become. He didn't even have to touch her, and she melted.

"Show me what you want," she said.

"Very well."

She followed him around the aisles of fabric, and nearly bumped into him when he stopped suddenly.

"This is perfect." He held up a rich, red velvet.

"Honestly, Derrick, I'll look like a harlot." She reached past him a grabbed a bolt of pink silk. "This is nice."

"Yes, lovely." He faked a yawn. "And boring." He grabbed hold of her hand and smoothed it across the bloodred fabric. "Do you feel that? How can you walk away from something that feels that good?"

"It does feel rather nice," she admitted.

"And when you wear it"—he leaned in closer to whisper—"I will not be able to keep my hands off you."

Sold. It was beyond beautiful; the bright, warm tone beckoned for a touch. It would make a glorious ball gown. Perfect for their wedding ball.

"We're not done." He moved through the store, then stopped and picked up a bolt of deep purple. It was silk and shimmered beneath the lights. He unrolled a portion, then slid it against the bare skin at her neck. Her nipples hardened in response. Gracious.

"What do you think?"

"I like it," her voice came out in barely a breath.

"I like it too. I think I will especially like the way it slithers off your body."

"You are incorrigible."

He gave her a toothy grin. "Can't help it. You bring out the worst in me."

"Are you sure about all of this? Not all women can wear such daring colors."

He turned to face her, tilted her chin so that she looked him in the eyes, and smiled. "Yes, I'm positive. Can you trust me on this?"

Could she? Perhaps everyone would think she looked like a harlot, but for all she knew, they all thought she was a harlot already. Her husband wanted her to wear bold colors; she owed it to him to do so. And truth be told, she rather liked the thought of slipping into that rich, red velvet.

"Yes, I will trust you on this."

They continued through the store, picking fabric upon fabric, reds, greens, blues, purples in velvet, silk, cashmere, muslin. She would have an entirely new wardrobe, and none of it was pink, she thought with a smile.

He seemed so positive that she was born to stand out, as if those words were absolute fact, not merely his opinion. She'd spent her entire life trying to melt into the crowd, yet he insisted she was an original.

While the dressmaker measured her, Derrick waited patiently. She'd never known of any man who went to the dressmaker with his wife. But there he sat, a giant among the tiny feminine chairs, hard and masculine amid the soft and lacy fabrics filling the room. He'd helped her select everything: fabric, patterns, hair ribbons, and even some new fans.

The entire experience had been one of the most sensual things she'd ever done. Every color, every texture, all meant to engage the senses. Up until today, she had known nothing about dressing. And she'd learned everything from a man.

She had picked out something all her own, though. When Derrick had been going over the patterns with Madam Silver, Claudia had picked out a sheer nightgown and matching robe and had them wrapped.

Two evenings later, Claudia took one last look at herself in the mirror before heading downstairs. She'd never had a ball hosted in her honor before, and it was both flattering and nerve-wracking. But Derrick's aunt had insisted. She'd said it would stop the gossips who were still twittering about their sudden nuptials.

She smoothed her hand along the red velvet bodice, loving the feel of the plush softness, then started down the stairs. For the first time in her life, she realized, she felt pretty. Beautiful, even. She tilted her chin and smiled as she descended the rest of the way to the first floor.

Her husband stood at the base of the stairs looking more handsome than she'd ever seen him. She hadn't thought that a possibility. But there he stood, dressed from head to toe in black, with the exception of his white shirt. He arched one eyebrow, and a sensual grin slid into place. Her heart beat wildly in her chest.

No other man had ever affected her the way Derrick did. She supposed that was how it should be between a husband and wife. But oh, how she wished there was more between them.

Love. Claudia wanted love. Her beloved friend Poppy had her heart broken, and she selfishly wanted more from her otherwise happy marriage.

She reached him, and he leaned down to place a hot kiss at her throat.

"You look stunning, as I knew you would in that dress. We might have to disappoint our guests and disappear for a while."

"Are you suggesting, dear husband, that we flee from our own ball, so you can toss up my skirts and please yourself?"

He clicked his tongue. "My, what a saucy wench my wife has become. I'll be tossing those skirts up tonight. You can count on that. But I shall not be the only one getting pleasure."

She had no doubt he was right. It would not surprise her in the least if she were the most pleasured lady in all of England.

"Shall we?" he asked, then held his arm out for her.

She linked her arm with his. "Yes."

They were announced amid applause and smiles. Whether or not people saw their union as fodder for the rumor mill, everyone was on his best behavior tonight. The cream of Society had turned out in force because of the simple words, "The dowager Duchess of Shelton requests your presence . . ."

The next two and a half hours sped past Claudia in a whirlwind. She danced with more men than she could count, and handfuls of others had offered to fetch her drinks or escort her here or there. As it was, right now she waltzed with a pleasant-looking man by the name of Lord Claybrooke, whom she remembered meeting several Seasons before.

"My dear Miss Prattley, or I suppose it is now Middleton, my apologies, I wish to congratulate you on your marriage."

"Thank you, Lord Claybrooke."

"I'm not certain if you recall, but we met before. We danced a few times several years ago."

"Of course I remember you."

"Excellent. I made my intentions known I wished to court you."

"You did?"

"Yes. I came to see your father."

She could see where this was going. He had declared his intentions to her father, and her father had ignored them. Blinded by his plans to see her wed to Richard. And she could have had a regular courtship by this very nice gentleman. Had there been any others whose requests had fallen on deaf ears?

"I see," she said. "I regret I never got such a message. You must have thought me most ungrateful. I wish I had known."

"It matters not now. I can see you and your husband are very happy. But I never got a chance to tell you what a charming woman I thought you were. I wanted to do so tonight."

"Thank you, Lord Claybrooke. That means more to me than you could know."

For years she'd made excuses for her father's harsh treatment of her, refusing to see the truth— he didn't love her and never had. There was no tenderness when he looked at her and saw a glimpse of her mother, no moments of pride at the woman she'd become. There was nothing that even resembled love, and Derrick was right, it was time she walked away.

She had a new family now. Someday she'd have her own children, and she'd make certain they knew every day that their mother and father loved them.

The dance ended, and Lord Claybrooke escorted her back to Derrick.

"May I say, Mr. Middleton, that you are a lucky man?" Lord Claybrooke asked.

"You may. And I agree. I am quite smitten with my wife." He hugged her close to him. Once they were alone, he whispered in her ear. "I do wish these people would leave. I'm crazy with want for you."

She smiled. "And I for you. But we must wait until our guests leave."

"What do you suppose they would say if I tossed you over my shoulder and hauled you upstairs?"

"That we had a scandalous marriage, and you are a complete cad."

"True enough."

"Behave."

"Lord Claybrooke seemed to be quite taken with you."

"Yes. As it turns out, he attempted to court me a

few years ago, and my father neglected to give me that information."

"Well, as much as I'm sorry your father did such a thing, I'm pleased by the outcome. I'd hate to think of Claybrooke lifting those tempting skirts of yours."

"Honestly, Derrick."

"This proves my point, though. You've always believed there was something wrong with you, something about you that prevented you from having a string of suitors. When in fact, it was only because your father is a bastard. I do apologize, my dear, but it's the truth."

"Let's not talk about him anymore this evening."

"I'm going to go find my aunt and make our excuses. I can take no more of this. We are going to bed."

Derrick waited in the parlor, knowing there was a good chance this was the worst mistake he'd ever make. He was putting his marriage on the line, gambling the newfound love he had with his wife. But if her father was guilty, it was a risk worth taking to ensure Claudia's safety.

He didn't have to wait too much longer before he heard the rapping of the cane down the hall, and then Lord Kennington entered.

"Middleton. What the hell do you want?"

"Are you this hospitable to all your guests?"

"You can save your sarcasm for someone who has the time."

"Fair enough. I've come with a business proposition for you."

"I'm not interested."

"Oh, but I think you will be."

He grumbled and found his way to a chair.

"Does the name Chester Edwards mean anything to you?"

A slight flicker in his eye, and then it was gone. "I'm familiar with him, yes. He was a patents officer. Offed himself as I recall."

"Yes, he did. But I think you knew him a little better than that."

"What are you after, Middleton?"

"I think you knew him well enough to blackmail him."

"That's preposterous." His color heightened, turning his cheeks and neck a cherry-red.

"Yes, I think you blackmailed him so that he would embezzle money for you from the patents office. And I think you used Richard Foxmore as your deliveryman. Only Richard didn't deliver your blackmail letters, did he? No, he must have relied on your threats, and he kept the letters himself, planning to turn the blackmailing tables on you. How am I doing so far?"

"You weave an entertaining tale. But you can prove nothing."

"Oh, but I believe I can. And I have more to tell. Richard, being the greedy, not quite so smart man that he was, fouled up his blackmail with you when he told you about the letters. That's when you decided to kill him. You simply were not aware that he'd already contacted me with the story. Of course my past with Richard and using him as a source is tainted, so I was reluctant to believe him. Until I saw the letters."

"Telling people you think you saw letters proving this ludicrous tale will only make you look the fool. People will believe me. I am an important man."

"Indeed you are. Which will make this scandal all the more explosive. So here is what I propose. You leave quietly. Retire from public life. Move to your country estate and cut all ties with the House of Lords. And cut all ties with Claudia."

"Are you mad?"

"No. It's a generous offer. Better than the alternative."

"Which is?"

"Prison. Don't think for a moment that a jury of your peers would not convict you for crimes against the crown. They might not care that you rid the world of Richard Foxmore, but stealing from the queen . . ." He clicked his tongue. "Shame on you."

"You cannot prove any of this."

"Oh, but I can. And I will. I have a story ready for my newspaper, as well as the hard proof ready to go to Her Majesty."

"Liar."

Derrick leaned forward. "Don't tempt me. I'm trying to save my wife some grief and leave her with some pleasant thoughts about her father. Would you ruin everything for her by making me print this story?"

"I care not a whit what my daughter thinks of me. She has betrayed me."

"Selfish, stubborn bastard. Well, that is my deal." He stood. "You have twenty-four hours to consider it and get back to me. If I don't hear from you, I will turn my evidence over to the queen and print the story. You have my word on that."

"Prove to me you have the evidence."

"Do you think I'm a fool that I would show you? That was Richard's mistake. You'll just have to trust."

"Like hell I will. You're bluffing."

"When it comes to my wife, be guaranteed that I don't bluff. Were it not for Claudia, there would be no deal. I would simply turn you over to the authorities. I'm doing this for her, because I don't want to see her hurt. But the bottom line is, you need to be stopped, and if you won't cooperate, I won't hesitate to bring this to the people."

"You can't threaten me."

"I can, and I did. Twenty-four hours. Your decision. The country with a nice quiet life, or life in a tiny, dirty cell in prison. It doesn't seem like much of a choice to me, but I'll let you think about it."

And with that he turned and left.

Chapter 21

⟨∾OO∾⟩

"It's an excellent drawing, Claudia," Poppy said.

Claudia glanced at the illustration, holding it up so she could inspect each detail. It might well be her best drawing yet. Pride swelled in her chest, and she smiled. A pictorial of her and Derrick. It would debut as the first full-colored illustration in the paper.

They looked happy. Like a happily married couple. She couldn't wait for Derrick to see it. After his reaction to the first drawing of the two of them, perhaps this one would please him. She looked at the image of herself, and it looked like her, not a caricature of what she thought people saw. Used to think, she corrected.

"Yes, it is, isn't it? I appreciate you letting me make this quick stop. I realize I could give it to him at home. I am still a paid employee. But this drawing is special, and I want to bring it to him."

"We don't have to go today. I'm not really in the mood for shopping anyhow," Poppy said.

"We are going shopping. It will take your mind off things. I won't be but a moment."

"I'll wait here."

"Perfect."

Claudia made her way up to his office and looked around, but Mason was nowhere to be seen, so she knocked on Derrick's door. No answer. She cracked the door and peeked inside. No Derrick.

She made her way to his desk and decided to leave him the illustration as well as a note, and they could discuss it later tonight, as she wasn't sure when he'd return.

She glanced around for some parchment and grabbed the quill. She set quill to paper to pen her note, but something caught her eye. Something with her father's name on it.

She picked it up and began to read. As she read, her world crumbled to her feet.

She sank into Derrick's chair and stared at the paper until the words blurred into a black smear. Embezzlement. Murder. Suicide. So her father had been the one Derrick had suspected. Two weeks ago she would have been positive her father wasn't capable of such atrocities, but now she wasn't so sure.

How could Derrick have written this without speaking to her first? He'd said he didn't want to accuse anyone until he was positive of his guilt. Surely he was positive, or he wouldn't have written this piece. But still he'd said nothing. He'd obviously had suspicions about this for a while now. Why hadn't he come to her first?

She grabbed the article and left his office. She stepped into the carriage and nearly burst into tears at the sight of her friend, but she swallowed hard and faked some courage.

"You look dreadful. What's the matter?"

Claudia recounted the article and all the details within.

"So what do you think of all of it?" Poppy asked.

"I'm not certain. I'm angry with Derrick for not coming to me first. I'm not positive all of his allegations are sound. And I'm frightened that they are, and my father is a horrible man.

"The embezzlement doesn't surprise me. But I

am hesitant to believe that he murdered Richard. I was so certain that it was a burglary." She looked up at Poppy. "You know the last time I saw my father alone, he tried to convince me that Derrick killed Richard. Which was ridiculous because Derrick and I had been together the entire time."

"If he's guilty, then it makes sense that he would try to throw you off his trail, so to speak."

"I suppose. But murder, Poppy. My goodness, I'd only recently come to terms with the fact that he'd never be proud of me. I've made peace with the fact that his standards were too high, that I was never going to be the daughter he wanted me to be. I never dreamed he'd kill someone."

"So you believe Derrick?"

"I know Derrick would never print a story without confirming the facts." And then it hit her. "Oh my goodness, this will clear his name, bring honor back to his father's name."

"What are you talking about?"

She shook her head. "It's a long story. Suffice it to say, Derrick and Richard had a past, and it looks like my father was to blame for a lot of things. I can't believe he wouldn't come to me to tell me what he'd found. He obviously doesn't trust me."

How could she have been so blind? He'd said he'd never lie to her again, and she'd foolishly believed him.

"Clearly Richard and my father were right. Derrick married me for the details of this story."

"This doesn't prove any such thing. Did you know anything about your father and embezzlement? No. Then how could marrying you help Derrick in his endeavor? Seriously, Claudia, do you think he had a master plan all along? Ruin you in public so you'd be forced to marry him, and then he could ruin your life by accusing your father of crimes against the crown? And you accused me of having an active imagination."

"You don't understand. He's spent the better part of our marriage teaching me to trust him. Yet he cannot offer trust in return. If he would have simply come to me with all of this . . ."

"You'd have done what?"

"I don't know."

"You'd have gone straight to your father. Don't you see, he kept this from you to keep you safe? To prevent you from getting hurt. He loves you, Claudia."

"No, he doesn't."

"You're so sure?"

"Yes."

"I've seen the way he looks at you. That night at your wedding ball. It was as if you were the only woman in the world. No matter how many men ask me to dance and try to steal kisses in the dark, no one has ever looked at me that way. Like they could really see me."

"If he loves me, then he would have told me."

"Have you told him?" Her voice was heavy with sarcasm.

"No," Claudia admitted.

Poppy didn't understand. Claudia looked down at her hands. Her wedding ring sparkled as if winking at her. Mocking her. Her husband didn't trust her, and he didn't love her.

"Why not? You love him. With your logic, if you love someone, you tell him. Right?"

"Why are you so angry with me?"

"You need to look around you. Stop being so blind to what is right in front of you. You have everything we've ever dreamed of." She shook her head. "I'm not certain why Derrick didn't tell you about the story first. I'm not certain why he hasn't told you he loves you. But I know he loves you, I've seen it. And I'm fairly certain that also means he trusts you. He's only trying to protect you."

The carriage stopped. Bond Street—their shopping trip.

Poppy opened the door. "Go home and talk to your husband. I'm sorry I can't offer you compassion, but I find myself lacking in sympathy today. Don't you see what you have? You have the kind of marriage I'll never have." Her eyes shone with tears.

"Give Derrick a chance to explain these things to you. Be patient with him, and be happy with your relationship. In time, I know he'll express his feelings for you. If you let this stand in the way of your happiness, you're a fool." She stepped out of the carriage. "I'll find my own way home."

Claudia sat back against the seat cushion and watched Poppy through the tiny window. They'd never before fought, and she wanted to be angry about Poppy's harsh treatment, but found she couldn't. The truth was, she was only hurt. Hurt by her father's betrayal. Hurt by Poppy's anger. And hurt by her husband's flagrant lack of trust in her, when he demanded time and again that she trust him.

There were things to be said. She needed to hear some things herself. She gave the driver the address. But first it was time for her father to be honest with her.

Chapter 22

❦

"Do I have any messages?" Derrick asked Mason as he stepped into his office.

Mason looked blithely up from his paperwork and shook his head. "No. Everything seems to be running smoothly today."

Derrick nodded, then entered his office. His meeting had lasted longer than he'd anticipated, and he was ready for the day to end. Ready to go home. To Claudia.

He sat at his desk to make a few notes for the following day, and that's when he saw it. Her illustration, an illustration of them from their wedding ball. He picked it up and admired her skill, and then his heart nearly stopped beating. Claudia had been in his office. He rummaged through the papers littering his desktop. Where was the article? He knew he'd left it right here on his desk; he'd planned to take it to Kennington tomorrow as a final threat. Derrick picked up her illustration and walked into the hall.

"How did this get here?" He held the illustration up for Mason.

Mason looked at him blankly. "I'm not certain."

"Did you see my wife?"

"No, but I was gone for a while."

"Bloody hell." She'd been here, and she had taken the article. He tossed the illustration on Mason's desk and tore down the stairs. He had to find her, needed to explain before she came to the wrong conclusion, which inevitably she would.

He ran into their house yelling her name, checked the parlor and the library with no luck. He was headed up the stairs when the housekeeper came in view, but she assured him that she hadn't seen Claudia all afternoon. That Claudia had left earlier to go see her friend.

It didn't take him long to get to Poppy's house, and he knocked none too gently on her front door. He was shown in and sent the servant to find her.

Poppy rounded the corner and spotted him. "She's not here, if you're looking for her."

"Have you seen her?"

"Yes, I was with her earlier. At your office."

"She has the article then?"

"Yes."

"Damnation." He rolled his neck in a vain attempt to relieve the stress.

"Exactly. I tried to make her see reason, but she wasn't interested in listening. Don't lose her, Derrick, she loves you."

He didn't respond, merely nodded and turned on his heel and left. There was only one other place she could have gone.

Kennington.

Derrick's blood ran cold. The bastard would likely kill her, if she accused him of such crimes. Derrick's heart slammed back and forth in his chest. He had to get to her. Now.

He had been drinking again. He stood at the window, and she could see it in his agitated manner and smell it in the room. His hands shook at his sides.

"Father, I've come to discuss something with you."

356

He turned as if she'd startled him. Red lines, like cobwebs, clouded the whites of his eyes. "We have nothing to discuss. Unless you've left that worthless husband of yours." He raised his eyebrows in question.

"I need to know what happened to Richard."

He shrugged and gave a little laugh. "How the hell should I know?"

"Well, if you won't tell me about him, then tell me about Chester Edwards."

He eyed her for a moment. "What do you want to know?"

"Did you have anything to do with the embezzlement he was accused of?"

"Where are you getting these ideas?" Then he released a laugh that snaked up her spine. "From your damned husband?"

She lifted her chin. *Be strong, Claudia.* "As a matter of fact." She retrieved the parchment from her bag. "He has this article ready for his paper that implicates you in quite a few crimes. I came to ask you if any of his allegations are true."

His eyes narrowed and focused on the paper she clutched to her chest. "So you don't believe him?"

She didn't want to answer that. She didn't want

to believe Derrick, but deep inside she knew the accusations were true. She felt it. But even that made her question. What if her instincts were wrong? Again.

She needed to give her father one last chance, an opportunity to be truthful with her. She could forgive his transgressions, if he cared for her enough to be honest.

"I merely wanted to hear your side of the story," she said.

"I have no side." He waved his hand in front of him and nearly lost his balance. "Your husband is a liar. He's trying to set me up. He printed that other story years ago, and Edwards offed himself because of it." He shrugged. "Now I suppose he's trying to get me to do the same thing. But it won't work." He pointed a bony finger at her. "No one will believe him."

She took a deep breath and swallowed the fear and anger that threatened to consume her. "His evidence is quite compelling."

"It's all lies." He stumbled across the room and poured himself another drink, half of which sloshed onto his desk. "Richard Foxmore was a liar too. He promised he'd marry you, the spineless cur. And you! I told you to do whatever you could to trap him, but no, you'd already lifted your skirt for that bastard Middleton. You just can't trust people to do things right. If you want something done, you're better off just doing it yourself."

She winced as her last threads of hope frayed away. Her father didn't love her. He never had. He wasn't looking out for her best interest. He was, and always had been, manipulating everyone around him to fit in some master plan. Derrick's story was right. Every word of it. Her father was a calculating murderer.

Footsteps sounded in •the hall. The door opened, and she saw Derrick out of the corner of her eye. Relief washed over her quickly, followed by a sickening fear that almost made her sink to the floor.

"Claudia, I'd like for you to come home with me now. There is much we need to discuss." His tone was even and soft.

"He's a bastard, that husband of yours," her father said, speaking of him as if Derrick hadn't just entered the room. "Clearly he married you just to print that rubbish. He needed you to validate his story. Without the connection to you, no one would ever believe him."

It was the same thing Richard had said that day in the garden. The very same thought that had raced through her head when she'd read the article. Derrick had used her to further his paper's reputation; to put himself back in the public as a serious writer. Regardless of her father's guilt or innocence, Derrick had used her, and it hurt. And here and now, Derrick said nothing to dispute it.

It had been easy to trust him, but he'd twisted that trust and convinced her to trust her instincts. She'd been such a fool. From the very beginning, she'd known that Derrick didn't want her, couldn't possibly want her. He had to have been after something. He'd admitted as much when they got married. But she'd foolishly thought the charade had ended there. She never imagined he'd orchestrated this elaborate plan.

She'd spent her entire life fighting her feelings, trying her damnedest to squelch her emotions and put on a more appropriate façade. And he'd come along and convinced her she didn't have to do that, convinced her simply to trust herself. She'd allowed it too, let go of propriety, turned her back on her father, and trusted her own instincts.

But now she wasn't so certain her instincts were wise. Because even now in the midst of Derrick's betrayal, her heart screamed for her to wait, not jump to conclusions, to give him the benefit of the doubt.

Tears stung the backs of her eyes, blurring her view of her father as he bent to retrieve something.

She needed to keep her father talking. She desperately wanted a confession out of him. "What does Derrick have to gain by ruining your reputation?" she asked.

"I'm an important man, Claudia. Calling into question my reputation would sell twice as many papers as he usually sells. Don't be so daft."

A flash of metal caught her eye, and she saw a pistol dangling from her father's right hand. She took a brief moment to absorb the situation— she'd never had to fear for her life before and was surprised that she was not afraid. There was no way for her to escape. If she turned to run, he could easily shoot her in the back. She hadn't a clue what kind of aim her father had, but she was so close, he would be hard pressed to miss.

She saw the sheen of metal as her father raised the gun and aimed it at Derrick, and her blood chilled. Despite her husband's betrayal, she loved him, and she would not allow her father to take him away.

"Claudia, come with me." Derrick held his hand out to her, but his eyes never left her father.

"She's not going anywhere," her father said.

Derrick took a step forward.

Her father moved the gun so that it pointed at her. "Don't take another step. I'll kill her."

"You don't want to kill her." Derrick's voice was even. "I'm the one you want."

What did she do now? Someone was going to get shot. She let the feelings wash over her, gauged her surroundings. Her father's face was contorted with rage. Derrick seemed calm, although his hands clenched at his sides.

She had to play this right, or her father would shoot Derrick. No matter if the gun was aimed at her or not, Derrick was the one in danger.

It was up to her to save him.

"Papa, listen to me. I see now that Derrick's story is full of lies. You were right. He married me to get to you. I understand that now." She kept her focus on her father's face, not wanting to see how her words affected Derrick. She reached one hand out. "Give me the gun."

He shook the pistol. "I'll kill you, girl. Don't play games with me."

"I'm not. Trust me. I should have listened to you and never married him. He's beneath us, not worthy of being associated with your good name." She took a step toward him, clutching the article tighter to keep her hands from shaking. "It's all lies, Papa, I know it is. I know you didn't black-mail anyone, and you didn't embezzle that money. And I know that you're not capable of murdering anyone. Isn't that right?"

She waited for him to answer. Sweat rolled like beads down his forehead. He glanced at Derrick and then back to her. It felt as though her heart were splintering. Regardless of her father's horrible deeds and Derrick's betrayal, she still loved them both.

"Tell me you're not capable of murder, Papa. Then I can know your side of the story is true."

He came around the desk toward her, all the while keeping the gun aimed at her. Out of the corner of her eye, she saw Derrick move toward her as well. She took a step closer to the fire and held the article near the flames. Both men moved closer. To the article, not her, she reminded herself.

And then in a brief second, both men were upon her. Derrick grabbed her and pulled her out of the way, while her father snatched the parchment from her hands. Derrick tackled her father, knocking him to the ground.

The gun slid across the floor.

"Find me something to tie him up with, then call for the magistrate," Derrick said.

She took one last look at her father and finally recognized the nagging feeling in her gut. Pity.

Derrick and Claudia had managed to keep her father controlled until the magistrate arrived and then answered a string of questions once they had. They hadn't spoken to each other since the authorities had taken her father. Now, on their way home, the darkness of the carriage surrounded her, and she could scarcely see her husband's form sitting across from her.

Claudia's mind swam with thoughts, trying to grasp all that had occurred in the span of one day. Her marriage was a charade, and her father, whom she'd spent her entire life trying to please, was a criminal.

Without him to trust, she felt as if she had no one. This morning, she'd trusted her husband and believed he trusted her as well, but now they would have to start all over again. Unless their marriage couldn't be repaired. How could she stay with a man who neither loved her nor trusted her?

It was evident that he cared for her. He'd at least shown that he was concerned for her safety, and she was grateful. But she loved him, and she could no longer ignore those feelings.

Her heart pounded so loudly, she was certain he could hear it. But regardless of her nerves, they had to talk; there were things she had to know.

"Derrick?"

"Yes?" His voice was soft with a hint of a question.

"I'm trying to understand everything that has occurred today, and I need your help with some of it." She tried to remain calm, but the myriad of emotions flowing through her blood made it an impossibility. "Can you please tell me how you thought it was acceptable to investigate my father and print an article about his crimes, without even once mentioning any of it to me?"

"You weren't supposed to see that article." He sounded tired, defeated.

"I gathered that much. But wouldn't I have noticed when it appeared in your paper?"

He closed the small distance between them and sat beside her. She felt him hesitate a moment, then he reached for her hands. He clasped his large hands around her smaller ones and shrouded them in warmth. She closed her eyes and tried to pretend for a moment that all would be well. But the sick feeling in her stomach questioned his every movement, every motive.

365

"I had no intention of actually printing it in the paper," he said. "I only wrote it to frighten your father. A few days ago I asked him to leave town, told him I wouldn't bring this to the authorities if he'd leave quietly. I wanted you safe. I needed to know you would be safe. I felt with him out of our lives for good, you would be. But your father refused to leave, so I penned the article and planned to send it to him as confirmation."

She opened her mouth to say something, but he put a finger to her lips. "Wait, let me finish. Today when I knew you'd seen those words, seen the accusations I'd made against your father without talking to you and informing you that I even had such information, I didn't know what to do. I knew I needed to get to you, to explain, before you thought the worst of me. I've never cared much for what people think of me, Claudia, but I couldn't live with you thinking the worst of me."

While she couldn't see his face clearly, she knew his eyes were pleading with her. She felt nothing but honesty and sorrow coming from him. He had wanted her safe. He'd done this for her, not for his career. Her heart leaped into her throat, and she fought the urge to throw her arms around his neck.

"The truth of the matter is I love you, Claudia. I

don't know exactly how it happened, and it scares the hell out of me, but I can't seem to make it go away." He cradled her face. "God, tonight when I almost lost you, I didn't think I could go on. Nor would I want to.

"Every morning when I wake up, I smile, knowing you're there next to me. That you'll be there when I get home. I want to tell you everything. It killed me to keep this from you, but I didn't feel as if I could tell you until I had absolute proof of your father's guilt."

He took a ragged breath before he continued. "I didn't want you to go and question him. I knew he'd hurt you. I tried to make the situation disappear without you knowing. Despite the wretched way he's treated you, I know you love him. I didn't want to be the one responsible for destroying the way you saw him. Can you understand that?"

She swallowed, trying to fight the tears, then gave up and let them go. "I'm sorry I doubted you. It's just that all my life I've doubted myself, doubted that I knew what was right for me. With you, though, I've felt more confidence. You've freed me to trust myself. Then when I found that article, it seemed that everything I believed about us was false."

He loved her. He'd said it. Out loud. She felt like screaming, like jumping out into the street and dancing. "But you love me," she repeated dumbly.

"Yes, I do." He squeezed her hands. "More than I thought possible."

She moved in and kissed him hard, fiercely, with all the intensity of the day's emotions pouring forward. He loved her. Her husband loved her. She smiled and laughed, despite their passionate kiss.

"What's funny?" he asked.

"You love me."

"And that's funny?"

"No. No, it's not funny. It's amazing."

"You're amazing." He hugged her to him. "I'm so relieved you're safe."

She listened to his breathing and felt the thud of his heart beating against her. All would be fine. She let the relief wash over her, then took a deep breath, and said, "I want you to print that article."

"What?"

"You heard me. It's the truth. The people of England have a right to know the truth. Chester Edwards's family deserves to know that he wasn't wholly to blame, that he was blackmailed into committing those crimes. And you deserve to have your name cleared. People should know you're a serious journalist who doesn't stop until he uncovers the truth."

"I can't do that." ·

"And why not?"

"Because people will assume that I married you just for this story. Merely to get to your father, to get close enough to validate my story. You heard him tonight. He won't be the only one to come to that conclusion. I refuse to allow people to think that about you. We might not have come to this marriage in a love match, but we found one. Didn't we?" He shook his head, his breath sounding ragged. "I understand if you don't love me; I've done nothing but deceive you from the beginning of our relationship. But that ends tonight. No more dishonesty. Ever."

What had she ever done to deserve such a man? This strong and courageous man humbling himself before her. No more questions. It didn't matter if she deserved him, she had him, and she would do everything in her power to ensure he was hers for the rest of their lives.

"Yes, we have a love match. I thought you knew. I've loved you forever, it seems. I honestly thought you knew." She leaned in and gave him a brief kiss. "I still want you to print the story. I don't care what people think. I know the truth."

"Which is?"

"That you desire me. That you love me. And that I desire and love you above all things."

The unthinkable had happened. She'd married the wrong man and found her love match.

"We have a real marriage, Derrick. We have real love. We know that. Who cares what anyone else thinks?"

Don't forget to stock up on these "school supplies" coming this September from Avon Romance . . .

Avon Romances
the best in
exceptional authors and unforgettable novels!

Avon Romantic Treasures

Unforgettable, enthralling love stories,
sparkling with passion and adventure
from Romance's bestselling authors

HIS EVERY KISS — *by Laura Lee Guhrke*
0-06-054175-X/$5.99 US/$7.99 Can

DUKE OF SIN — *by Adele Ashworh*
0-06-052840-0/$5.99 US/$7.99 Can

MY OWN PRIVATE HERO — *by Julianne MacLean*
0-06-059728-3/$5.99 US/$7.99 Can

SIN AND SENSIBILITY — *by Suzanne Enoch*
0-06-054325-6/$5.99 US/$7.99 Can

SOMETHING ABOUT EMMALINE — *by Elizabeth Boyle*
0-06-054931-9/$5.99 US/$7.99 Can

JUST ONE TOUCH — *by Debra Mullins*
0-06-056167-X/$5.99 US/$7.99 Can

AS AN EARL DESIRES — *by Lorraine Heath*
0-06-052947-4/$5.99 US/$7.99 Can

TILL NEXT WE MEET — *by Karen Ranney*
0-06-075737-X/$5.99 US/$7.99 Can

MARRY THE MAN TODAY — *by Linda Needham*
0-06-051414-0/$5.99 US/$7.99 Can

THE MARRIAGE BED — *by Laura Lee Guhrke*
0-06-077473-8/$5.99 US/$7.99 Can

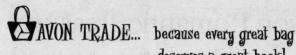